"B...

nee...

I'm in big trouble.

I had a familiar knot in my gut. Or was it a rush of adrenaline? I knew exactly where the conversation was leading.

"Bel, I need your help. I need evidence to take to the police. If I go to them without any proof, I'll lose my job and gain nothing. Will you help me this time? Or are you still too busy?"

So there it was, a double whammy. I had seen her request for help coming, but I was totally blindsided by the bitter zinger she threw in as a coda. I had been right all along. Ashley hadn't forgotten the unwritten letter of recommendation anymore than I had. She was still hurt and had just saved it for a rainy day. And it was pouring now.

"I've been assigned to Chris's old territory to finish what he started," she said. "I need you to help me finger Chris's killer before he kills me, too."

———

"The gifted Jane Isenberg writes with wit and compassion about life transitions that range from menopause to murder."
Susan Conant, author of the
Barker Street Regulars mysteries

Other Bel Barrett Mysteries by
Jane Isenberg
from Avon Books

THE "M" WORD
DEATH IN A HOT FLASH
MOOD SWINGS TO MURDER

JANE ISENBERG

Midlife Can Be Murder

AVON BOOKS
An Imprint of HarperCollinsPublishers

AVON BOOKS
An Imprint of HarperCollins*Publishers*
10 East 53rd Street
New York, New York 10022-5299

Copyright © 2001 by Jane Isenberg
ISBN: 0-380-81886-8
www.avonbooks.com

First Avon Books paperback printing: October 2001

Avon Trademark Reg. U.S. Pat. Off. and in Other Countries, Marca Registrada, Hecho en U.S.A.
HarperCollins ® is a trademark of HarperCollins Publishers Inc.

Printed in the U.S.A.

10 9 8 7 6 5 4 3 2 1

To the United Synagogue of Hoboken with affection,
the City Congregation of New York in appreciation,
and the Jewish Community of Amherst in anticipation

Acknowledgments

If you're crazy enough to write a book while you're moving, you need a lot of support. That's what I got, first, from a lineup of New Jersey and New York stalwarts. I'm very grateful to Jimmy Shamburg, Jersey City's Deputy Police Director for information on police procedures; Professors Elaine Foster, Liliane MacPherson, Joan Rafter, and Mojdeh Tabatabaie for restaurant research; and Marge and Bill Graham for introducing me to klezmer music and inviting me to Marge's adult bat mitzvah. Ruth Tait and Dr. Annette Hollander are always a phone call away with advice and encouragement, just as Denise Swanson provides the same crucial help via e-mail from the midwest.

I continue to appreciate my agent, Laura Blake Peterson, and my editor, Jennifer Sawyer Fisher, the former for her negotiating skills and the latter for her ability to tweak a manuscript into shape without bending its author out of shape. My writing group members share this gift: Pat Juell, Susan Babinski, and Rebecca

Mlynarczk have been my muses and critics for almost ten years, and I'm still thankful for their insight, patience, tact, and friendship. And five stars to both Tom and Pat Juel, who provide me with bed and board when I visit New York for our meetings.

People in Massachusetts have proved no less helpful. I'm indebted to Rabbi Sheila Weinberg of the Jewish Community of Amherst for explicating the adult bat mitzvah and Shirley and Saul Gladstone for introducing me to the complexities of Hebrew study. Janice Brickley probably saved my life by referring me to John Jackson, who willingly and eloquently shared his rock climbing expertise, thus sparing me the perils of on-site research. And to Lisa Kleinholz and other members of the New England Chapter of Sisters in Crime who have welcomed me to Amherst and to the northeast, I also say thank you from the bottom of my newcomer's heart.

Brian Stoner, my son-in-law, has generously offered his observations of dot com culture and Rachel Stoner, my daughter, packed and labeled hundreds of boxes when we moved. My son, Daniel Isenberg, and our friend Shilyh Warren have also earned my affectionate appreciation by staying safe and continuing to e-mail all the way from Morocco the words and phrases of their generation that I need to know when I write. My husband, Phil Tompkins, has evolved from proofreader to web designer (*www.JaneIsenberg.com*) and maintainer into on-line researcher and now public relations whiz. What I am most grateful for, though, are his calm courage and good humor in the face of life's blocks, revisions, and deadlines.

 **Chapter 1**

To: Bbarrett@circle.com
From: Sandig@calgal.com
Re: Surprise! Surprise!
Date: 8/25/99 16:34:08

Hi there Super Roomie!

Before you even start, I know I promised to touch base right after
Rebecca's wedding (And what a stunning MOB you were, dear
Bel. It was worth the trip to Seattle in January to see you in a silver feather boa. You've come a long way from that circle pin on
your Peter Pan collar, baby!) But when you hear all that's happened to your long-lost Vassar roommate you'll understand.

Here's my first surprise. I've left Jerry. Okay, so you're not that
surprised. I finally got tired of supporting him, just as you predicted I would. But the real shocker is . . . are you ready? I've
left California! I decided to make a clean break. Now sit down.
I'm apartment sitting in the West Village for an alum who ad-
vertised in the *Vassar Quarterly*. That's right! This slightly over-

the-Berkeley-Hills California girl has rented out her empty nest and taken a leave of absence from work. So now you and I are practically neighbors, which is just perfect because I've got a terrific idea for a project for us. You'll love it. I'll give you the details when we meet for dinner. Should I come to Hoboken? How about tomorrow night? Or the next night? Call me.

Sandi

"Sandi couldn't just leave her husband. No. She has to leave her job and her house too. That woman never could do anything halfway," I said to Sol, shaking my head at my former roommate's grand gestures as I recounted the essence of Sandi's message. I was folding laundry while I spoke.

"I guess nobody ever advised Sandi to make just one big decision at a time," said Sol, affection deepening his already bass voice. Like everybody else, he had been smitten with Sandi as soon as he met her. Sandi Golden was a BIG blond with a heart to match. She was generous to a fault. Her stack of pastel cashmere sweater sets had been at my disposal for four whole years, as had her organic chemistry notes, her boundless enthusiasm, and her infectious laughter. Sandi was so much fun that I hadn't minded stumbling over her books, her laundry, and her love letters that had littered the floor of our shared quarters throughout my entire undergraduate career.

"She wouldn't have listened anyway," I commented, still shaking my head.

"Isn't this husband number three?" Sol asked from the slanted depths of our bedroom closet where he was stashing shirts and slacks.

"Well, no. I don't think she ever actually married Carlos. But she did live with him for around ten years. He was a wonderful stepdad to Josh. The kid adores him," I said, already looking forward to seeing Sandi, who could make me giggle uncontrollably by just looking at me and raising one eyebrow in imitation of our long dead French prof. Actually, Sandi's e-mail was a welcome diversion from the prospect of fall registration the very next day at River Edge Community College, where, as a full-time English professor, I was contractually mandated to materialize and enroll students for classes. "Want to meet her for a late dinner after registration?" I asked, knowing that the prospect of dinner with Sandi and Sol would get me through a day of explaining to students why they had to take developmental courses instead of the college level courses they really wanted or why the one course they needed for graduation wasn't being offered until the following semester.

"You go. I'm not sure I want to sit through the whole Jerry saga. Or listen to her try to sell you the Oakland Bay Bridge either," Sol said with a grin. "I'll see her next time, okay? Tell her we'll have a cookout California style." Sol was probably right. As a retired economics professor and financial consultant to fledgling democracies, he was often right. It was one of the few infuriating things about him. But I had to agree that Sandi would want to rehash the demise of her latest long-term relationship.

And then she had this "project" to pitch to me. Decades ago Sandi had persuaded me to hitchhike to New Haven on a Tuesday night to surprise our boyfriends, to take organic chemistry to "expand our horizons," and to taste an avocado to understand California—challenges that had, in retrospect, enlivened my college experience no end. She'd even tried to persuade me not to marry Leonard Barrett. In fact, she had been the only one of my friends who didn't think marrying the newly minted Colgate-educated economics major with the white Triumph and the whiter teeth was a brilliant coup. I should have listened to her that time. Yes, Sol was right. After Sandi had told her story and sold me whatever bill of goods she was marketing now, she'd be much better company. I'd meet her for dinner alone.

"Well, you can take the girl out of California, but you can't take California out of the girl," I said with a chuckle as Sandi and I embraced before seating ourselves at Zafra's, a tiny new pan-Latin bistro that had just opened in Hoboken.

"Well if you think *I'm* going to run around looking as if I'm sitting shiva for my best friend like everybody else out here, think again," retorted Sandi, smoothing her sea green linen shell over her zaftig hips encased in matching linen capri pants. The fact that she was the only woman in the crowded eatery not wearing the standard-issue black uniform of fashionable denizens of the metropolitan area seemed to delight her. She winked at me. I grinned. My grin belied the fact that I was concerned to note dark smudges beneath my friend's eyes and a slight pallor in lieu of her customary tan. New lines creased her forehead while others radiated from the corners of her mouth when she smiled. Jerry may have been a feckless freeloader, but he had also been Sandi's partner and companion for the past five years. She had anticipated growing old with him.

"I'll give you three months and you'll be indistinguishable from an undertaker just like the rest of us," I challenged, waving my pinky in the air between us. Sandi linked hers through it, sealing the wager, as we used to do decades ago when I bet her that I wouldn't meet anyone at the Yale mixer she dragged me to or that I was going to fail the impending organic chem exam. After searching the wine list in vain for a California red, Sandi broke down and ordered a bottle of Chilean merlot.

"So tell me," I began, settling back into my chair after we had ordered. "What did Jerry do? What was the straw that broke the camel's back?"

"Same old same old," answered Sandi with a twisted grin. "But even less of it. I was slaving away as usual at Kirkland, Inc., putting in really long hours, under a lot of typical postmerger stress." Sandi sighed, recalling the rigors of her work as human resources director of one of the nation's largest HMOs. According to her, the only thing harder than being an HMO patient was being an HMO executive. "I came home one night just a couple of weeks ago and there was no dinner, no food in the house, his golfing gear was all over the place. *And* the slug was on the phone arranging a foursome for himself and three buddies for the next day. He wasn't even apologetic." Sandi shrugged her shoulders.

"But I didn't lose it, Bel. You'd have been proud of me. I just told him to pack and be out by the end of the week." Sandi blinked rapidly a few times as she continued. "While he was standing there with his mouth open, I picked up the phone and called a realtor I know and told her to find a tenant for the house, so Jerry knew I meant business. Jeez, Bel, he had stopped even trying to find steady work, and he wasn't freelancing much anymore either. He wouldn't see a shrink. I was living with a golfer and I wanted a go-getter. Or at least a gofer." Her grin reappeared. "You were right about Jerry, Bel. And he wasn't even Jewish."

I smiled at Sandi's final condemnatory line, uttered with a snort. Sandi and I, two nice Jewish girls accepted to Vassar in those bygone days as part of the alleged annual 25 percent quota of Jewish applicants admitted then, had spent hours when we should have been studying organic chemistry trying to figure out what Judaism meant to each of us. We knew only that we'd each requested Jewish roommates, wanted to marry Jewish men, and planned to give our kids Old Testament names. Sandi had married Harold Golden and they had Joshua. I had married Leonard Barrett and we had Rebecca and then, in a triumph of biblical ignorance over intentions, Mark. Since neither Sandi nor I nor our families was religious let alone observant, as undergraduates we had had no ready explanations for these preferences.

"Well, I guess you and Jerry had a few good years anyway," I said, wanting to give Sandi a chance to mourn the end of a relationship that once had mattered a great deal to her. My shrimp ceviche and Sandi's empanadas arrived, and we began to load samples of our goodies onto each other's bread and butter plates in what had become a ritual of food sharing that had evolved over time from bartering the Toll House cookies and brownies in our mothers' care packages.

"Things were good while he still worked for the paper full-time, but when MacLeod took over, Jerry was made part-time, let go really, and he never recovered. That was a while back. I should have asked him to leave a year ago, but I felt sorry for him. I still do, in a way . . ." Sandi paused, twirling her wineglass and letting a tear fall from one eye onto her wrist. "But keeping him like an expensive pet wasn't doing anything for either one of us. So good luck, Jerry." Swallowing hard, she raised her glass and I clicked it against mine in a solemn toast.

"I guess you fled your precious California so you wouldn't be tempted to take him back?" I probed tentatively. Sandi's affection for her native state had been legendary at college. And the passing years had only deepened her love for that arid, earthquake-prone part of the world. "Bury me in my Birkenstocks near a vineyard," she'd said once when Sol had asked her if she'd ever consider living elsewhere.

"Yes. You know me too well. I'm so easy. And this way, I'll have a New York adventure while I'm still able to survive the damn humidity. Look." Draining her wineglass, Sandi raised her hand to her head and pulled back the strand of blond hair that always fell into her face. If I leaned across the table, I could barely distinguish a border of gray framing her temple.

"Oh Sandi, you look fabulous," I said. "First, you're practically a poster woman for the perfect menopause. No hot flashes, no insomnia, no weight gain, no dry

eyes. Honestly, you make me sick. And don't you think
it's a little tactless to bitch to *me* about a couple of gray
hairs?" I reached up to fluff my salt and a little pepper
frizz just as our waitress arrived with our entrees. We
were both having snapper, broiled with julienned trop-
ical veggies stacked like rainbow-colored pick-up sticks
in a tower on each plate.

Had I not been distracted by our statuesque food,
maybe I wouldn't have been so taken aback by Sandi's
next words, "So what you and I have to do is study for
adult bat mitzvahs. Should we use the synagogue here
or should we find one in New York?"

"Hold on, Sandi," I practically shrieked over the pil-
lars of food between us. "Just hold on. You lost me.
You dump your loser goy boyfriend, rent out your gorgeous house, leave your dream job, get a few gray
hairs, and I have to go to Hebrew school? What am I
missing here?"

Sandi put her fork down and leaned toward me to
answer. "It's spiritual values, Bel. That's what you're
missing." By the time I had recovered from this not so
subtle barb, Sandi was saying, "You and I may have
been Vassar's chosen of the chosen people, but let's
face it, between the two of us, we don't know *bubkes*
about Judaism. We're both as secular as you can get
and always have been. Our mothers and my dad were
into assimilation, not roots, remember? And your dad
was a Yiddish-speaking atheist commie type. You think
you're in touch with your spiritual heritage if you have
somebody step on a glass at your daughter's wedding.
I try to buy my way into some kind of Jewish community by giving money to UJA." Sandi was sputtering

with indignation at our belated and misguided efforts to act out our Jewishness. She stopped long enough to pour us both more wine and continued. "And we both thought making decent chicken soup, driving our kids to Hebrew school, and worrying about their every breath made us good Jewish mothers. But it didn't. My own kid called me a hypocrite right before his bar mitzvah. And I bet you haven't learned anything about Jewish history since you were in Sunday school." Sandi plunged her fork into her fish as if the snapper itself were responsible for my failures of spirit and knowledge.

"No, I haven't," I answered lamely. "But then why should I? I'm a secular, humanistic, and, you know, cultural Jew. Maybe that's enough."

"No, it's not. Not in your case. How do you know you're not rejecting something valid, something you really need if you haven't learned anything about it since you were a kid? You know, Bel, there's a prof out in California who calls that 'pediatric Judaism'!" Sandi had a California guru on every subject from child raising to financial planning. I wasn't really surprised to learn that she had found one to support her latest enthusiasm. She continued. "And how can you be a 'cultural Jew,' as you so smugly put it, if you don't know anything about your own culture, Ms. Multicultural Professor?" She posed this question with all the solemnity of the righteous after the righteous has just polished off half a bottle of Chilean red. I felt myself starting to pay attention to her. The wine was getting to me too.

"And aren't you even curious about how feminism

has influenced Judaism?" Sandi persisted, brushing back a lock of hair from her flushed cheek. "You're supposed to be such a serious feminist, yet you don't even know how the women's movement has affected your own religion. Do you really want to go through your whole life thinking Marjorie Morningstar was the last word in Jewish womanhood?" Sandi paused to take a gulp of water and signal our waitress.

I was grateful for the resulting silence because Sandi had, as usual, rung my chimes. Her words called up snatches of the few high holy day services at the Jewish Community of Hoboken that I had actually attended recently, services where the masculine pronoun for the deity was avoided, where women stood on the *bimah* and read from the Torah, where, thanks in part to that "nice" Jewish girl, Betty Friedan, there was actually a woman rabbi. At that service, sitting in a pew, pretending to understand the Hebrew words while repressing my guilt about not being more observant, I had not dwelt on these changes, but they had registered.

But before I could formulate a response, Sandi suddenly took a different tack, heading toward the same destination. "Listen, Bel. Think how much fun it would be. Remember those long conversations we used to have about being Jewish? Remember how we used to argue? And we didn't even know what we were talking about then. Literally. But now, we could really study, and we could have informed conversations. It would be like in college only better. We're at that time of life when we need to explore and affirm our spiritual identity."

I was at that time of life when I needed to relax, but listening between the lines, something I've become quite adept at as an English prof, I heard my old friend saying, "Hey, I'm out of love, out of work, out of California, and getting older. I'm looking for a way to meet people, establish connections, move on. I don't want to do it alone." I felt a rush of empathy for her, remembering how, after my divorce, Sandi had hauled me off to a Calistoga mud bath to recover. Now Sandi needed me to join her in her quest for her own spiritual identity, to play Sancho Panza to her Don Quixote, to help her make the transition she needed. An adult bat mitzvah study group, which I envisioned as an orgy of immersion, bonding, and renewal, could be construed as the East Coast's answer to the mud bath. Hanging out with Sandi and studying Judaism had real appeal, not least because it would be a kind of midlife mitzvah, a combination of a commandment and a good deed. And even I knew that doing mitzvahs was central to one's life as a Jew. I chuckled to myself at how I was already connecting to my heritage, was already a bat mitzvah or daughter of the commandments although I hadn't even set foot inside a synagogue yet.

There was just one problem though, and it was a biggie. When would I find the time? Teaching, advising, committee work, and grad school took most of my available hours and all my energy. But I knew I was hooked when I heard myself asking out loud, "But when will I find the time? You know how busy I am, especially since I started grad school."

"It'll be easy. I'll come into Hoboken. I don't have a job yet, so that's no problem. And the classes won't

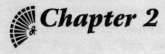 *Chapter 2*

Jewish Community of Hoboken
Adult Bat Mitzvah Program Outline

Requirements for participation

1. Learn to read Hebrew.
2. Learn blessings for being called to the Torah (aliyah) and learn to chant three sentences in Hebrew.
3. Attend a minimum of twenty Sabbath services.
4. Take on as a personal practice the study and performance of at least one new regular mitzvah.
5. Compose a talk, prayer, or poem integrating your Torah studies and prayers with your life (dvar Torah) to be shared at your bat mitzvah.
6. Meet twice a month as a group with the rabbi.

7. Choose a book of the Old Testament to ana-
   lyze and report on.

8. Required reading . . .

I was sputtering with rage when I glanced at the syllabus Rabbi Ornstein-Klein had distributed. Once
more siren Sandi had seduced me into doing something that I was neither prepared for nor capable of. It
was organic chemistry all over again. My therapeutic
mud bath had just morphed into a mudslide that threatened to drown me. But I had only myself and that
Chilean merlot to blame. Now, sober and tired from the
first days of the new semester, I resolved to extricate
myself from this doomed undertaking. I would chat
with the rabbi after the session was over. I had waited
over half a century to explore my roots. Surely they
would keep at least until I finished grad school.

But as the class continued, I had to admit that I was
enjoying myself. And when the rabbi explained that
the program extended over two years rather than over
the semester I was so used to measuring my life in, I
reconsidered my initial response. Surely with some
juggling, I could learn a little Hebrew, read five or six
books, and show up for a few services over a two-year
period. After all, according to my daughter Rebecca, I
was the mother of all multitaskers. And I'd completed
the coursework for grad school and turned in my dissertation proposal. If that was approved, all I had to do
was write my dissertation, and in the time-honored
tradition of doctoral students, the world's greatest pro-
crastinators, I'd do anything to avoid starting on that.
Besides, by keeping Sandi company in this undertaking, I was already doing a "new and regular" mitzvah.

Part of my pleasure derived from working with Rabbi Ornstein-Klein. I'd watched her in action when I'd made my annual appearance at synagogue on the high holidays and knew her to be a dynamic and learned speaker. She had also helped plan a meaningful memorial service for my dad. It evoked my mother's many happy memories and vanquished some of the ghosts that had plagued her after Dad's death while at the same time comforting my children and me. And while we collaborated on that ceremony, Rabbi Ornstein-Klein won my undying affection by never once suggesting that I increase my attendance at services, even to say Kaddish, the mourning prayer, for my dad. Unlike many rabbis, she did not believe that the path to God was paved with guilt. Rather, judging by her demanding syllabus, slave labor was her thing, but the extended time period rendered her high expectations reasonable.

Another thing that made me feel so good in the study group was that it was small. Besides Sandi and me, there were only three other women. Each of us was there for a highly individual reason, and yet all of us were there for the same reason. There was Mildred Kooper, a stocky forty-ish concert violinist whose serious demeanor was in keeping with her gray slacks and plain white shirt. She came from a family of secular Jews in a small town in Maine where there had been no other Jews. After a nearly fatal car accident had left her limping but still able to play and teach, Millie said she felt an urge to "claim my heritage." Janet Schecter was another member of our coterie. Pale, drawn, and extremely thin, Janet looked about fifty. She had worked as a nurse in the neurological intensive care unit of our local hospital for many years and when we met was still wearing her baggy hospital greens. During our introductory session she candidly explained that Rabbi Ornstein-Klein had counseled her into our study group in the hope that it would serve as an antidote for the burnout and depression that had plagued Janet lately. Actually, the way Janet put it was, "It's either kill myself or study Judaism." The grin she suddenly flashed as she said these words signaled to me that Rabbi Ornstein-Klein had been right. The medicine she had prescribed was working already.

Our third classmate was Ashley Solomon, a self-described "market analyst." Even if she hadn't told us she was in her mid-twenties, and so the "baby" of the class, her close-cropped black hair, seamless skin, and sculpted muscles screamed youth. And her taupe suede slacks, taupe silk blouse, taupe flats, and perfectly manicured taupe nails screamed princess. Sandi and I automatically exchanged the look, a glance we'd perfected years ago in response to debutantes wearing full-length raccoon coats over jeans. Our radar was rusty, though, because Ashley Solomon was of neither Jewish nor of royal descent. In her own softly spoken words, she was "born in Indiana to an alcoholic mother who was a lapsed Methodist and a dad who had simply lapsed." Ashley left home at seventeen after her mom died and worked her way east waiting on tables. She put herself through college, where she met her future husband, Howard Solomon. The young woman actually blushed when she spoke his name. Ashley converted to Judaism shortly before they married. Since she and Howard hoped to have children, Ashley wanted to continue her Jewish education so as to be a "perfect Jewish mother." Like many converts and unlike the rest of us, Ashley knew some Hebrew and was observant to a fault. She looked vaguely familiar, but I couldn't place her.

That's why I really hadn't been surprised when, at the end of the class, Ashley approached me and said, "You don't remember me, Professor Barrett, but years ago when I was young, I was in your Intro to Lit class. I was still a blond then, so that's why you don't recognize me. It was years before I married Howard. My name was Ashley Roberts." We chatted for a few minutes before I left with Sandi.

"She did look familiar," I remarked to Sandi near the end of a quick bowl of pasta at Cucina Roma later. "I run into my former students all over the place . . . at the supermarket, in the doctor's office, in line at the bank, in restaurants, everywhere. It really gets to Sol."

"It must feel good to be recognized and remembered so fondly. Ashley seemed pleased to see you. Maybe Sol's just jealous," Sandi speculated.

"No. Well, maybe, but not of the recognition. It's more that I spend so much time and energy at RECC that he sees my students popping up everywhere we go as a further intrusion of work into our life, an invasion of our privacy. In a way, he's right," I added.

"Well, is Ashley Solomon's appearance in our study group intrusive?" asked Sandi, signaling for the check.

"Funny you should ask," I said, taking a deep breath. "Yes, sort of. Actually, Ashley is one of the few students for whom I've ever refused to write a recommendation to a four-year college." I tried not to sound

pompous when I made this pronouncement, but I
wanted Sandi to understand that my refusal to tout
Ashley to another academic institution had been a
serious matter to me and, for that matter, to Ashley.
"She probably hates me," I added sourly.

"She sure didn't seem to," countered Sandi. "She
went out of her way to come over and say hello. She
even said you had been one of her favorite profs. Why
on earth wouldn't you write her a letter of recommendation? Wasn't she a good student? She seems so re-
sourceful and bright."

I had to remember that Sandi was a human resources
pro who ran seminars teaching managers the fine art of
evaluating employees. Naturally she'd be curious.
"Ashley is bright. She was actually one of the best students I've ever had," I said with an exasperated sigh.
The shortcomings of the very intelligent bothered me
more than those of the less intellectually gifted. After
all, if you've got it and you waste it or abuse it, at least
you're making some kind of choice. But if you never
had it, well . . .

"So . . . I guess she was lazy," Sandi suggested,
clearly eager to learn about our classmate.

"No, not at all. She worked hard," I answered, taking a perverse pleasure in withholding the details of
my relationship with Ashley.

"Jesus, Bel. This conversation is beginning to remind me of when I was off campus one night and that
dorm burned to the ground. Remember? Davison, I
think it was. The one in the quad right next to ours?
And when I got back, you took forty-five minutes to
tell me that somebody had plugged in an illegal elec-

tric coffee coil and left it on her bed while she took a phone call, and that had started the fire. What bugged you about Ashley? Tell me." Sandi was practically whining.

"I do like watching you get all red in the face," I joked. "Come on. I'll walk you to the PATH train and tell you on the way." We left the restaurant and set out in the direction of the subway to New York on the south end of Hoboken, joining the throngs of yuppies strolling from bar to bar or en route home from the gym or a late dinner in Manhattan. "Ashley wrote a paper for my Intro to Lit class in which she did a brilliant analysis of three poems by Emily Dickinson," I stated flatly, not unaware of how enigmatic I was still being.

"So? Is it a crime in New Jersey to be brilliant?" asked Sandi. Her lemon yellow pants and matching knit top made her look like a walking sunbeam, at odds with the darkly draped figures around us.

I ignored her slur against my home state for the time being. Sooner or later an opportunity to retaliate with an anti-California barb would present itself and I would strike. It was a familiar pattern. "No, but in my class it was a crime not to turn in drafts of the paper and go over them with me in conferences. That's how I give feedback and that's how they learn how to develop, support, and organize their ideas. That's also how they learn to revise and proofread—"

"Spare me. I've heard this rant from you before. So why wouldn't she do the drafts?" Sandy persisted, interrupting my lecture on the pedagogical importance of revising.

"As I recall, she was working and didn't have time to draft anything for me to go over. She just did her paper the night before." I shrugged my shoulders.

"Was it any good?" Sandi asked.

"Yes. That was the problem. Her analysis was so insightful and her writing was so sophisticated that I assumed she had plagiarized the paper. But I couldn't prove it. I spent hours checking all her sources, and I couldn't find a shred of evidence to support my hunch." I shrugged again.

"Was her normal writing so dismal? Was this paper a real departure from her usual work?" Sandi asked reasonably.

"No, not exactly. She was a good, clear writer. But this was really brilliant work and . . ." I hesitated. "I had always perceived Ashley as very competitive and also very low profile . . ." I hesitated again, wanting to find just the right word. "You know, kind of like Martha Gibbons, that girl from Ohio who lived in a single at the end of our hall sophomore year? Remember? The one you said should be in the CIA because of the way she always walked around indoors in a trench coat? The skinny one who always picked up our books to see what we were reading? You remember." Maybe if I insisted, I could browbeat Sandi into recalling what I wanted her to. "Martha Gibbons used to hang around in the dorm parlor on Saturday night so she could see what people's dates looked like." Sandi still looked blank. Rolling my eyes, I made one more attempt to guide my old friend down the long lane littered with our mutual memories. "Remember how Marty used to stand behind us when we played bridge? She didn't want to play, just to see what we were doing. Come on, you have to remember her." I felt like stamping my foot in frustration.

But finally Sandi rewarded my efforts to trigger her memory by grabbing my arm. "Of course. Marty Gibbons. I always wondered about her. She was just so curious about everything," Sandi exclaimed, and without even turning to look at her I could picture her shaking her head as we walked. "But why are we talking about Marty Gibbons?"

I had to chuckle. We could conjure up the details of our long lost salad days, but we sure had trouble remembering the last five minutes. Without belaboring the all too obvious effect of short-term memory loss on one's ability to carry on a lucid conversation, I said, "It's because Ashley Solomon reminds me of her. After every test, Ashley wanted to know how many other A's I had given. She was always peering over my shoulder at my grade book or asking other students to let her see their notes. And when I held in-class conferences at my desk, she sat up front pretending to read, but really, I thought she was eavesdropping. I never could understand why." I sighed and continued, resignation flattening my voice. "So when I read this insightful and original paper, I was not at all certain Ashley had authored it herself. See, if I keep track of a student's writing process over a couple of drafts and revisions, I know that there's no plagiarism involved. But . . ."

"Oh. I get it. Having students write drafts not only helps them improve their composition, but it also enables the prof to be reasonably certain the paper is original. Pretty shrewd," Sandi acknowledged. "So did you confront Ashley about the paper?"

"Of course I asked her about it, and of course she insisted she had written it, and when I checked all her sources, I couldn't prove she hadn't. As best I recall, I gave her a B+ on the paper because she hadn't fulfilled the requirement to submit the drafts and an A– in the course. But I still couldn't bring myself to recommend her. When she asked, I refused." I had rushed the last part of the story, not eager to relive what I still saw as one of the less satisfying episodes of my teaching career.

"Did you tell her why you refused?" Sandi was beginning to remind me of my son Mark when he was little, asking why and responding to each answer with another why.

"No, Sandi. I did not. We'd been over all that territory. I just told her that I had already committed myself to writing too many letters that term. I suggested that she ask one of her other profs." Sandi couldn't miss the impatience in my voice, but it hadn't put her off forty years ago, and it didn't even slow her down now.

"So is having her in our study group going to spoil the whole thing for you?" Bless her, Sandi sounded genuinely concerned.

I thought a moment before answering. "No. That was years ago. As I said, she's very bright and seems highly motivated to learn everything she can. It'll be fine."

"Do you think *she'll* stay in the group if you're in it?" Sandi persisted. Her question took me aback.

"You mean because I didn't write her the recommendation?" I asked, contemplating for the first time how *my* presence might be affecting Ashley.

"No, because you're a known chocoholic who would savage her own mother for a square of fudge. Of course I mean because you didn't write her the letter. Is your presence going to be a real downer for her?" Now it was Sandi's turn to sound exasperated.

"I couldn't tell you," I said. But when Ashley didn't show up for the next session, I feared it was because of me.

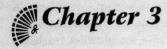 **Chapter 3**

To: Bbarrett@circle.com
From: Rbarrett@uwash.edu
Re: Oy vey
Date: 09/08/99 16:04:40

Mom,

Give me a break. I can't believe you're making time to go back to Hebrew school. Is this some sort of new menopausal thing? You've got an estrogen patch, so now you want a God patch or something like that? And Mark says you and Sandi are actually planning to have a bat mitzvah. I can see it now. All of us fly into Hoboken for the big event. We're sitting in the front row of the shul with Sandi's family while up on the bemah you and Sandi struggle to remember your Torah reading. You can't, so you bag it and just start reminiscing about college like you two always do whenever you get together. (By the way, I keep meaning to tell you. Everybody said the rendition of "Scotch and Soda" you guys performed in the parking lot after our wedding reception was . . . awesome. Keith and I heard all about your impromptu duet as soon as we got back from our honeymoon.) Seriously, it's cool that Sandi is in NY and everything, but you're so overextended now that if you actually do this, you'll collapse from exhaustion. Speaking of exhaustion, I gotta go feed your precious grandchild and pump out an extra bottle so I can leave for class as soon as Keith gets home. I'm working at the restaurant again tonight.

Shalom,
Rebecca

Rebecca's less than enthusiastic response to my belated attempt to acquire a meaningful Jewish education had not dampened my determination to do so. Besides, who was Rebecca, mothering a new baby, going to grad school, and waiting tables, to lecture *me* about being overextended? In fact, if anything, my daughter's cautionary tone honed my resolve to learn as much as I could and to enjoy the process. Graduate school had already taught me to appreciate being back on the other side of the desk in the role of the student with limited responsibilities and expectations. Compared to teaching at RECC, being a student anywhere was the proverbial piece of cake, and I loved it. What's more, I admired Rabbi Ornstein-Klein's structured and rigorous approach to our work. And I had resolved to appreciate the strengths of each of my new classmates, including Ashley.

That's why when Ashley didn't show up for the second session, I felt cheated as well as guilty. Rabbi OK, which is what we and other members of JCH's largely yuppie congregation dubbed her, said, "Well, we'd best begin. I don't know where Ashley is. She didn't call, and that's not like her. I worked with her as she prepared for her conversion, and she seldom missed a class. She must be ill. I'll phone her tonight." I made a private resolve to do the same, imagining that Ashley would rather risk her future as a Jewish mother than be in a study group with me, the bitch from hell who had been too busy to write her a letter of recommendation.

As soon as class was over, I got Ashley's number from Rabbi OK and called Ashley from my cell phone, leaving a message when she didn't answer. I wasn't exactly sure how I would phrase my concern, how I would reassure her that I posed no threat in our new context. Maybe I'd even apologize for my former suspicions. "How do you know she didn't show up because of you?" Sol asked after I updated him on the situation that night. "Maybe she had to work late. Maybe she's sick. Maybe her husband's sick. Why blame yourself? Your beef with her was years ago, and she's obviously gone on with her life. You said she finished her degree at St. Peter's. She has a good job, a guy who cares for her. Not having a letter of reference from Professor Bel Barrett didn't hold her back. And you said she actually seemed glad to see you." Sol, who'd enjoyed a really thorough Jewish education himself, had been enthusiastic about my participation in this group from the get-go. He didn't want some former student to prevent what he saw as my belated reunion with my birthright.

"Of course she was polite. What else could she do?" My voice was sharp. I was annoyed with Sol for not understanding the pivotal role community college faculty members play in our students' lives. We're mentors, role models, gatekeepers, surrogate parents, advocates, and friends. It's a huge responsibility. I had been hard on Ashley, maybe too hard. But now I had a chance to make amends and that would be a real mitzvah, another good deed. I was sure as hell going to try. I hoped she would return my call. When I heard the phone, I answered before the end of the first ring.

"Professor Barrett? It's Ashley Solomon. Can we talk? Can you meet me at Starbucks in about fifteen minutes? Please. It's important." The younger woman's voice was nasal and her words rushed out in spurts as if she were trying to swallow sobs.

"Okay. Sure. The downtown Starbucks, fifteen minutes. I'll be there." I shot Sol a triumphant look as I strapped on my sandals and grabbed my purse. "See. She's really upset. We're going to talk it out. I'll probably be about an hour," I called over my shoulder as I dashed out the door and began to stride rapidly toward the Starbucks four blocks away.

Even as I hurried, I had to marvel at the fact that in Hoboken, a town measuring only one square mile, there were now two Starbucks. Like many Hoboken buildings, the one housing Starbucks used to be something else. Once an ornate deco bank, it had recently been eviscerated and reborn as a branch of the ubiquitous Seattle coffee franchise. All over town, banks, churches, synagogues, stores, gin mills, row houses, and factories had metamorphosed into cafes, bistros, and, of course, condos. In fact, there was no edifice too grand or too humble to be considered as a candidate for a condo conversion. As I approached the downtown corner straddled by Starbucks, I refocused my thoughts on my relationship with Ashley, anticipating with some trepidation my contrite apology and the rewarding new bond that would result.

"Oh, Professor Barrett, I mean Bel, thanks for coming." Jolted at first by Ashley's use of my given name, I quickly recalled that we were no longer teacher and student, but peers studying together under the tutelage of Rabbi OK. In fact, when Ashley had addressed me as Professor Barrett during our tête-à-tête after our first session, I had reflexively suggested that she call me Bel. I sat down opposite her. "I needed to talk to somebody, and you were so sweet last time . . . When I got your message I remembered I could talk to you . . ." I put my hand on Ashley's arm to stem the rush of words, went up to the counter, and ordered us both herbal teas.

When I returned to the table carrying the tea, Ashley began speaking again before I could even set down the hot containers and reclaim my seat across from her. "It's Chris. Chris Johanson," she said. When she saw my features contort in confusion, she interrupted herself to explain, "My friend, my best friend really, even though he's a man." When this thumbnail sketch did not suffice to smooth my face into a facsimile of comprehension, Ashley began to cry quietly into her napkin. Then, straightening up, she looked across the table at me and said, "I'm sorry, but I just learned that Chris is dead. I had to talk to somebody. I can't believe it. We worked together for years. We had breakfast together at least twice a week, we shared office space, we talked about everything . . ."

While the young woman struggled to articulate the nature of her relationship with the late Chris Johanson, I struggled to regroup so as to participate in the conversation Ashley and I were actually having there in real time rather than the one we were still having in my head. This sad tête-à-tête was very different from the one I had left home, Sol, and unread student papers to have. Once again Sol had been right. Ashley's absence from the bat mitzvah study group earlier tonight had nothing whatsoever to do with whether I had or had not written her a letter of recommendation years ago. In fact, it had absolutely nothing to do with me at all. She hadn't shown up because she was grieving for her friend. But Ashley *had* returned my call, so I still had the chance to do a mitzvah, to listen and try to help her come to terms with the loss of that friend. "You weren't the star of the show, but you could still play a supporting role," was how Sol would put it an hour later when I finally got home and told him that Ashley had needed a shoulder to cry on and my number had been on her machine.

Meanwhile Ashley was saying, "I just came from his house, from seeing Norma, his wife. She's devastated. Where he was working they have an indoor rock climbing wall." Ashley said this matter-of-factly, as if having a rock climbing wall in one's office were no different from having a water cooler or a Xerox machine. "He slipped while he was rock climbing with the CEO there and fell. Broke his neck. DOA. Never even knew what happened, the doctor told her." Ashley stopped talking and played with the tea bag still soaking in her untouched paper cup. For a moment I felt numbed by the sight of this slender young woman across from me. It seemed as if I had spent years of my life sitting across tables from distraught people—students, friends, relatives—all sobbing over something or someone. What was I, a one-woman hotline? A millennial midlife Miss Lonely Hearts? Then I flashed on all the friends who had listened to my sad stories over the years and felt ashamed of my momentary resentment. Comforting Ashley was, after all, a mitzvah, and I should be grateful to have the chance to perform it. The mitzvah concept had my name on it.

I reached across the table and patted Ashley's arm again. It was as if I had signaled her to continue. "You know, the work Chris and I do . . . did . . ." Ashley bit her lip as she corrected her verb tense.

"No. Actually, I'm not at all clear on what you do, Ashley," I said gently. "I've been meaning to ask you what a market analyst does."

Ashley ran the fingers of both hands through her hair and kept her hands on the back of her lowered head for a moment. Looking up, she sighed and said, "The short answer is that what we do is like troubleshooting but undercover. I'll give you the specifics another time. What's important to understand is that the work is high stress. It's a little like being in the army. You can get real close to the people in the trenches with you. Over the years I realized that Chris was somebody I could vent to, confide in, joke around with. He felt the same way about me."

Ashley paused. I patted her arm again. On cue, she resumed her monologue. "I think some people in the office thought Chris and I were, you know, hooked up.

But we were both happily married. He adored Norma. He wanted to have kids. And Howard and me, we're really solid. But it's funny. In some ways, even though we never had sex, Chris and I were closer than a lot of married people. We were really tight . . . It's hard to explain, hard to talk about, even with Howard or Rabbi OK. That's why as soon as I heard your message, I returned your call. I knew you'd understand. You were amazing at RECC. I always sat up front, so I couldn't help overhearing your conferences. You always listened to everybody's problems, no matter how weird. That's the one thing I remember most about you." Her voice faded.

By the time Ashley and I left Starbucks, she had promised to discuss her loss with Rabbi OK and had agreed to let me call her a cab so she wouldn't have to walk across town alone. I used the short walk home to contemplate the vagaries of a world in which one person remembers a letter not written and the other recalls a woman who lent a nonjudgmental ear.

When I explained to Sol what Ashley and I had talked about, I had to marvel at his discretion. He did not say, "I told you so." What he finally did say as he put his arm around my shoulder and pulled me to him was, "It's late. You're tired. Come to bed. There are never any former students there."

 **Chapter 4**

Class Notes

One of our "lost" classmates Bel (Sybil Bickoff) Bar-
rett has finally turned up in a note from Sandi (Hal-
prin) Golden, her VC roommate. Sandi reports, "Bel is
living in Hoboken, NJ, with partner Sol Hecht, teach-
ing English at River Edge Community College in Jer-
sey City, and working toward a Ph.D. in English Ed at
Eleanor Roosevelt U. I shared an umbrella with class-
mates Hillary (Smythe) Dupres and Trish Walker at the
Seattle wedding of Bel's daughter Rebecca and Keith
Roche last January." Sandi herself has left her beloved
Berkeley Hills (remember, it was Sandi who taught
many of us Easterners that not all good wine was
French) and taken a leave of absence from Kirkland,
Inc., to spend a year in Manhattan and join Bel on a
"quest for the meaning of our Jewish heritage and its
place in our lives as millennial midlife women. Bel and
I are preparing for adult bat mitzvahs." Welcome to the

Big Apple, Sandi, and please invite your class corre-
spondent when you and Bel celebrate your coming of
age.

By the time I saw the piece in the *Vassar Quarterly,*
the high holidays had come and gone. On the eve of
Yom Kippur, the Day of Atonement when Jews everywhere reflect on their behavior and ask forgiveness of
God and the rest of us, Sandi joined Sol, Ma, and me
for a preholiday meal. Then, sated and fortified against
the twenty-five-hour fast that tradition demands and
that none of us expected to complete, we made our annual pilgrimage just a few blocks down the street to the
Jewish Community of Hoboken. We entered the lovely
old white stone building whose minarets set it apart
from the row houses on the block and climbed the
stairs to the sanctuary. "This is a charming old shul,"
Sandi whispered.

Sol nodded and said, "You know, there used to be
five Jewish congregations in Hoboken in the forties
and fifties. Gradually though, like lots of other groups,
the Jews migrated to the suburbs."

They sure did, I thought, recalling the Jewish Community of Hoboken as it had been in the seventies
when Lenny and the kids and I moved to town. I remembered a drizzly March afternoon when Rebecca
came home from second grade and asked, "Mommy,
can I go to catechism with Maria? She invited me.
Please." The same unexamined atavistic urge that had
led unbelieving and nonobservant me to opt for a Jewish roommate and a Jewish husband suddenly electri-
fied me. My fingers flew through the Yellow Pages,

and that very evening I had brought Rebecca here for the first time. We joined a dozen elderly congregants to listen to the rabbi read the Scroll of Esther, for it was Purim. Neither of us understood a word of the reading, which details the story of how the Jewess Queen Esther saved her people from death at the hand of the wicked Persian prelate Haman. At every mention of Haman's name, the congregation rattled noisemakers to drown out the odious syllables. Rebecca got into the spirit of this pretty quickly, and so began her life as a Jew.

The old guard saw us, correctly, as the first of the tidal wave of newcomers who would, depending on one's perspective, improve or destroy their town and their synagogue. For in the ensuing twenty years, the congregation had mirrored the gentrification of Hoboken, growing younger and more affluent, and exchanging the liturgy and rituals of Orthodox Judaism for those of the conservative movement. Before I had a chance to wax nostalgic over Rebecca's bat mitzvah, Ma's elbow in my ribs jolted me back to the present. It was time to stand as the cantor prepared to chant the Kol Nidre, a beautiful and solemn song of praise. While I listened, put off by the Hebrew words but drawn in by the haunting melody, I caught a glimpse of Ashley. For the duration of the service, I focused on asking her for forgiveness for what I still saw as my abuse of power years ago.

There was plenty of opportunity for me to do that since I was now seeing Ashley on a regular basis. The study group had agreed to change our meeting day and times to early Sunday afternoons. Even Janet had been able to use her seniority at the hospital to assure that she would not be working every second Sunday. After our third session, I had suggested that we all go out for a late lunch, but Millie and Janet had made other plans. However, even though she kept kosher and probably wouldn't eat anything, Ashley seemed glad to join Sandi and me. Since black clouds overhead threatened a deluge, we walked quickly to the new Indian bistro on Washington Street. Soon Sandi and I were relishing tandoori chicken and some marvelously spicy vegetables. I decided to take a break from the chat we were having about the resurgences of paganism and goddess worship in biblical times and the neo paganism of today's wiccans to ask Ashley, "So tell us, what exactly does a market analyst do?"

"That's a kind of code for 'competitive intelligence professional.' That's what I really am. That's what Chris was too." Ashely's face darkened as it always did when something reminded her of her friend. "Just don't spread it around," Ashley said with a tired sigh.

"So you're a silicon spy, right? For e-media.com?" Sandi asked, naming the hottest dot com company to locate in Jersey City's Silicon Slum, a reduced-rent spinoff from Manhattan's Silicon Alley. The area was a run-down former industrial site that was supposed to have been rezoned to accommodate live-in studios for artists and, in the process, had acquired considerable cachet. But the process had dragged on, and e-media.com and other new high-tech startups had jumped on the large low-rent spaces. The five-square-block zone had probably earned its "slum" status simply because it was in New Jersey. Apparently, being a cyber-savvy, dot com techno nerd billionaire didn't preclude New Jersey bashing. e-media.com was fast becoming Silicon Slum's Netscape, with a converted warehouse "campus" rumored to be an urban version of the software giant's Silicon Valley home.

Ashley nodded. Then, ignoring my dropped jaw and furrowed brow, she added, "What Chris and I did, what I still do, is research rival companies."

I recalled Ashley's stellar research ability and also my long ago impression of her as competitive and extremely curious. "Uh, how do you mean 'research'?" I asked, sipping my mango lassi.

"Well, we eavesdrop, we wheedle, we observe, we sometimes go undercover, as temps usually, or we might even go so far as to pay somebody else, like a consultant you could say, to get friendly with our target and then get him or her to talk." Responding, no doubt, to the look of incredulity on my face, Ashley continued, "Seriously, you'd be surprised what people will tell you. You just have to get the right targets, secretaries, techies, mailroom types, sales reps, anybody really. Sometimes I just get them to brag or to complain and next thing you know, they're giving me all kinds of useful information," Ashley said with a touch of pride as if she were describing a successful career in sales or engineering. I continued to stare at her with the blend of horror and fascination I generally reserve for jars containing coiled cobras.

"What's a nice Jewish girl like you doing in a job like that?" I heard the words and felt them leave my lips. Oops. I hadn't meant to disparage the younger woman's career choice, or, for that matter, question her commitment to her new religion, but damn it, I really *was* curious now.

"I'm good at it and I don't do anything illegal, Bel," Ashley said simply, although a bit defensively, responding no doubt to the criticism embedded in my flip query. "And I like the rush," she added softly.

When I looked perplexed, Ashley elaborated. "The adrenaline rush. It's risky. It's exciting. And, of course," she added with lowered eyes, "it pays extremely well. Howard and I want to have a baby before too much longer, so I need to maximize my earnings now."

Sandi was nodding, not appearing the least shocked by Ashley's revelations. I guess in human resources you get used to people doing things you were raised to think of as unethical if not downright sleazy. So Sandi was all ears when, turning to look at her, Ashley continued. "As a matter of fact, Sandi, are you serious about finding work in New York?"

Sandi had mentioned at our very first study group meeting that she had initiated a rather low-key job search by putting out a few tentative feelers to professional contacts in Manhattan. She nodded again. "Yes. I'm settled in now, and I have a mess of bills to pay. Of course I am." Sandi made no mention of the substantial trust fund left to her as a child by her grandfather. She had never lived on it, but rather used it as a cushion. That was the cushion that had enabled her to take an indefinite leave of absence from her job at Kirkland and from the executive paycheck that went with it.

"Are you dead set on working at another HMO or would you consider a different setting?" I heard Ash-

ley asking, as she continued to make eye contact with
Sandi.

"I'd actually enjoy a change. Hiring and firing health
care bureaucrats can get to be a drag. Why this sudden
interest in *my* career?" Sandi asked.

"At work the other day at a trade show, I, uh, heard
about an opening for an experienced HR person at
Classic Media. It hasn't been posted yet. Probably
won't be. But here's the name of the dude you should
contact." Ashley handed Sandi a piece of paper, which
Sandi filed somewhere in the recesses of her large
shoulder bag. I couldn't help but appreciate Ashley's
willingness and ability to help Sandi.

Then Sandi placed a few bills in my hand to cover
her lunch and stood, saying, "Well, thanks, Ashley. I'll
let you know what happens. I've got to take the train
back to Manhattan now. A neighbor of mine is joining
me for dinner, so I have to do a little shopping and,
yikes, a little cooking. Ciao!" Sandi made the kind of
face women our age generally make when someone
mentions the "C" word, blew me an air kiss, and left the
restaurant, her peach skirt bright beneath the denim
jacket that she pulled over her head, slight shelter from
the driving rain that had begun to fall shortly after we
sat down.

As Ashley and I waited for the check, she grew
quiet. I assumed she was contemplating the ethical and
moral quandaries posed by her work. So I wasn't
caught completely off guard when she looked up at me
and said, "Bel, I'm sorry, but I really need to unload on
you again. I'm in big trouble." Just then the waitress
brought our bill, and, as if by agreement, Ashley and I

let it sit on the table. I waited, making my silence an invitation for Ashley to speak.

"You know, Bel, my friend Chris was very, very good at what he did." Again Ashley hesitated, chewing on her lower lip. When she resumed talking, I had to lean across the table to catch her whispered words. "He was also a very good rock climber. The dude used to teach that stuff. He won awards." Again she hesitated. Again she gnawed on her lower lip. Finally she resumed her sotto voce soliloquy. "I think somebody blew Chris's cover. And then the target, the one he got something out of . . ." This time before she went on Ashley attacked her lower lip until I feared it would bleed. "What I think happened is the target realized he had given away the store and stood to lose everything when Chris reported in, so he killed Chris before Chris, you know, came home."

Ashley's narrative of *The Spy Who Came in from the Cold* meets Outward Bound had rendered me momentarily speechless. But it had not rendered me senseless. I intuited that there was more to come, and I had a familiar knot in my gut. Or was it a rush of adrenaline? This time I knew exactly where the conversation was leading. I kept quiet, waiting. "Bel, I've been assigned Chris's old territory at scoop.com. That's where he was working when he died. What if . . ." The thought that would have completed her sentence remained unarticulated. Now I was sure of what was coming next. I waited again. "Bel, I need your help. My friend Cynthia Nugent adjuncts in marketing at RECC, and she told me a while ago that you've got quite a reputation for helping people in fixes like this. I've been assigned

Chris's old territory to finish what he started. I need you to help me finger Chris's killer before he kills me too. I need evidence to take to the police. If I go to them without any proof, I'll lose my job and gain nothing. And right now I have nothing to go on, but I just know I'm right. Will you help me this time? Or are you still too busy?" So there it was. I had seen her request for help coming, but I was totally blindsided by the bitter zinger she threw in as a coda. I had been right all along. Ashley hadn't forgotten the unwritten letter of recommendation any more than I had. She was still hurt and had just saved it for a rainy day. And it was pouring now.

# Chapter 5

To: Professor Bel Barrett, Department of English and Humanities
From: Dr. Ron Woodman, President, River Edge Community College
Re: Committee to Review Aims and Priorities
Date: 09/20/99

Congratulations, Professor Barrett! As you no doubt recall from my April memo to faculty and staff, one of the major outcomes of the RECC Board of Trustees' spring retreat was the establishment of the Committee to Review Aims and Priorities to reconsider our mission statement in anticipation of preparing the self-study document necessary for our next visit from the state accrediting agency. Charged with selecting an effective chair for this crucial committee and reluctant to add to the burden of our already overcommitted administrative staff, I have decided to honor you with this opportunity to serve the institution we love so well. I know you will do your usual admirable job. I am attaching a list of those members of the RECC community who have been recruited to serve with you on this important committee. Please convene the group at your earliest convenience, so that you are prepared to report to the board before their winter retreat.

When I found this memo from hell in my mailbox at RECC the next day, I was so furious that for a few minutes I forgot all about Ashley's disturbing story and her even more disturbing request. Even the initials ER at the bottom accompanied by a smiley face did not do much to quell my rage.

Elizabeth Ramsey, executive assistant to RECC's president, happens to be one of my closest friends. She had undoubtedly had a chuckle when she initialed this missive from on high, knowing how I would explode at being told, not even asked, to chair yet another dumb-ass committee. I picked up the phone and dialed the president's office. "Betty!" I practically screamed as I heard her businesslike voice on the end of the line. "How could you let him do this to me? 'Overcommitted administrative staff'? Are you serious? How could you let this death threat get out of the office? Everyone on the faculty calls this the CRAP Committee and not just because it's an acronym either. Is there a conspiracy afoot to drive me to early retirement?"

"Of course, Professor Barrett," said Betty in that superprofessional don't-mess-with-me voice she uses at work. "I'll be happy to tell the president you have to think about accepting his offer. Or would you like to speak with him about it now? He's right here. Oh, you have a class? Of course, I'll see that he gets the message."

"You do that. Meanwhile, can you get together with Illuminada and me at my house tonight for take-out?

It's important." I spoke quickly, knowing that in the presidential shadow, Betty would be brief. "I'm calling her now."

"Yes, of course, Professor Barrett. I'll do that. And you have a great day too." Then she hung up.

Illuminada Gutierrez, private investigator and adjunct in criminal justice at RECC, was already there when Betty arrived at my house that evening. Years ago the three of us had connected to figure out who killed Ron Woodman's predecessor, Dr. Altagracia Garcia, RECC's first and only woman president, and we just never disconnected. Like Sandi, Betty and Illuminada had moved into a privileged area of my emotional landscape reserved for certain women friends, and like Sandi, they were stuck there, specially selected and forever special, the sisters I never had.

Illuminada was perched on a stool at our sink island, scratching the head of my black cat, Virginia Woolf, with one delicate, well-manicured hand and holding her cell phone with the other. She had been talking to someone in rapid Spanish when she rang the doorbell, so I hadn't even greeted her myself yet. Illuminada's thriving PI agency did business throughout the tri-state area now, and her husband, Raoul, joked that he had forbidden her to bring her cell phone to bed. Betty was livid as usual when she stormed in. "Damn it, girl, when are you going to move someplace civilized? I've been circling this town for half an hour trying to park," she exclaimed. In Hoboken, people measured their lives in how long it took to find a parking space and, for this reason, inviting over out-of-towners really tested relationships.

"Serves you right," I said, giving her a hug and offering her a handful of take-out menus to look over, an activity the three of us had refined to a science during many evenings of dialing for dinner, "letting that fool try to manipulate me into chairing that dead-end deadhead committee. I don't think so. No way, Betty. Not. As in it's not going to happen."

"I am sorry about that. I had nothing to do with it, though, believe me. I didn't even see it until Gina had typed it. I just initialed it. So how are you going to get out of it?" Betty had scanned the fistful of menus and selected one from a local Mexican place. I stuck it under Illuminada's nose and she absently nodded her okay. I checked off each of our favorite dishes, phoned the restaurant, and sat down with Betty to wait for Illuminada to finish her conversation and for the food to arrive.

"I'm not telling you, but you better believe that I *am* getting out of it. Twenty years ago I'd have been flattered to be asked to chair that committee, and I'd have done it. Fifteen years ago I'd have felt guilty about refusing, so I'd have chaired it. Ten years ago, after we finally got tenure here, I'd have said no to the chair but offered to serve and ended up doing all the work anyway. But not anymore, you'll see. I've got a foolproof memo going in the mail on Monday. He'll buy it. He'll have to." Even though I was tired, the thought of my brilliant ploy exhilarated me. Betty was practically twitching with curiosity. "Listen, I know your inner control freak must be going crazy, but you'll enjoy it more if you just come across my memo when you preview your boss's incoming mail on Monday. I wouldn't want to spoil your pleasure."

"Okay. I don't have the energy to argue with you anyway. Long day," Betty sighed as she kicked off her shoes and collapsed onto the couch across from me, putting her feet up and resting her head on the sofa's arm so her dreads flopped over the side. From a similar position on the other end of the couch all I could see was her chin.

"*Dios mio,* is this the morgue or what?" exclaimed Illuminada, stepping out of her pumps and plopping down in the easy chair across from the coffee table.

"No, Illuminada, we just got bored listening to you *habla*-ing *español* a mile a minute, so we decided to have a little night-night," Betty said, sitting up and tickling my feet. I too pulled myself up, saying, "Mexican goodies are on the way. Meanwhile, can I interest either of you in a beer or a soft drink?" The question was really rhetorical, so nobody answered it. I went into the kitchen, grabbed three Coronas, and handed them around.

"So Bel, what's going on? I haven't heard a word from you since school started and then all of a sudden, I get this call. When I called back I got Sol who said something about your having a bar mitzvah?"

Illuminada's last sentence was a question, not a statement, but before I got a chance to answer it, Betty spoke for me, one of her less endearing habits. "She can't have a bar mitzvah, she's a girl! And not only that, she's allergic to religion."

Illuminada and Betty had met Sandi at Rebecca's wedding, so they were interested in hearing about her. By the time I had recapped the story of Sandi's arrival on the East Coast and her request and explained what

I knew about adult bat mitzvahs, we had worked our
way through several quesadillas and burritos. "Girl,
I'm happy for you, seriously. It's time you did something about your faith. I'm all for it. It's worth the time
and energy. You'll see. Now you'll have something nobody can take away from you." Betty spoke from her
heart and her own deep belief, I knew. A devout
churchgoing Catholic, she found my secular humanistic Judaism incomprehensible. I used to tease her that
the only reason she believed in God was that if she
couldn't run the world herself, He might as well do it.
Betty was so devout that she just could not accept the
fact that I could be Jewish and yet be nonobservant
and, worse yet, nonbelieving. It was bad enough I
didn't accept the divinity of Christ or the Holy Trinity
as she did, but to reject even the God of my own faith
and yet to profess to be part of that faith was beyond
her. She had expressed her views on this subject often,
and lately, having failed to win me over, she reiterated
them with sadness.

"*Caramba*, Bel! Are you crazy? You know you don't
buy into that stuff and I know it too, so what's going
on? And don't give me the good deed argument either.
You do more good deeds than most religious people.
Listen to me, Bel. Take your friend Sandi to a spa, go
shopping with her, give her a party, but don't take on
another course. That's what this will be like, another
grad school course. Do you really have time for that?
You could study until Bush ends the Cuban embargo,
but you still won't believe in God, so what are you
trying to prove? Did your estrogen patch fall off in
the shower again, or what?" Illuminada weighed in as

expected. Her mother's blend of pious Catholicism
spiced with Santeria had left Illuminada with little but
contempt for religious belief of any kind. Like me, Illuminada thought that a combination of luck, human
effort, and nature was the primal cause of everything.
A firm belief in the healing power of chocolate was the
closest I got to faith in the supernatural, and Illuminada, whose consuming passion was popcorn, didn't
even buy into that.

"Your mother must be delighted. Are you doing this
for Sadie? Is that it?" It was Illuminada again, projecting her own mother's script onto my mom in her effort
to understand.

"No. Sadie still thinks that if we give our real last
name to a restaurant, we won't get a reservation.
Sadie wanted me to be American first, Jewish second. She thought it was enough to send me to Sunday school. She didn't say much when I told her
about my bat mitzvah. I think she's a believer, but
she doesn't know it. I think all gamblers are. When
she throws the dice or plays the slots, she talks to
God. That's the only time I've ever heard my mother
pray," I replied, getting up to put on some decaf and
water for tea. I didn't mention my father's stance.
Also nonobservant, he had spoken Yiddish and, before they moved south, had played gin with a group
of other Marxist Jewish men who enjoyed talking
politics, listening to jazz, and eating kosher salami.
They called themselves Altecockers Anonymous. He
teased my mother about what he called her desire to
be like the goyim.

"Well, let us know the date, so we can come. I've

never been to a bat mitzvah," said Betty, ignoring Illuminada's outburst and my response.

"Me too, I wouldn't want to miss this. Will there be
a big party?" Illuminada's sarcasm was somewhat mit-
igated by her grin. I could tell she was having trouble
absorbing the fact that taking a course in Judaism was
not the same thing as believing in God, any more than
taking sex education was the same thing as having sex.
"So did you really invite us over here to tell us that you
are being born again as a thirteen-year-old?" Illuminada asked now, with an unmistakable edge to her
voice that was only partially softened by her grin this
time. "I don't think so."

I poured the hot beverages and brought out a plate of
brownies. As I took off the Saran Wrap, Illuminada
said, "*Dios mio!* Now I'm really worried. First you're
getting religion and now you're baking. Or am I hallu-
cinating these brownies?"

"Sadie made them, right?" Betty asked, helping herself and passing the plate.

"You got it." My mother's brownies had to be the result of alchemy, they were that good. The combination
of dark chocolate and the company of my friends was
practically a religious experience, and I felt fortunate
to have both. Inspired by my blessings, I resolved to
discuss Ashley's request before I allowed myself a second brownie. I took a deep breath and began. "There's
a former student of mine in our bat mitzvah study
group . . ."

Finally, my story over and my hand already reaching for the brownie I had promised myself, I said, "So
I think I want to take this on but I need your help."

"But just explain to us why you want to get involved with this. Ashley sounds like she's used to taking care of herself. Why do you want to help her? That part was a little vague," said Betty, who, to her credit, had listened to my lengthy explication without interrupting.

"That's what Sol asked me," I answered. "He says I'm doing it because I see myself as personally responsible for enforcing the commandment 'Thou shalt not kill,' but that's really not where I'm coming from, and he knows it. He just likes to yank my chain. It's hard to explain. Ashley's right. I do owe her something. As far as I know, she wrote every clever word of that paper, and the only reason I didn't write her the letter was that she didn't write the drafts. It was more like a power struggle, a control thing. That's not right. I can see now that she was just another working student with too little time and too many responsibilities. I can see now how good-hearted she is. She's all broken up over her friend. She's helping Sandi to find work. She's offered to help all of us with our Hebrew. And also," I hesitated here, anticipating an argument, and trying to phrase my thought in the strongest possible way, "it would be a mitzvah to do something just because it needs to be done. I may never believe in God, but doing mitzvahs is a part of my responsibility as a Jew. It always has been."

They could see that I was nearly in tears when I finished, so Illuminada didn't make any smartass comments. They both knew that the postmenopausal me was as lachrymose as an infant, weeping my way through cell phone commercials, graduations, parades, weddings, and now, it seemed, through my revived religious identification. In the silence that greeted my speech, I added, "Besides, if I refuse to help her and something happens to that young woman, I'll never forgive myself."

"Amen," intoned Betty. Illuminada rolled her eyes.

done is depriving others of the opportunity to do the amount of committee work necessary to be considered favorably by the Tenure Review Committee. I have even heard it bruited about that some of these individuals perceive themselves to be victims of gender bias and are considering consulting with the attorney for the RECC Professional Association. Of course, these are all rumors, but in the interests of serving "the institution we love so well," I pass them on to you in confidence, certain that you will use your customary sensitivity and judgment when, and if, you act on them.

Betty was the first to arrive in my office where I had asked her and Illuminada to meet me for a very brief strategy session. She practically flew in the door, dreads streaming behind her like a fringed flag, and collapsed on Wendy's chair, guffawing. "You really are something else, girl. What did you put in that memo anyway? I saw you had marked it confidential on the envelope, so I just put it with Woodman's other mail and stood around while he opened it. After he read it, his whole body stiffened, and he turned whiter than usual and ripped it up into tiny strips. I swear, he went at that piece of paper as if he was a human shredder! Then right away he asked for a list of faculty up for tenure this year. When I gave it to him, he scanned it, picked up the phone himself, mind you, and called Fatwah Fatal. Woodman more or less told poor Fatwah he was chairing the CRAP Committee." Dr. Fatwah Fatal, associate professor of physics, is RECC's resident Einstein. During the four years he had graced the RECC faculty with his learned presence I'd never seen him at a single committee meeting.

"Good! Serves him right." I chuckled. "I believe in sharing the wealth."

"So what did you say? How did you do it?" Betty was still smiling.

"I just mentioned the magic word *attorney,* that's all. You know Woodman would burn down the college to avoid any more litigation. After the last three lawsuits, our leader has developed a real phobia about the legal profession, and I can't say I blame him." When Betty flashed me a thumbs-up in appreciation of my ploy, I returned the salute.

Illuminada found us in this conspiratorial mode when she arrived looking uncharacteristically frazzled. Her lipstick was a faint blur, as if she had not bothered to reapply it after lunch, and her hair, which lately she had been wearing in a sleek black blunt cut, was matted behind her ears. Her gray silk shirt was rumpled above the waist of her skirt and her eyes were red. I'd never known Illuminada to cry, so I was instantly alarmed. Betty snuck a glance at me, and I could tell she shared my concern. We didn't have to wait long for an explanation. "Before we even talk about this Ashley business, just let me sound off for two minutes." Illuminada ran her fingers through her hair in a nervous gesture that was new to her and explained the way her hair looked. Betty and I exchanged glances again. "*Como mierda,* it's Lourdes. She's dropped out of school." Illuminada's voice was somewhere between a scream and a sob. "Can you believe that? My daughter, the most driven, hardworking, straight-A student a mother could ask for, has just walked out of Rutgers School of Pharmacy in the middle of the semester."

Betty and I again exchanged glances, and this time our looks conveyed relief. "Jesus, Illuminada, when you mentioned Lourdes's name, we both feared the worst," I said.

"Yeah," Betty echoed. "You know, the good stuff. Illness, drug addiction, a car or plane accident, mugging, rape, pregnancy, or maybe arrest." Betty ticked off these parental plagues on her fingers as she cited them.

"Or all of the above. Or the kid could have been taken hostage by terrorists or become a terrorist," I added, trying to put Lourdes's behavior into perspective. "You know, we thought you were dealing with something really awful."

"Yeah, something, you know, cosmic. We were afraid something had happened that would leave the poor kid scarred, traumatized, maimed, or, in a worst-case scenario, dead," Betty explained.

"*Caramba!* When I get through with her, she'll be scarred and traumatized," exclaimed Illuminada. "Maimed too."

"Cool it, girl. Like you once told Bel, dropping out of school falls somewhere between normal and nuisance on the list of parental worries. I'm quoting you," said Betty.

"Yeah. Think about Mark. Not to mention Rebecca," I chimed in. "My precious baby boy dropped out of undergraduate school three times before he finally finished. Now it looks as if he's approaching grad school on the same timetable. And you know he travels a lot, but only in countries where terrorism is the national sport." I paused for breath. "Then there's *my* daughter.

Rebecca wrote the book on maternity bridal wear and shotgun wedding protocol. Now she's waiting tables and breast pumping her way through grad school. Give me a break, Illuminada."

"Yeah, and while you're at it, look at Randy. How many cars has he totaled? Do you think I wanted to become an authority on emergency room medicine all over the damn East Coast?" Betty looked sharply at Illuminada as she posed that highly rhetorical question.

Now that Betty and I had put Illuminada's crisis in context, I moved the conversation back to Lourdes. "Let's face it, the only thing Lourdes, a paragon of overachievement, ever did that upset you was date a Filipino boy. And you were just bothered then because your mother was. As I recall, Milagros got over that eventually."

"Lourdes can always go back to school." Betty, ever the pragmatist, steered the conversation from the anecdotal to the practical. "What's she going to do? Did she say?"

"She's got a job. Tending bar. Can you believe that? From pharmacy school to bartending." Illuminada looked a little less distraught now. Contemplating the exploits of Randy, Mark, and Rebecca had obviously enabled her to see Lourdes's defection from the chem labs of academe in a slightly less desperate light. "She's working in Jersey City, near Silicon Slum as a matter of fact, at some fancy new place."

"Where's she planning to live?" I queried, knowing the answer.

"She's got an apartment in downtown Jersey City with three friends." It seemed sometimes as if everybody's kid had an apartment in Brooklyn or downtown Jersey City with three friends. "She had this all set up," Illuminada went on. "Can you imagine how that's going to sit with my mother? *Como mierda!*" Illuminada brushed back her hair again, the prospect of her mother's reaction to Lourdes's treason upsetting her further. "Raoul says she has to pay back every cent of this semester's tuition, so she'll have to mix a lot of drinks. I guess that's the accountant in him," Illuminada said, finally smiling a little at the thought of her handsome husband, who had insisted that she herself get a college education years ago. "He's taking this better than I am."

I knew Illuminada was over the worst of it when she glanced at her watch, an action that, in recent years, had become almost a reflex. Her booming investigative business and her class at RECC kept her on the run. "*Dios mio,* it's almost time for my class. Stay tuned for the next chapter." Illuminada allowed herself one final sigh and then said in her usual matter-of-fact tone, "But I know you didn't invite me here to share my little daytime drama with you. What's up, Bel?" As she spoke, Illuminada whipped a small green suede cosmetic kit from her purse and began effecting a makeover before our very eyes.

"It's just that I've got an appointment with Ashley Solomon later tonight, and I wanted to run by you what I'm going to tell her," I said, pausing for a moment.

Betty jumped in, saying, "You're going to tell her that you'll try to help her to gather evidence."

"I couldn't have put it better myself, even if you had let me," I said sweetly to Betty. "Yes. I'm going to tell her that all I want to do at first is talk to the players involved under some pretext or other. We can take it from there."

"And you're going to tell her that you have two dynamite partners who'll help." Betty was pushing her luck.

"Yes, dear," I said in my best imitation of resigned compliance.

"No. Don't say anything about us to her," Illuminada chimed in sharply while running a comb through her hair so that it fell at once into the familiar jet black wings that framed her face when she was not dealing with a family crisis. "I know you think she's an angel, but you've such a bias about all your former students, especially when you're feeling guilty about how you treated them." Illuminada stood and adjusted her blouse with a quick wiggle and a tug, gathered her books and jacket, and opened the door. She was herself again, poised and soigné, a far cry from the morose mom who had entered just a few minutes ago. "The less she knows about us the better." Then she arched her dark eyebrows, cocked her head, and said, "We're your secret weapon."

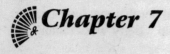# Chapter 7

To: Bbarrett@circle.com
From: Sandig@calgal.com
Re: The hand of God
Date: 09/27/99 08:23:34

Hi Bel!

Guess what! I got the job! I'm employed again, running HR at Classic Media, where the chances of my meeting a buttoned-down, middle-aged, single Jewish male are less than nil. Both interviews went very well (obviously). (Okay, I did wear a slate gray suit, but just for the first interview.) I start Monday. Please send me Ashley's e-mail address so I can thank her for the lead. It was so sweet of her to pass it on to me. Just think, if we hadn't joined the study group, I'd never have met her, and I'd still be pounding the pavement. From Ashley's mouth to God's ears. See you Sunday.

Love,
Sandi

Of course, Ashley's hotline to God was only partially responsible for Sandi getting hired. Sandi was a damn good HR person and had never been out of work for long. But I didn't have much time to reflect on the reasons for her success. After my last class of the day, I was scheduled to meet Ashley and give her my answer. I had suggested we meet at her office so I could check out the place and the people.

When I arrived, the switchboard operator paged Ashley, who looked drawn and red-eyed. Nevertheless, she greeted me with an attempt at a smile. "Bel, meet Cindy, our temp. She's filling in today for our receptionist. Cindy, please give my guest a visitor's pass," Ashley said. In return for my driver's license, Cindy handed me a laminated card that Ashley clipped to my collar. Then she led me through the looking glass.

e-media.com was unlike any workplace I'd ever seen. My first thought was that I'd wandered into a preschool during time-out. A second look made me think I was a fly on the wall at an NBA practice session on a bad day. In one corner of the huge loft space in the converted warehouse were rows of cubicles in which I could see several young people in jeans and T-shirts staring at computer screens. "That's the cube farm. It's full of Dilbert boxes," Ashley said, waving her arm in the direction of the cubicles. As we passed, one ponytailed young man tossed a teddy bear into a trash basket. Then he stood, stretched, walked over to retrieve it, and repeated the entire sequence. Another sauntered over to a large fridge and extracted a beverage and an apple, went back to his cubicle, and began scrawling something on one wall that was, apparently, a white board. Nearby a young woman wearing a *salwar kemeez* was holding her cell phone in one hand and chatting in an Indian dialect. With her other brightly manicured hand, she threw darts at a target, rarely missing the bull's-eye.

Some of the cubicles appeared deserted. Through the open door of one of these I could see what looked like a snowdrift. Leaving Ashley's side, I walked over to the door and peered in. Following me Ashley said, "That's Carl's cube. He's away at a trade show. When he gets back, he's going to discover that somebody filled his cubicle with pieces of Styrofoam. That's the level of humor you get here," Ashley snorted, clearly contemptuous of her colleagues' sophomoric antics. Then I eyed four or five young men and women in shorts playing basketball on a good-sized court at the other end of the huge space. In the farthest corner were a tier of bunk beds, a sofa, and another fridge. "If you don't give them bunk beds, they just curl up on the floor, like ferrets," Ashley said even before I could stop gaping and ask.

Ashley and Chris had shared a large cubicle behind the bank of computers. "See, our walls are higher, for privacy," Ashley explained. "The walls on the Dilbert cages are lower to encourage collaboration." Confounded as I felt in this weird wired world, I could tell that Ashley saw her higher and larger cubicle as vastly superior to those of the techies. Ashley and Chris's space also had a wall of white board covered with what looked like scribbles. But the adjacent wall was different. "See. Isn't this awesome?" Ashley pointed to the metal surface pockmarked with magnets holding more notes and a large photo of a traditional young bride, russet hair upswept, amber eyes shining, and white dress billowing. Next to it was a photo of Ashley and a bespectacled young man, both wearing walking shorts and both grinning at the camera. The other two walls were standard burlap-covered wood. Tacked onto one of them, almost as an afterthought, was an unframed snapshot of a young man glommed onto a sheer wall of rock with, it seemed, only his daredevil grin and a filament of rope between him and his mother's worst fears.

In Ashley and Chris's space I also saw two desks, two PCs, two wastebaskets, two phones, a printer, a small DVD player, and some drawers and shelves. One desk was heaped with printouts and other papers. "That was Chris's in box," Ashley said with a sad smile. Between the desks was a compact fridge with the words *Ashley's Kosher Kitchen* spelled out in magnetic letters. "Cool, huh?" asked Ashley as she offered me what must have been Chris's chair. Even though she seemed on the verge of tears, it was obvious that she was proud of her unconventional work site.

It was also obvious that, in spite of the pleasure she took in showing off her office, Ashley was even more upset than she had been on Sunday. As soon as we reached the relative seclusion of the cubicle, her shoulders heaved and she pressed the back of her fist to her mouth to stifle a sob. She stood inside the cubicle for a moment, breathing deeply. Then she squared her shoulders and blew her nose and began to stage what, at first, looked like a one-woman demolition. Removing the photo of the bride, Ashley placed it carefully

into a large Banana Republic shopping bag that she
had apparently earmarked for this purpose. Next, taking short deep breaths like a woman in labor, she
pulled open a desk drawer. I interrupted her, saying,
"Ashley, take it easy. Sit down. Listen to me." To my
amazement, she sat. I took the other chair. "Listen,
Ashley, I'll do what I can to help you sort out what
happened to your friend Chris. It's kind of a mitzvah
for me."

Ashley nodded at me. Looking me in the eye, she
said softly, "Thanks. I appreciate that. I really do."
Then with a quiver in her voice, she went on, "Would
you mind starting right now? Our boss Greg's kind of
a wild man, but he's probably worth three or four million by now. Anyway, he's out in California this week
at that trade show." I was having trouble following
Ashley's disjointed appeal, but decided against ques-
tioning her. I figured she needed to vent and sooner or
later she'd tell me how I could help.

"So Greg asked *me* to clean out Chris's desk and
take all his personal stuff to Norma. And no one says
no to Greg. Except, of course, for Chris. Chris was the
only one in this whole outfit who didn't jump when
Greg said jump." Ashley's voice became almost rever-
ential as she recalled Chris's temerity. Her eyes filled
again and she seemed lost in thought. I waited. "I don't
want to go alone, Bel. I can't." She reached into the
open desk drawer and pulled out a dog-eared copy of
Winnie ille Pooh, a few pens and pencils, a set of what
looked like car keys, boxes of paper clips, staples, and
a bottle of prescription pills. "His allergy meds," said
Ashley as she flipped the vial into the bag. Next she

picked up the Milne book and stashed it in her purse. I shot her a look, the same look that had inspired hundreds of students to keep their eyes on their own papers during tests.

Ashley looked up at me and explained, "*I* gave him this for his birthday. *I'm* taking it back. He'd want *me* to have it." Again I said nothing, feeling very much the spectator at this sad scavenger hunt. I saw Ashley brush away tears, but still I held my tongue. I was imagining myself going through the desk of my office mate Wendy and then taking her personal effects home to her grieving husband. This exercise in empathy rendered me close to tears myself.

Having emptied the top drawer, Ashley opened the file drawer below and pulled out a pair of smooth-soled sneakers and a handful of metal loops. "His climbing shoes and other gear," she said, holding the footwear at arm's length by the purple laces. As she continued to rummage about in the drawer, a cloud of white dust rose from its depths, causing her to draw back suddenly, exclaiming, "What on earth . . ."

After teaching for decades in pre–white board classrooms, I'd have recognized that smell anywhere, so I broke my silence. "Chalk dust. It's chalk dust. He must have some chalk in there."

Acknowledging my explanation with a sigh of relief, Ashley reached back into the drawer and, sure enough, retrieved a grubby sock that simply oozed chalk dust. "Must go with the rock climbing stuff," she said, wrinkling her nose and brushing off the front of her suit. Finally she pulled out a red helmet and several old newspapers. After putting the sock in a Ziploc bag and sealing it, Ashley plunked everything but the papers into the larger bag. The papers she threw in the trash. The last drawer contained hard copy files and a few loose disks. After a perfunctory look, Ashley said, "This is all work-related. It stays here." She closed the drawer.

"Do you think I should have a look at some of those files," I asked, "as long as I'm here?" It seemed quite reasonable to suspect that work-related documents might hold clues to Chris's work-related death.

"That stuff won't mean much to you," Ashley replied. "Besides, I've already gone through it. I don't want to overwork you," she said, making an effort to smile. We left the building carrying the bag of Chris's things between us. I wanted to examine Chris's personal effects too, so when we got outside, I asked Ashley to wait while I looked them over quickly. Nothing struck me as unusual about any of the items in the bag, but I wished I'd brought a camera. I would have liked to photograph them so they wouldn't disappear into the void of a senior moment. "Will you get a second chance to go through the work-related stuff we left there?" I asked.

"Sure. It's all mine now. I told you, I've been assigned his territory. I'll let you know what I come up with, if anything," Ashley answered, sounding tired. Then in a whisper that made her request as irresistible as a child's prayer, she said, "Bel, please come to Chris's apartment with me? Please? I can't face seeing Norma again. She's so broken up. And I really don't know her well. It's so hard to know what to say. What is there to say?"

In spite of how tired I was I couldn't refuse her. "Okay, sure. I'll go with you. Besides, I want to check out Chris's widow anyway." We walked the few blocks to the new high-rise apartment that Chris had shared with his wife. It was in one of the luxury buildings that had suddenly risen, phoenix-like, from the industrial residue on the Jersey City waterfront. Here a two-bedroom apartment now rented for $2,500 a month, a previously unheard-of figure for the area. I marveled that someone Chris's age could afford such a rent.

I also marveled at the fact that such luxury could exist just a few blocks from a run-down housing project in a neighborhood of dilapidated and condemned buildings. A Republican mayor with a Wall Street résumé in synch with a booming economy had created Jersey City's famed Gold Coast, which was, in fact, a narrow strip of newly constructed high-rise offices, condos, and hotels along the river. Meanwhile, much of the rest of the seedy old city, bedeviled by crime, unemployment, and failing schools, sat, like the ugly fairy-tale frog, awaiting the transforming kiss of a princess.

The doorman telephoned up to announce our arrival and, apparently getting Norma's approval, nodded across the vaulted pink marble lobby in the direction of the elevator. Even carrying the large Banana Republic shopping bag, Ashley did not look like a typical shopper. Tension and misery had hunched her shoulders and narrowed her lips into a grim stripe. "I still can't believe Chris won't show up in the office tomorrow," she said with her head down. "Even after getting this stuff together, I just can't get it into my head that he's totally gone." I reached across the elevator and squeezed her arm.

We got out at the twenty-fifth floor and walked down the hall to apartment twenty-five eighteen. When we rang, the door opened within a few seconds. I barely glanced at the slight woman who had answered it. Instead I stared over her head at the panoramic view of the Hudson River from the George Washington Bridge to the Statue of Liberty. These two landmarks bookended the strip of skyscrapers that is Manhattan. I was used to seeing this vista from area parks, and the spectacle had never failed to move me. But now I was viewing it at sundown from the twenty-fifth floor, and it was like an Imax movie, up close, all around, and literally breathtaking. For a few seconds I gaped, contemplating what bank to rob so that I too could wake up to this miracle every day. Meanwhile Ashley was introducing me to Chris's widow. "Norma, this is my friend Bel Barrett. She didn't want me to come alone."

The hand that reached out to take mine was small and cold. Norma's icy touch jolted me back from my covetous reverie. "So terribly sorry about your loss," I murmured, like Ashley, newly conscious of the inadequacy of the stock words and phrases available in the face of death. I felt the hand retract and looked into the eyes of the woman in the photo I'd seen earlier. Now her hair hung in rust-colored strings and those amber eyes were ringed with red. Grief and shock had marked her. An older woman, her mom or perhaps an aunt, stood behind her, watchful, protective.

"Thanks for coming, Ashley, and you too, Bel." Norma nodded politely in my direction. "Mom, Ashley is Chris's friend from work." Norma took the bag and handed it to her mother, who accepted it and stood there awkwardly holding the detritus of her dead son-in-law's professional life in one hand.

"Where do you want this, sweetheart?" The older woman spoke softly.

"In the study where you're sleeping, Mom. Just leave it on the desk. I don't want to look at it for a while." Norma's mom left the room with the bag. "There's coffee over there. Help yourself," said Norma, again playing hostess. Her voice, deep and resonant, like a female version of Sol's, sounded like the voice of a much larger woman. She sank onto the sofa, motioning us to sit beside her. Ignoring the coffee, Ashley sat down next to Norma and I positioned myself on a chair across from them.

"Thank you for bringing Chris's gear, Ashley. I didn't really get a chance to talk to you at the wake what with all the people there. Even though Chris hardly ever talked shop, I know how tight you two were, so I know this has to be tough on you too." I watched Norma as she spoke. Was there a tinge of sarcasm in her words? Was she being ironic or sardonic? How did she really feel about this other young woman who had been her husband's best friend?

Norma swallowed hard and continued, "Greg was over last week too. He said a lot of nice things about Chris, of course." She lowered her head modestly, as if Chris's virtues were somehow hers and so required a self-deprecating response. "He asked me if I need anything . . . Troy Tarnoff came by too." She sighed and went on. "Everybody's being so nice." Norma's mother had returned and I saw her nod in silent affirmation of Norma's statement. At the thought of everybody's kindness in the aftermath of her loss, Norma's face crumpled, and the sob she had been holding back finally erupted in a series of muffled gulps. In a second her mother was beside her.

"Sweetheart, why don't you take one of those pills Dr. Madison sent?" Turning to us, the older woman added unnecessarily, "Her doctor ordered something so she could get a little sleep. She hasn't slept at all lately." At Norma's nod, her mother left the room again, presumably in search of the bottled bromide that promised to bring her daughter a few hours of relief from her new and lonely reality.

But when her mother returned with the pills and a glass, Norma waved away the offered medication. "No. That's okay, Mom. I'll be okay." Looking at us, she said, "I don't want to get hooked on those things. I'll be okay," she repeated. When she attempted to flash her mom a reassuring smile, I saw a vestige of the pretty bride in the photo on the wall of Chris's cubicle. Her mother quietly receded, taking the bottle and glass with her. I didn't know whom I sympathized with more, the grieving young woman whose life companion had suddenly died or the worried mom who had to bear witness to a beloved child's suffering.

"Maybe a run would help," Ashley offered. I had to hand it to Ashley. She was really trying to relate to this woman and her loss, all the while feeling pretty down herself. "Chris always bragged about what a dedicated runner you were. Norma finished the New York

Marathon last year," she added, directing this explanatory comment to me.

"Maybe," Norma said listlessly. "I'll try. Maybe tomorrow."

"Good. And I'll stop by again to see how you're doing," said Ashley, standing up to signal that we were leaving. I followed suit, making it a point to sneak one more glance at the towers of Manhattan now, in early evening, a light show like no other.

Ashley and I didn't speak until we had left the elevator and entered the marble lobby. I really felt sorry for her now, so I asked, "How are you? Widows and other relatives get all the sympathy. Friends are just expected to suck up and deal. It doesn't seem fair."

"Thanks, Bel," Ashley said. "I never thought about it that way before, but you're right. I don't see why you wanted to meet Norma though. She's totally out of the work loop. Like she said, Chris rarely talked shop at home." Ashley trudged along beside me. Putting her hands in her coat pocket, she continued. "He told me they had a fight over buying a house in Morristown or staying here. Norma wanted to have a yard and a lawn right away." The way Ashley drawled this last sentence made Norma's rather ordinary desire for suburban sprawl sound a little unreasonable. "But, of course, Chris wanted to live near the office for now. I'm sure he was just kidding, but he once said they hadn't had sex for months over this. He was so comical. He said it came down to 'No grass, no ass.' But the dude idolized her anyway." Ashley shrugged her shoulders. I reminded myself that she was still young enough to be surprised by the many vagaries of the male mind.

The idea of two *pishers* barely wet behind the ears having the means to afford either a $2,500-a-month apartment or a house in upscale Morristown was in itself ludicrous. But the Internet had made millionaires out of kids who hadn't yet learned that money can't buy happiness or that you can have too much of a good thing. These *nouveaux riche* techno nerds were actually in therapy learning how to overcome the symptoms of Sudden Wealth Syndrome. I shook my head at the absurdity of it all as Ashley and I, each lost in thought, slowly made our way to my car.

Finally, adopting a let's-get-down-to-business tone that I sometimes borrowed from Betty, I broke the silence. "Ashley, one of these days I'm going to show up at e-media.com as a reporter from the local paper and interview Greg for a feature article on Silicon Slum. If you're around when I get there, don't let on that you know me." I caught the skeptical look that momentarily furrowed her brow.

"But Bel, the problem isn't at e-media.com. Don't you understand? It's at scoop.com where Chris was working and where I'm assigned now. That's where you should be focusing your effort." Ashley turned to face me, frustration apparent in the unfamiliar stridency of her tone and the jut of her chin. "I'm positive that when Troy Tarnoff, Chris's target at scoop, learned that Chris was a plant, he killed him." Now her usually soft voice rose a little and she enunciated her words slowly as if speaking to a child. "Because he must have given up something to Chris that Chris could use and he didn't want anyone at scoop to know. That's why." Ashley had answered my question before I could ask it. She looked rather startled by her own outburst and lapsed into silence again. I thought the discussion was over.

That's why I was surprised when suddenly she took my arm and said, "Bel, I know Troy Tarnoff. He and Greg have been friends forever and were roommates at Brown. They both dropped out after sophomore year and founded e-media.com together. Troy worked there until paranoid Greg accused him of planning to launch a spinoff company of his own. As payback, Greg muscled him out of some shares right before their IPO, and Troy was really steamed. He sold his remaining shares and started scoop.com, our biggest competitor. Troy's done really well there acting as CEO and directing special projects. And now he'd do anything to protect that position and that organization. He owns a lot of shares there now."

"It may not make sense to you, Ashley, but I need to get a better handle on e-media.com before I look at scoop. Trust me. I know what I'm doing," I responded. "One step at a time. That's how I operate." I accompanied these words with a reassuring smile.

"I guess it's a generational thing, Bel. I like to move fast." Whenever Rebecca disagreed with me lately, she said it was a "generational thing," so I was used to being called old in what a younger person thought was a tactful way. Ashley went on, "But anyway, suppose you do ask for an interview with Greg. How do you know he'll buy into that? He's so busy. He's always traveling. And he's totally paranoid about security. He's paranoid about a lot of things."

"Don't worry. I'll call first and set up an appoint-

ment. He'll buy it. Nobody can resist a little PR, even
if it's only in the local rag," I said. I recalled a very successful bit of "reporting" I'd done with the help of my
friend Sarah, who really was with the local paper, an
editor, in fact. Together we'd gotten evidence that had
helped pinpoint the killer of a local Frank Sinatra im-
personator. Memory of this triumph lent confidence to
my voice.

Ashley smiled for the first time that day and gave
me a big hug. Then, her smile becoming an impish
grin, she said, "It's really a shame you're too high-
minded for corporate intelligence work, Bel. I have a
feeling you'd be awesome at it."

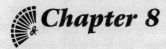# *Chapter 8*

To: Bbarrett@circle.com
From: Futura@recc.nj.edu
Re: Internship essay
Date: 09/27/99 08:11:45

Dear Professor B,

You said after class to set up a conference with you to discuss my
internship analysis, but I haven't got a internship. See, the place
I started my internship in just got bought out or merged, I'm not
sure which. All I know is, Mr. Abraham, that cool old dude who
was mentoring me, got canned. And the woman who took over
his job says she's sorry, but they didn't agree to keep no interns.
That's too bad 'cause she was wack:-). So I need a new placement. Professor Jones looking for one, but so far he hasn't found
nothing. He say we always short of internships for RECC business
majors. I hope this don't mess me up for the semester.

Your favorite student:-)
Nathan Futura

Nathan's e-mail was waiting for me when I got home after visiting Ashley at e-media.com and meeting Norma. Nathan was a student of mine in Composition III, a pilot course with three prerequisites: students had to be business majors doing their internships who had passed Comp II, but with a grade lower than B. Comp III was designed to help these students through the process of writing the internship analysis essay, an extended critical composition required of all RECC business majors. This paper often proved a stumbling block for developing writers. As the designer of the new course, I was teaching it this semester.

Nathan's message infuriated me. RECC students were almost always the first in their family to attend college and didn't have a network of relatives working in white-collar jobs to mentor them. That's why the internship was a crucial crash course in office culture and contacts. The infusion of high-tech startups and investment firms on Jersey City's Gold Coast should mean that RECC students didn't have to go begging for placements. I went straight to the phone.

She must have gotten home at the same time I did because she picked up on the second ring. I cut to the chase. "Ashley, Bel here. Listen, you know the regular mitzvah we're supposed to perform? Well, your little project is mine, and now I've found one for you. I've got a bright, highly motivated, and very personable student who's majoring in business and needs an internship ASAP. He lives right here in Jersey City. Can you place him with a mentor at e-media.com? He has to spend a few hours a week there making himself useful and gaining an understanding of workplace culture and demands." I paused, giving her a chance to put aside her own problems and focus on my request. Then, in the tradition of those Vassar classmates who call me every year, I added, "This is a great opportunity to give back to your alma mater." Ashley could easily get Nathan an internship at e-media.com, and he'd sure learn a lot watching the current generation of cyber jocks do business.

"Sure, Bel. No problem. Maybe Greg'll act as mentor himself. Greg talks a lot about community service, so now he can put his money where his mouth is. What's the young man's name?"

Flush with my small triumph, I resolved to ask Sandi to take on a RECC intern or two the following semester. I turned back to my keyboard to e-mail Nathan the good news. I knew Professor Jones would also be relieved that his student had found a placement.

Later I called Betty to schedule an update. "How's Friday night?" she asked.

"Sandi, Sol, and I are going to Friday evening Sabbath services, so I can't make it then," I responded. "We have to go to twenty of these things and we need to start sometime. Besides I promised Sandi."

"So come over here after you're done," Betty suggested. "We'll save you some supper."

"That won't work either. You know the Sabbath goes from sundown on Friday to sundown on Saturday. Sol's making us a Sabbath meal first. Sofia and my mother are joining us for that. Anyway, the whole point is observant Jews aren't supposed to do any work on the Sabbath. And since solving this murder is most definitely work, it won't feel right to talk about it then. Besides, I've never observed the Sabbath, so it won't kill me to try it."

"Wait a minute. Are you telling me that on Saturday you're not going to do any work? How are you going to get all those student essays you're always complaining about done? And when are you going to start writing your dissertation?" Betty sounded genuinely worried. After years of trying to run my life, she knew exactly how tightly scheduled my weekends were.

I sighed. "No. I'm not going to Saturday services this time and I am going to read student essays, but I'm at least keeping Friday night free. I want to see what that feels like. Listen, how about you go to early Mass on Sunday and we get together after that for breakfast at the Truckstop? There's even parking there." Though this was not her idea, Betty agreed to go along with it. The prospect of a pricey but delicious breakfast *and* a parking space near the diner on the western fringe of town was too good to resist.

"That'll work for me. Vic too. He's got a funeral later that morning. He won't miss me too much." Betty spent most of her free time with her new love, busy funeral director Victor Vallone, so she often found herself competing with corpses for his attention. "It's kinky, but it works for this girl," was her response when we teased her about this. We preferred Vic's comeback, which was, "Betty's the only warm body in my life."

"I'll be there. I'll get in touch with Illuminada. Listen girl, I didn't realize that when you got religion, I'd have to change my lifestyle." I could hear Betty chortling as I put the phone down.

Sol had gone all out. He'd roasted a chicken and some potatoes, baked an acorn squash, and made a salad. He'd even bought a loaf of challah, the egg bread that traditionally accompanies the Sabbath meal. Sofia Dellafemina, my mother's eighty-something-year- old housemate, and Ma sat at opposite ends of the table while Sol and I took places across from Sandi. Our company candlesticks graced the center of the table. The tableau made by the gleaming silver candlesticks and braided challah served to expunge all thoughts of Ashley and her dead friend from my mind. It was as if I had received permission to relax, to live in the moment of this ritual meal. Just then the Sabbath seemed to combine the pleasures of yoga with those of the table. I hoped the other requirements for bat mitzvah would be this therapeutic.

To my amazement, Sol turned to my mother and said, "Sadie, will you please light and bless the candles?" Then for Sofia's benefit, he added, "This is a very brief ritual that the woman of the house usually performs at sundown to welcome the Sabbath."

"It's too early and I don't remember the words, but if you help, I'll try," my mother answered. Ever since she and Sol had buried the hatchet a few years ago, she had gone out of her way to oblige him. That's why I wasn't surprised by her game response even though I had never heard her bless anything but a deck of cards in my life. But I also knew that she didn't want to embarrass herself in front of Sofia, whom she frequently accompanied to church on Sunday mornings, so I figured she knew what she was doing.

Sadie pulled her large Vera scarf up from behind and draped it over the back of her head. The simple gesture instantly transformed her from a retired court stenographer who worshipped at the casinos in Atlantic City to a Traditional Jewish Mother. Before I had a chance to wonder if she'd worn that scarf purposely so she'd be prepared to cover her head, Sol began chanting slowly, *"Baruch atoh . . "* and my mother joined him a syllable behind at first and then, her face alight with pleasure, her voice strong, she caught up. Sol's deep voice ceased and Sadie finished the blessing alone. *"My* mother used to say that blessing sometimes," she said. "Before we moved from Brooklyn." By the time we actually began to eat, Sadie had blessed the wine, a California Chardonnay that Sandi had insisted on bringing, and the challah, and was busy translating the Hebrew for Sofia.

Then, having discharged her religious duties, she turned her attention to Sandi while Sol and I served the meal. "So Sandi, it's been a long time? It's good that you came East so we can catch up. You know, I still remember what my Ike said when we brought Bel up to Vassar for the first time. We got in the car to go home, and he said, 'I like that girl, that Sandele.' Right away he called you 'Sandele,' like he adopted you. 'She'll be good to Bel. They'll take care of each other.' My Ike was right, wasn't he?" Sandi nodded and Ma continued, "How's that handsome son of yours? Is he still a surfer? Sybil nearly went out of her mind when Mark was skateboarding. She would have had a heart attack if he'd gone in the ocean with those big waves, right Sybil?"

Sandi giggled a little at Ma's use of my full name. She knew it drove me crazy. Then she said, "Yes, actually Josh still surfs when he can. But most of the time he's a woodworker, you know, a cabinet maker," Sandi said with that mix of pride, surprise, and concern that many parents reserve for discussing their adult children's career choices. "He and two friends bought an old run-down farm a few years ago and turned it into a woodworking cooperative."

Before I could dwell on how different Josh's career choice was from that of Ashley or poor Chris Johanson, I heard my mother ask, "So how's he doing? Is he busy?" Sadie was never known for her reticence.

But Sandi was a match for her. "You can ask him yourself. I invited him to Bel and Sol's for Thanksgiving, and he's coming. He's going to talk with a few buyers out here. I sent him a ticket today. That's his Chri . . . I mean Chanukah present." We all had to laugh at Sandi's slip with the "C" word. I was happy for her. *She* would at least get to spend Thanksgiving with her only child. Sol's daughter had already told him that she and her husband Xie and their little girl planned to spend the holiday with Xie's family in Oregon. Mark was teaching English in Buenos Aires and would probably not even remember Thanksgiving, and Rebecca, Keith, and my granddaughter Abigail Jane . . . Well, even if they had the money or I sent them tickets, they wouldn't be able to take the time off.

"Here's our baby." My mother whipped out the small white calfskin album Sofia had presented to her on the birth of Abbie J, Ma's first and only great-grandchild. Ma carried the album with her everywhere. Sol and I suspected her of sleeping with it. There were photos of Abbie J doing all the adorable things that babies do. I had to admit, she was perfect. With a pang I found myself realizing that parenthood and grandparenthood were pleasures the late Chris Johanson would never know. No sooner had I banished that un-Sabbath-like thought from my mind when Sofia, not to be outdone, got out her album, and we passed it around too. Between mouthfuls of food and sips of wine, we all made the silly noises even sensible grown-ups make when looking at photos of babies. With all the sighs and oohs and aahs, we sounded a little like the soundtrack for a porno movie rather than Sabbath celebrants.

Oddly enough, Ma was the first to break the mood. "You know, whenever I see that precious little face, I remember I have to redo my will. I know it's a nuisance, but I should do it." Sandi and I exchanged a look. Ma obviously saw nothing untoward about making the transition from goo-gooing over baby pictures to preparing for death.

"You better do it. Anything could happen," said Sofia, easily welcoming the grim reaper into the conversation. I recalled that she had, with great hoopla, redone her will each time a new great-grandchild was born. I guess when you are in your eighties, death is an intimate to be included rather than a stranger to be avoided. I myself wasn't ready to go there yet. I found myself wondering if Ashley's friend Chris had been ready. Had he written a will? He was so young.

"And you too, Bel," Sol chimed in, forcing me to re-focus my drifting thoughts.

"My will's okay," I said defensively. A fine Sabbath conversation this was turning out to be. I was sure wills weren't on the approved list of Sabbath-appropriate chitchat.

"You know what I mean," Sol pressed. That man could be so annoying sometimes. "We both have to do our advanced directives. You know, our pull the plug papers."

Sandi and Sofia looked bewildered. "He means the papers that say if you're in a coma, pull the plug," said Ma, trying to be helpful. "Sybil thinks she's going to live forever. She doesn't even have a lawyer." Ma jerked her head in my direction as if there were any doubt as to whom she meant and as if I were simultaneously not there and two years old.

"Yikes!" exclaimed Sandi. "Does everybody on the East Coast discuss their worst-case health scenarios at Sabbath dinner?" That's why I love that woman. She and I think alike. "What time do we have to be at services?" I loved her even more for this clumsy effort to change the subject.

"We have time for some of Ma's brownies," I said, not giving any indication that I was contemplating matricide as I spoke. Sandi had developed a craving for my mother's brownies the year a pre-med student from Princeton broke a date with her for the Yale-Princeton game. That weekend I gave her the whole care package, figuring she needed it more than I did. I had just met Lenny, whom I was convinced was the answer to a Jewish Ivy League coed's prayers. What did I know?

With a brownie in her hand and another on her plate, Sandi turned to me and asked, "Didn't Ashley Solomon say that her husband, Howard, was a lawyer? You could try him out." I saw Sol jot down the name.

vocabulary? I didn't want to be one of those people who read Hebrew without understanding it. And what about Torah chanting? I harbored no illusions about my ability to carry a tune and I knew I would need lots more than a shamus or guide to help me unlock the secrets of the Torah. For the enigmatic scroll includes no vowels or notes. I might as well try to learn Chinese.

And Hebrew wasn't the only new language I had to learn. In Silicon Slum with Ashley I had felt like a tourist in a foreign country where the natives were all millionaire whiz kids under thirty and the lingua franca and the customs were utterly alien. That's why I planned to return for another look, this time in the guise of a reporter and in the company of my old friend *Jersey City Herald* managing editor Sarah Wolf. With a press card as passport, I'd get to tape conversations so I wouldn't have to take notes or rely on my midlife memory. For reasons I never understood, people revealed themselves to the press, off the record and on. Sarah would pose as a photographer, so we'd get photos. I'd pose as a freelance feature reporter and Sarah would actually run the article, so there would be no cover needed and no cover to blow. I'd use my own name. It was a foolproof strategy.

When I met Sarah for lunch later that week, she was game to cooperate. "I hope you're planning to reward me with a story," she sassed as we loaded the camera and tape recorder into the backseat of her car. "I could use another promotion." Sarah's tone was light, but we both knew that her biggest promotion to date followed her scoop naming the murderer of RECC president Dr.

Altagracia Garcia. Sarah and I had met in an aerobics class in the eighties. We used to go out for coffee afterward, and our friendship continued long after I had traded in my step and Spandex for a yoga mat and sweats.

"Let's get a snack at the Hard Grove Café right now. Then I can brief you."

"Deal. I can't wait to hear what you're sticking your busybody nose into now." Sarah always badmouthed my detecting efforts while at the same time helping me with them. I think she enjoyed getting out of the editorial office and being a reporter again. She had been among the best in the business.

The Hard Grove Café with its campy plastic palm trees and dangling fake fruit is downtown Jersey City's answer to *la vida loca*. While Sarah and I savored our decidedly nonkosher Cuban sandwiches of roast pork and cheese, I explained to her what e-media.com was and why we were going there. "Everybody who works there is the opposite of a slacker. It's like a camp for young, talented workaholics."

Sarah was enthusiastic. "Sounds like a timely feature story. We should have been chronicling those dot com startups in Silicon Slum from the get-go. We'll definitely run this one. But listen, Bel. No tears this time."

I smiled, recalling how during our visit to the parents of a murdered singer, Sarah'd had to kick me hard to stem my tears of sympathy. "Not this time," I said. "No way."

e-media.com looked the same as it had the week before, except, as Ashley had assured me, Cindy was gone and the regular receptionist, a young dark-haired woman, was back. I'd called ahead, so she was expecting us. In a flash, she'd issued us visitors' passes, insisted that we fasten them to our clothes, gave us nondisclosure agreements to sign, and paged not Greg Mollifer, the CEO, as I'd requested, but someone named Mattie Mollifer. "Mattie is our director of sales and marketing. She's going to show you around. Greg's at a meeting now. He'll see you later for a brief chat." Before I had a chance to think how nice it was that Greg had hired his sister, a graying fifty-ish woman wearing a stunning burgundy cashmere suit emerged from a large cubicle in the area Ashley had said was the turf of marketing and sales. Reading glasses hung from a silver chain around her neck, and she was sweating visibly. We stood there, three women, older by a quarter of a century than everyone around us. It was a moment for smiles of complicity, but this walking anomaly extended her hand and, in a no-nonsense voice, introduced herself. "Mattie Mollifer, here. Welcome to e-media.com." When I heard that clean-your-room-or-there'll-be-no-TV-tonight tone, it dawned on me that Greg Mollifer had hired his mother.

After greeting her, Sarah looked around the loft and said in her best gee-whiz manner, "Wow! This is some setup. Would you mind if I just walk around and shoot some candids while Bel here interviews you? That's how we usually work it. It saves time."

"You may walk around, but not unattended. Jill!" she bellowed. A young woman whose dress-for-success gray suit and black pumps contrasted dramatically with the grunge getups of the techies emerged from a cubicle. "Jill is my assistant. She'll accompany you." Then, dismissing Sarah and Jill, Mattie directed her attention to me.

"Do you mind if I tape you? It's so much easier." I was getting out my tape recorder as I spoke.

"Not at all. And remind me to give you some brochures before you leave," Mattie answered, suddenly gracious as she led me toward a bank of low cubicles. "Here's where the engineers and sysadmins dream up solutions to problems and new product."

"Sysadmins?" I interrupted.

"Systems administrators," she decoded and then continued where she had left off. "e-media.com attracts talent from all over the world. We sell service B2B, that's business to business, on the Net." I smiled my appreciation for the unsolicited translation. "These folks here are in the front lines of product development, support, and troubleshooting." As she went through her well-rehearsed spiel, I noticed the teddy bear lying on the floor beside the trash can. The young man who'd been using the stuffed animal as a basketball and the trash can as a basket on my earlier visit now sat hunched over his PC studying what looked like a grid. Next to him the Indian woman, today clad in cords and a sweater, was typing text, possibly an e-mail message. As we strolled by, another young Turk stood and, picking up the teddy bear, ambled over to the bunk beds mumbling, "Later," to anyone within earshot. In a minute he was prone, his snores audible across the room.

"These young people live for their work. They need their rest. We try to make the office user-friendly," Mattie explained.

At the last computer station in the row I saw Nathan. I'd forgotten about him, but thank God he couldn't blow my cover. He looked happy enough. After I'd described the informality of e-media.com's physical plant and the apparent lack of a dress code, Nathan had agonized over what to wear on his first day. He'd finally decided to show up in a suit and tie and after that to play it by ear. I had wondered if he'd dress in his hip-hop baggies or go the preppy route. Now I knew. He had opted for a hip-hop fashion statement, baggy jeans, a long baggy black sweatshirt, and a backward baseball cap. He was dressed for cyber success all right, and I hoped he'd find it. Nathan deserved a reward for crossing the digital divide to become fairly computer literate without owning a PC. He was the first one in the RECC computer lab every day and often closed it down on the nights he didn't have to work.

Nathan's eyes widened when he spotted me and he rushed over to say hello. "How's that downloading going, Nate?" asked Mattie. "You two have met?" She looked troubled by the fact that Nathan and I obviously knew each other. But I didn't have to explain because Nathan, never one to avoid a conversational opportunity, jumped in.

"Cool, Mrs. M, real cool. She my prof at the college," said Nathan, proud of being a college student, of having a prof. "You come to check up on me, Professor Barrett?" The twinkle in his eye made it very clear that he did not find the prospect of my surveillance very threatening. And I didn't find his presence problematic either. But I was glad I'd not mentioned to him who I knew or how I'd lined him up for the internship he was currently enjoying.

"No, Nathan. Actually I'm here for my other job. I sometimes moonlight as a freelance reporter for the *Jersey City Herald*. The photographer and I are doing an article on Silicon Slum and all the new businesses opening up down here." I assumed that that rather literal explanation would suffice and it did. Nathan gave me a thumbs up and returned to his work. I couldn't wait to read the journal he was required to keep in preparation for writing his paper.

"He's a good kid, and we're happy to have him. We need a community service connection, and he fits right in here," said Mattie. She seemed oblivious to the fact that at twenty-four Nathan was probably no younger than most of the men and women in the other cubicles and might find the appellation "kid" demeaning.

There was no one playing basketball. Ashley and Chris's cubicle was deserted, and our tour ended with a quick visit to the bank of PCs belonging to the PR and marketing teams. There was only one member of these groups present besides Jill, and she was talking on a cell phone. "The rest of the crew is on the road, so Angie's real busy. Otherwise I'd have her talk to you. The young people spin e-media.com a lot better than I do even though it's my son's company," Mattie said in a confusing burst of both false modesty and real maternal pride.

"Oh no. You're doing a great job. Really. This is a whole new world to me." I addressed her false modesty first. I'd suck up to her maternal pride later. Mattie paused in front of what appeared to be her office, a

large cubicle lined with bookshelves and enclosing a
couple of reclining chairs and a table. It was the neat-
est office in the place. There was a vase of flowers in
the center of the table. Photos of children were pushpinned into the burlap wall opposite her desk. Once inside, Mattie removed her jacket and wiped her face.

Encouraged by the ego massage I had just given her,
she elaborated, "We're trying to affiliate with a bricks
business. Bricks 'n' clicks are great combos, you
know." When my face registered the fact that, in reality,
I didn't know what she was talking about, she translated patiently. "We're a 'clicks' or dot com company.
See?' Reaching across the table, she grabbed the
mouse at the PC there and clicked it. "A 'bricks' company is a more traditional organization like Time-
Warner or Hearst." Seeing me nod, she continued, "So
I've got a team out sniffing to see if we can get a brick-
based business to come to our party."

I moved closer to the wall and inspected the photos,
most of which appeared to be of the same little boy.
"What an adorable child! Could you tell early on that
he was going to be in the vanguard of the information
revolution?" I was laying it on. No stranger to maternal pride myself, I knew she'd drop her lady executive
persona long enough to brag about her boy genius.

"Actually, yes. Greg was always special, bored in
school, precocious you might say. His teachers didn't
really understand him. He took to the computer right
away." Now Mattie was beaming again and gestured
me to sit down. "Do you know Greg had his own on-
line business designing websites when he was a fresh-
man in high school?" She pointed at a photo of a

grinning adolescent geek holding up what looked like a check. "I took that photo when he got his first check." Mattie sighed and continued her maternal musings. "He had so much work he had to bring his buddy Troy on board to handle the overflow." Shaking her head in mock amazement, she said, "I really shouldn't have been surprised when the two of them dropped out of Brown." She looked down for a minute, then squared her shoulders and wiped her brow again. I resisted the urge to advise her to get an estrogen patch.

She continued, "You know what my Greg said? He said they were losing money by staying in college. He couldn't afford to finish is how he put it. And Greg was really the ringleader, so once he decided to leave, Troy just followed. The two of them really stuck together back then." Mattie shook her head, perhaps wondering about the forces that had separated two childhood friends. But when she resumed speaking, she talked about herself. "Greg's dropping out of Brown was hard for me to accept. He left school about the time of my divorce. It was another blow," she repeated.

I knew all about midlife divorce and about the disappointment parents suffer when a child wants out of college. I wondered what Illuminada would make of this saga. Putting that thought on hold, I focused on Mattie, who was grinning now. "But I needn't have worried. Next thing you know, he and Troy are partners in e-media.com and getting ready for an IPO." I nodded to reassure her that even I knew the abbreviation for an initial public offering on the stock market. I noted that at this point in the conversation, another woman would inquire whether I had any children, would give me my turn to brag. That's the way the game was usually played. But Mattie didn't seem to know the rules. Instead she said, "Maybe he can see you now." Clearly she wanted me to experience her prodigy in person.

Picking up her cell phone, she punched in some numbers, and I heard the phone ring in the adjacent cubicle. I stifled a giggle. Mattie spoke into the phone for a moment and then said, "Yes. He'll see you." She used the same reverent tone a devout Catholic would use when announcing an audience with His Eminence, the Pope.

Greg, a sandy-haired green-eyed young man, stood when we entered, towering over his mother and me. He wore jeans and a plain gray sweatshirt and, of course, a baseball cap. When he reached out to shake my hand, I noticed that he also wore a Rolex. After the quick handshake, he sat down and said, "Excuse me, but I just got back from Manhattan," and reached down to remove his Rollerblades. His next line was: "Can I offer you some lunch? I'm about to send out for a sandwich."

"Thanks, but no. Sarah and I had lunch before we got here," I answered.

"Mom?" He looked inquiringly at his mother, who nodded her head. "Great. Order me a sandwich too. The usual." e-media.com's director of sales and marketing did not seem to expect her CEO, whose behind she had often diapered, to say *please* or *thank you* to her. Oblivious to this incivility, she planted a big smooch on the cheek of this same CEO, gave me a quick smile, and left. Shaking his head as if to apologize for her affectionate gesture, Greg leaned back in his chair until the front of the swivel base was off the floor, turned to me, and asked, "So what can I tell you? My mother's such a spinmeister I can't believe she left anything out. What do you want to know?"

"Well, for starters, tell me what it's like to be in a position to hire your mom." I figured on that question getting to the heart of the lad's own success story.

"Isn't that cool?" Greg asked. "She did marketing and sales for years so they'd have enough money to put me through college. She used to win all these prizes. Then I dropped out of Brown and my folks did the divorce thing." Did I see a trace of a grimace? "I don't know which upset my mom more, the divorce or me dropping out of college, but she kept calling me up and asking me to come home to Philadelphia. Meanwhile, our marketing person decided to stay home with her baby." Greg looked askance at this notion as if the young mother had decided to wrestle alligators. "And then I remembered Mom's background. So I called her up one day and the rest is history." Greg's grin had, perhaps, a trace of smugness. Clearly he was pleased with his performance in the dual roles of prince and problem solver. "Mom's totally awesome at both sales and marketing," he stated. "That woman can get people to move product. Beside, I never have to worry about her backstabbing me." He grinned and then sighed with satisfaction at how well things had worked out.

"How old are you anyway?" I asked, my curiosity driving me to blurt out my query rather than to frame it tactfully.

"I turned twenty-five last weekend," Greg said, not at all put off by my bluntness. I guess it's only older folks who get bent out of shape by direct inquiries about their age.

"Wow. Happy birthday. It must feel good to be running your own company and still be so young," I responded.

"Yup. It does." I had just broken one of my cardinal rules for extracting information from students by asking a yes or no question. I resolved to expand the scope of my inquiries.

"Greg, exactly what does e-media.com do or make or sell?" I asked. "I'm embarrassed to say that even though your mom explained it, I'm not sure I understand."

This was only partially true, but I knew he'd like to expand on this topic, and I wanted to hear his version. The young man spoke quickly, easily, an indication that he was used to answering this particular query. "e-media.com designs websites and brokers Internet access. And then there's mediamerchant.com, our first spinoff. We have forty vendors that pay us to do business with each other." I widened my eyes, feigning total ignorance. "Like say you're a phone company and you join mediamerchant. Some other member vendor, say a company selling office supplies, wants phone service. They buy it from you at a discount that we negotiate, and we get a commission. See?" I nodded. "So far we're mostly operating B2B with media-related companies. But we're expanding our scope of services. A lot depends on what else is happening out there." I pictured Ashley, perhaps eavesdropping at scoop.com even as we spoke, in an effort to determine exactly what the competition was doing.

Thinking of Ashley jolted me back to my real purpose in talking with Greg. In the hope of catching him off guard, I omitted a transition and said, "I understand that a former employee died last week, Chris Johanson. Care to comment on that?"

Before he answered, Greg lowered his head and sat in silence for a moment. Then, looking directly at me, he said, "Chris's death is a tragedy, a terrible tragedy. That man was the consummate modern media professional. He was technologically savvy and hip to what was going on in the industry. You could say Chris was the personification of everything e-media.com stands for." Greg lowered his head again. When he raised it this time, he spoke very softly, so I inched the mike closer to his mouth. "Plus he was my friend. I really cared about that dude."

This elegiac moment was interrupted by the arrival of Mom Friday bearing a brown paper bag. "Here you are, dear. What would you like to drink with it?" Turning to me and winking conspiratorially, now totally mom-to-mom, she said, "It's a silly question. He's always had the same thing to drink with every meal since he was a little boy." Then addressing herself to Greg again, she promised, "I'll be right back, sweetie," and hurried off in the direction of the fridge.

"Do you mind? I'm starving." When I offered no opposition, Greg carefully peeled foil off what looked like a grilled vegetable wrap and began to make it disappear in great sloppy chunks. He dabbed at the drippings with a napkin. I fought the urge to walk over and tie a bib around his neck. By the time his real mom appeared with a can of Sprite, the sandwich was almost gone. She set the drink down on the desk, squeezed his shoulder, and left. I wondered if she would stop back with milk and graham crackers at three. Greg washed down the last of his meal with a few long swigs of soda, dexterously and meticulously folded the foil wrapper into a disk the size of a quarter, popped it back into the bag, and dumped the bag into the trash. Next he tossed the now empty soda can into what I presumed was a recycling bin. His mom may have catered lunch, but she didn't have to clean up after he ate it. His attention to neatness was at odds with the frat-boy squalor of his desktop, which, like Chris's, was hidden beneath piles of paper. Greg leaned back again, a smile of satiety brightening his features.

I stuck my head out the office door, caught Sarah's eye, and signaled for her to join us. "Greg, just one more question and then I'd like to get a few photos of you and we'll be out of your way," I said. "Tell me, how do you like doing business in New Jersey, in Jersey City to be exact?"

This time Greg stroked his chin. Then with surprising enthusiasm he said, "Sweet, sweet deal. I can be in New York in fifteen minutes on the PATH. And the real estate here is *relatively* affordable compared to the Valley." As he spoke, Greg stretched out his arms as if to remind me of the enormity of the space we were in. "We got a grant to hot wire this place. And when our lease is up, if we decide to buy, well, there will be tax abatements up the ying yang." He added the next sentence quickly, perhaps to convince me that he was more than just an underage moneymaking machine. "Not only that, but I like the diversity here, the energy."

When Sarah walked in, I glanced at my watch, skipped the introductions, and ordered, "Sarah, get a shot of Greg here and Mattie Mollifer. She's his mom. And then get one of the young man over there who looks like Dilbert as homey rapper. He's a student intern from RECC's business department." A photo of him would earn Greg points among the locals and it would tickle Nathan no end.

Sarah arranged Greg and his beaming mother so that she stood behind him as he sat at his PC. I smothered a smirk as I envisioned the caption, "Behind every great techno nerd there's a good woman." Then Sarah took one of Nathan and Greg beneath the e-media.com logo. We left in a flurry, packing up the photo equipment, stowing the tape recorder, and saying our good-byes all at once.

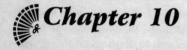

Chapter 10

Nathan Futura
College Composition III
October 7, 1999
Prof. Barrett

Journal

Yo Profesor B, this placement you got me, it phat. It ain't nothing like where I was at before. You want me to write about corporate culture, well what I'm about to tell you, it the truth but you may not believe it.

Everybody here be totally psyched about they jobs. They don't never look at the clock. Everybody come in early and stay late, especially the technodudes and, man, every day is dress down Friday for them. Greg, my mentor, you saw him. He a millionaire and he dress worse than the homeless dudes in Journal Square. The folks in sales and marketing dress more presentable.

Back to how they working all the time. They even got a washer and dryer here so they can wash they own pitiful close and not have to leave. And a dentist came the other day so the programmer with the toothache didn't have to leave the job he was running! See, Professor B, I knew you wouldn't believe it!

So far they treat me real good. I can help myself to the stuff in the frige (they got mostly fruit and fruit juice though. What these dudes got against a little sugar?) I can use the computer to do my homework if there's nothing else for me to do. They give me mostly copying and downloading to work on and they say maybe they gonna teach me to run the switchboard and let me sit in on some of there meetings. I try to tell them I do some programming, but Greg say I have to wait. It's a security issue he say cause I got no clearance yet. He say they work-ing on it. He give me some stuff to read about the product and the company.

The management style here is way different than even what's in our textbook. It whack. They got teams for everything, mar-keting, sales, tech support, tech development, everything. And the teams got captains. The captain is like a supervisor only real nice. The captains write up reports on the team members to see who gets a raise and whatnot. But nobody say nothing if you get up and shoot a few hoops in the middle of the morning or if you crash after lunch. (I think if they ate more sugar, maybe they wouldn't be so tired all the time. What you think? I seen those M&Ms in your office:-).) That don't feel right to me though. I'm only here two afternoons a week and I want to get the most out of it I can. Like I was saying onceandawhile the captains meet with Greg to go over problems. I think that's when they do their planning too. Everybody seem real mellow.

Maybe that's why the place look so nasty. Except for Mattie, don't nobody pick up after hisself. You could probably grow a lotta corporate cultures right there on Greg's desk:-)!

Gotta go get my sister now. I don't like her to get out and

there be nobody waiting. Thanks again for getting me this placement. I be writing more next week.

"Security is tight in these places. It may not be easy for us to get into either one of these companies to look around," Betty remarked, tossing the copy of Nathan's journal back to me. Betty, Illuminada, and I had converged upon my tiny office at RECC right after convocation for an impromptu strategy session.

"Yeah, your Brenda Starr impersonation is getting old," said Illuminada. Since Lourdes had dropped out of Rutgers, Illuminada had been uncharacteristically edgy and snide. Even though I understood that the disapproval in her tone was not really directed at me, I bridled.

"Don't knock my reporting," I answered, making a conscious effort to keep the defensiveness I felt out of my voice. "At least I was able to meet the players. I got some good press for RECC too. And Nathan was thrilled to see his photo in the paper. His little sister hung it up in her room." I smoothed out Nathan's journal on the desk in front of me as I spoke and, with my hand on the paper, I suddenly realized how we could gain access to scoop.com. The glow from the light bulb going off in my head must have lit up my face.

"*Dios mio,* I know that look," cracked Illuminada. "Bel's just had an idea. I can see her brow wrinkling and hear the wheels cranking in there."

Ignoring her totally this time, I said, "We can disguise ourselves as cleaning women, you know, pretend we work for a cleaning service, and get in that way.

Nathan says e-media.com is a mess, and he's right. scoop.com is probably just as bad."

"If the place is such a sty, they probably don't have a cleaning service," said Betty. "But they must, at least for the bathrooms and the common spaces. They have to." She was thinking out loud.

"I'll talk to Delores," said Illuminada. When Betty and I simultaneously arched our eyebrows, she explained. "Delores Melendez. She runs Delores Does Dusting. She started out as a one-woman operation cleaning condos in West New York, and now she's got a crew of fifty women cleaning offices and apartments all over the county. I bet both those companies use her. She's got an excellent security rating." Illuminada's chin lifted ever so slightly as she spoke, so I assumed that she had had not a little to do with the high security rating of Ms. Melendez's firm. Illuminada's own business had expanded exponentially in recent years, and a fair amount of it came from local businesses that contracted with her to do background checks on candidates for employment. Glancing reflexively at her watch, Illuminada reached for the doorknob. "I'll get back to you," she called over her shoulder as she opened the door and eased herself out of my monk's cell of an office before Betty or I could respond.

"I could just ask Ashley to find out if either company uses a cleaning service and if so, which one," I said to Illuminada's back and to Betty, who was standing now too, with her arms crossed in front of her chest.

"Oh no, you don't!" Betty snapped, her voice sharp in the small enclosure. "Remember, Illuminada said not to let her in on what we're doing. The fewer people who are involved, the better." Betty uncrossed her arms, picked up her purse, and turned to leave. "Well, girl, after all the offices my mom cleaned to get me educated, it looks like I'm going right back in the family business," was her cryptic comment as she edged around my desk toward the open door. Only a quick hug as she left reminded me that, unlike Illuminada, at least Betty wasn't holding me personally responsible for what was bothering her.

The rush to get through a stack of speech outlines and another of journals, two demanding classes, and an unusually deadly committee meeting later in the day prevented me from thinking further about the implications of my plan. I was drained when I got home and found a barely audible phone message from someone whispering something about Ruth and Samuel and an oral presentation. I assumed this soft-spoken caller was a student in one of my speech classes confused about an assignment and intimidated by my answering machine. I spent a few minutes muttering to myself about how the RECC English faculty should incorporate telephone skills into the speech syllabus so students would learn how to leave audible and coherent messages. I was hunched over the machine listening to the third replay when I finally realized that the mystery caller was, in fact, Mildred Kooper, from my bat mitzvah study group. Apparently proficiency on the violin did not translate into proficiency on the phone.

Given this new context, I decoded the message easily. Mildred wanted to know if I would mind switching presentation topics with her. Each of us was expected to report on and interpret a different book in the Old

Testament. I'd drawn the Book of Ruth, while Mildred had gotten the Book of Samuel. Like I knew the difference or it mattered. Happy to oblige and chuckling at my own ignorance, I returned Mildred's call at once, as always, eager for closure to the day's obligations. Rather smugly, I left what I thought was a very clear and accessible message to the effect that I'd never read either of the biblical texts in question and had no objections to making the switch she proposed. I hoped she'd use my sharp diction and projected volume as models of message-leaving protocol.

It was only after I put down the phone that I thought to consult the course calendar Rabbi OK had provided. The presentation on the Book of Ruth was not for several months but the one on the Book of Samuel was two weeks away. Later that evening over a glass of Chianti and a slice of Patsy's pizza embellished with fresh mozzarella, roasted red peppers, and basil, I told Sol about this most recent lesson in my Jewish education. He said, "Well, your friend Mildred may be a wipe-out on the message machine, but the woman sure as hell can read a calendar."

Chapter 11

19 And Elka'nah knew Hannah his wife and the Lord remembered her: 20 And in due time Hannah conceived and bore a son, and she called his name Samuel, for she said, I have asked him of the Lord.

1 SAMUEL 1

19 And Samuel grew, and the Lord was with him and let none of his words fall to the ground. 20 And all Israel from Dan to Beer-sheba knew that Samuel was established as a prophet of the Lord. 21 And the Lord appeared again at Shiloh, for the Lord revealed himself to Samuel at Shiloh by the word of the Lord.

1 SAMUEL 3

1 And the word of Samuel came to all Israel. Now Israel went out to battle against the Philistines; they encamped at Ebene'zer, and the Philistines encamped at Aphek.

4 SAMUEL 4

104

"What's a nice Jewish bubba like you doing with a shiner like that?" That was the question everyone in our bat mitzvah study group was too polite to ask when I showed up on Sunday. Instead, Rabbi OK jotted something in the margin of her lecture notes, Sandi's brows contracted with concern and curiosity, and Mildred frowned and blew me a kiss. Ashley held her own head in a pantomime of concern. Fortunately the fact that with my black eye and bandaged ear, I looked like the big loser in a skirmish with Mike Tyson, never really required an explanation, at least not then. We were too busy trying to follow the threads of Rabbi OK's lecture on the history of the Old Testament that began as a far-flung assortment of ancient Hebrew scrolls, recording the earliest history of the Israelites. This was the story of the book so crucial to those who long ago came to be known as "the people of the Book." Engrossed in the saga of the Dead Sea Scrolls, the tribulations of various translators, and the dating of the Pentateuch or Five Books of Moses, we did not notice the time pass. We were all a bit startled when Rabbi OK apologized for keeping us late, and rushed off to meet with someone waiting in her office.

No sooner had she left than Mildred came over to where I sat, slowly closing my notebook and reminding myself that one cannot live on revelation alone. It was long past time for lunch. She put her hand on my upper arm. I saw red. Under my black turtleneck, a purple and navy blue bruise extended from my shoulder to my elbow. I stiffened, drew back, and winced. Intent on her own agenda, Mildred was oblivious to my body language. Fortunately she withdrew her hand to adjust the strap of her shoulder bag before she gushed, "Bel, I can't thank you enough. I'm auditioning for a spot in a feminist klezmer jazz band, the Klezmamas, next week, and I need to practice every minute between now and then. I even canceled a couple of regularly scheduled violin lessons. Joining this group would be a chance to integrate my feminism, my music, and my religion, not to mention it would mean a little additional income too." Mildred rubbed her thumb and forefinger together on that last line. "I certainly wouldn't have had time to do justice to Samuel now, but by the time we get around to Ruth, I'll be able to immerse myself in it." Her narrow face was rounded by her smile. Obviously the prospect of cuddling up with the faithful Ruth delighted Mildred. I couldn't help returning her smile.

"Glad to help. It's a mitzvah," I replied, taking quiet pleasure in what an accomplished liar I was. "I don't know how much time I can give Samuel either. We're getting close to midterms." I didn't want Mildred to think that she was the only one with anything to do. I was dying to tell her that I was moonlighting once a week as a slave for Delores Does Dusting but discretion triumphed and I added simply, "But I'll do what I can." In spite of my determination not to blame Mildred for what was my own fault, my inner martyr, chafing at the unfamiliar gag order I'd imposed on her, had injected a nasal whine into my voice. Striving for a warmer tone, I asked, "Can you spare a few minutes and join us for a quick lunch today?"

"No. Not until after the audition. But then it'll be my treat, okay? Meanwhile, I hope your eye feels better."

I couldn't stay mad at Mildred. She was very earnest
about reconnecting with her roots, and her zeal, like
her smile, brightened our discussions and sparked enthusiasm that was often latent in each of us. And I appreciated her solicitude about my eye. I hadn't felt this
bad since some thug on a bike tried to make roadkill
out of me when I was looking into Dr. Garcia's death.
I needed all the sympathy I could get.

"I will. Thanks. Meanwhile, good luck. I'll keep my
fingers crossed for you."

"Yes, me too," echoed Sandi as she pulled me in the
direction of the synagogue door. "Good luck." Then,
turning to our other classmates, Sandi asked, "Ashley,
Janet, either of you up for a late lunch type experience
today?"

"No. Thanks. I'm meeting Howard." Ashley's voice
softened as it always did when she mentioned her husband's name. "But later I'm going to see about getting
us a Hebrew tutor like Rabbi OK suggested. I'll e-mail
you." Ashley didn't mention my shiner at all, but she
too patted me on the arm as she left. "Take care," she
said gently. She turned away and so did not see me
flinch.

"Thanks," Sandi called after her.

"Sorry, I can't go either," said Janet. "I have to cover
for a friend tonight at the hospital, so I'm going home
to sleep for a few hours. Maybe you should get a little
rest too," Janet said tactfully to me. Compared to the
people she treated every day in neuro ICU, I probably
looked pretty good.

Even though Janet's remark made me realize that I
had no monopoly on the mitzvah market, I had started

at Ashley's mention of a Hebrew tutor, though Lord knew we all needed one. "Yeah. I just about have time for Hebrew lessons on top of everything else," I muttered as Sandi and I walked out together. By the time we got to the street, I was fully into a self-directed sotto voce riff on how I could fit Hebrew lessons into my twenty-minute lunch break or while driving my mother to the doctor's office for one of her numerous medical consultations.

"Remember when you used to study out loud, Bel? You'd list all the characteristics of Impressionist painting or chant the prologue to *The Canterbury Tales* in Middle English while you were in the shower. And right before comps, you took to reciting lines from *The Waste Land* every time you dealt a bridge hand." Sandi's voice was good-humored as she recalled one of my least endearing collegiate quirks. "So what the hell are you muttering about now? Does it by any chance have something to do with the fact that you look like a poster person for a battered woman's shelter?"

"Well, no, actually. It doesn't." It would serve Sandi right for getting me into all this in the first place if I kept her in suspense about how I earned these battle scars for a few minutes. Sounding exactly like one of my own students, I griped, "Not only did Mildred con me into giving my presentation months early, but the Book of Ruth is about five pages long and Samuel is two books. It's over eighty pages! I started it yesterday. It's full of guys fighting, mostly the Israelites and the Philistines. And when it's not about fighting, it's about whose wife's able to conceive or who's going to be king. It's kind of like Spartacus has his wife get divine in vitro and then he goes to the democratic caucus where a little divine intervention also goes a long way. It gets a little juicier when David finally comes on the scene. Unless I'm reading it wrong, he's a studly bisexual who's ambitious as all get out. But just when he's getting ready to hit on Bathsheba, I had to stop to respond to some papers for class tomorrow."

I groaned before droning on, "And there are too many names. I can't remember who's related to whom for two seconds. I've just got one estrogen patch. For me to remember all those names I'd have to walk around with an entire estrogen quilt plastered to my butt. And I have no time to read any commentary either." As my lamentation went on, I realized I had fallen into an old pattern, and boy, did it feel good.

Sandi recognized it too and, on cue, assumed her role in our familiar if dated dialogue. "Now listen. You're going to do just fine. You know you're a quick study. And you can make up your own commentary. Remember, Bel, underneath that frizzy fluff you actually paid someone an outrageous amount of money to style for you is the feminist brain of an estrogen-enhanced candidate for a doctorate in applied linguistics. Just don't be intimidated by the fact that it's a biblical text. Deconstruct it." Sandi stopped for a minute and then added, "Seriously, Bel. Remember, you're the one who thinks on her feet and can talk her way out of a glue barrel."

I gave Sandi's arm a little squeeze as I followed her into Benny Tudino's. She turned and winked at me. She could still pump me up. I really don't know if I'd have made it through college without her cheering me on. I know I wouldn't have made it through organic chemistry. We took seats in a booth in the back room of the old pizzeria. It had to be the least trendy place in Hoboken. There was a conspicuous lack of fresh air let alone fresh basil, but there was no doubt among generations of pizza aficionados that Benny's pizza was to die for. It was always Rebecca's first stop when she came home to visit.

"Actually, I don't know what you're complaining about. I'm stuck with reading the whole megillah," said Sandi, dragging out the syllables of the Hebrew word for the Book of Esther. But she was smiling. "I read a few pages every night. It's fascinating, almost as fascinating as the shiner you've got."

"That's fine if your schedule allows," I said, ignoring her reference to my eye, not quite ready to relinquish my role as the complainer. "I don't have many nights left now," I whined in my best imitation of a Jewish Joan of Arc contemplating the flames. Relaxed in the cushioned seat of the booth, I was finally ready to tell Sandi how I got hurt.

"I didn't think you had any evening classes this semester," Sandi said. "Or is Sol taking Viagra and keeping you up all night?" I stuck my tongue out at her. "Or have you just been banging your head against a wall? Aren't you ever going to tell me how you got a makeover that makes you look like you just did ten rounds with Hulk Hogan? Please."

Our slices arrived just then and I realized it was hard to play the martyr when eating Benny's pizza. The stuff is just so good. But I was determined to give it my best shot, so I continued, "You know how Illuminada and Betty and I are trying to get a handle on who killed Ashley's friend?"

Sandi nodded, looking at me over her slice. "Well, we've been working . . ." The buzz of Sandi's cell phone cut me off. She reached in her capacious bag, found it, and held it to her ear. "This afternoon? Well, why not? Sure. I can just make it. Four-thirty at the Angelika. First one there gets on line for tickets, right? Sure. I know the drill. I'm a fast learner." Dumping the phone back in her purse, Sandi pulled out a few bills and said, "Sorry to rush off. I'll explain another time."

In seconds she was on her feet and blowing me air kisses on the way out the door. As she left in a whirl of blond hair and lime green chenille, she called, "I know I swore I'd never dump you for a guy, Bel. But for a really good foreign movie *and* a guy? I'm outta here. Put ice on that eye. I'll call you."

Chapter 12

To: Bbarrett@circle.com
From: Rbarrett@Uwash.edu
Re: Now what?
Date: 10/12/99 18:09:56

Mom, now what are you into? I called the other night like we agreed, and you weren't home. Sol answered though, and he told me you were out cleaning somebody's office as part of another "murder investigation." My friends' mothers play golf or do volunteer work or maybe garden in their spare time. But not my mom. She's either looking for God or running around at all hours playing Cagney and Lacey with her girlfriends.

Hello, Mom, we had a telephone date for ten, East Coast time. How could you forget? I just can't believe you blew off your only daughter and your only grandchild (who stayed up specially to gurgle to you) so you could clean somebody's office. That is just so lame. I got a little steamed, so Sol told me Betty and Illuminada were with you. I think he thought that would make me chill, but I told him sometimes all three of you have no more sense than Abbie J. I'd tell you to plaster another estrogen patch on the other half of your butt if I honestly thought it would restore your memory or your common sense. Sometimes I think Dad's right, and you're not wrapped too tight.

Anyway, did Sol tell you that the other day Abbie J sat up all by herself? And I passed my statistics exam? But what do you care about that, right? And you're probably not interested in Keith's promotion, are you? (By the way, he says hi.)

Gotta nurse Abbie J now and then I promised her a bath. I would never stand up MY daughter for some dead guy.

Love anyway,
Rebecca

Before I had too much time to marvel at how my mother's talent for inducing guilt had skipped a generation only to resurface in her granddaughter, I had to turn off the computer and get ready for another night with Delores Does Dusting. My life had somehow turned into a rerun of the old Hazel comic strip. As I buttoned the brown polyester shirt with the words *Delores Does Dusting* embroidered in gold over my left boob and wedged my hips into matching brown pants, I winced. My left side was still sore in a few places. I sure didn't feel like doing two hours of domestic drudgery at scoop.com tonight, especially after what happened the last time.

It had started out okay when Delores picked us up in her van at Illuminada's house a little before nine. Before she got there, Betty reached into a large shopping bag she had brought and pulled out three wigs, and we all shared a giggle. "Vic says we should wear these in case we run into somebody from the college who knows us," she explained. We immediately recognized the wisdom of his suggestion since RECC students popped up everywhere. Vic, proud proprietor of Vallone and Sons Funeral Home, had provided us with disguises before. He had on hand a fairly respectable selection of wigs, clothing, accessories, and makeup for those of his clients who needed a little sartorial and cosmetic assistance before making their last public appearance. "Here's yours, Bel," said Betty, handing me the sleek blond tresses I remembered wearing the night we nailed Louie Palumbo's killer. Illuminada got a blond one too, a halo of golden curls with a lavender plastic butterfly clip nesting in them. Around her own trademark dreads, Betty tied a purple silk scarf with burnished red tendrils peeking out to frame her dark face.

I guess we passed muster because the two other workers in the van didn't stop chatting and laughing in Spanish except to nod a greeting. Illuminada spoke to us in Spanish, and, according to plan, Betty and I mumbled, *"Si"* and *"Dios mio"* when it seemed appropriate. As soon as Delores dropped off the other two women and their cleaning equipment at a condo in downtown Jersey City, she turned the car in the direction of Silicon Slum. Once parked outside the huge old warehouse that was home to scoop.com, Delores turned to face us, gave Illuminada a set of keys, and explained in English where the lights were. We got out of the van and Delores shepherded us past the security guard. He recognized her and waved us in without even eyeballing the plastic card she offered him. Then Delores turned and left. We were on our own.

We stepped into a black hole. Betty grabbed my hand and we froze while behind us the door creaked shut and in front of us Illuminada groped along the wall for the light panel. It wasn't long before she found it and flipped a switch. Betty and I both gasped. We were face to face with a sheer wall of slate gray fake rock soaring two stories into the warehouse's upper regions before extending parallel with the ceiling and the building's concrete floor. Looking eerily like Notre Dame meets the Flintstones, the wall arched over a segment of the space, casting shadows over several cubicles and what should have been the vestibule.

This had to be where Chris Johanson had fallen to his death. What I saw next validated this impression. Beneath the wall was what I took to be a simple shrine made out of a helmet with a single white chrysanthemum protruding from one of the vents. Standing in the shadow of the monolithic facade in the dim and nearly deserted old building, I suddenly felt queasy. Betty was on the same wavelength because she muttered, "Welcome to Fred's place," and squeezed my hand. "These dudes have the same decorator as the Flintstones." As soon as Betty spoke, Illuminada turned around with her finger to her lips, reminding us of our vow of silence.

We had agreed to pretend to be non–English speakers so that people working late would communicate freely in front of us. This meant that Betty and I would continue to say *"Si"* and *"Dios mio"* and *"No comprende"* if we spoke at all. I could tell that Betty, who lived to control things, felt smothered by the rules of this charade. I, who lived to talk, also hated having to muzzle my motor mouth. Illuminada could speak as long as she spoke Spanish, but she pointed out that once we began working, we'd be too far apart to talk anyway because the place was so big.

And we had to work. That had been Delores's only condition. If we didn't clean the place, she'd lose the contract. Looking us up and down, she had said that three young women usually managed to do a pretty good job on the bathrooms, kitchen, and common spaces in a couple of hours. We didn't have to clean the cubicles because they were "private." Accepting the challenge inherent in her comment, we had agreed among ourselves to focus only on cleaning the first night so as to familiarize ourselves with the office's layout.

To that end, we circled the floor, our eyes everywhere. Like e-media.com, scoop.com boasted kitchen equipment, nap areas, a unisex bathroom at each end of the cavernous space, and lots of cubicles. I saw Betty and Illuminada's noses wrinkle at the sight of the workstations piled high with paper and the overflowing trash cans. At one point we stopped short at the sight of a barefoot, long-haired young woman in jeans and a T-shirt performing what looked like a robotic dance solo in a darkened lounge area. Tiptoeing closer, we realized that she was doing tai chi. She was the only person we saw on that side of the office. As we turned the corner, we came upon a bank of cubicles and noticed one that was dimly illuminated. Approaching it, we became aware of soft snuffling noises.

We peered in and saw that the room was lit only by the glow of the monitor. Beneath the desk, curled in a nest of printouts, a young man snored. Over the rhythmic sounds of his sleep, I heard Betty catch her breath.

The door to the last cubicle in the row was open exposing a space empty of everything but a black canvas butterfly chair exactly like the one Sandi and I had had in our room at Vassar for four years. Even without the overlay of plaid kilt skirts and jeans I would have known it anywhere. In the corner behind the chair stood a life-sized inflatable plastic cactus with a black cowboy hat placed rakishly atop its highest branch. A large purple button with '98 printed on it in gold was pinned to the hatband. Some spray painter had spangled pink polka dots over every paintable surface, creating a strange diorama of Seurat meets Barbie. Clearly the denizens of scoop.com shared the penchant for practical jokes of their peers at e-media.com. The requisite piles of paper carpeted the floor, and the little room had been empty long enough for everything in it to have acquired a patina of grime. My dusting arm twitched at the sight. Shaking our heads in amazement we continued. At the end of our circuit, we stopped in the open doorway of another cubicle. Illuminada reached in and turned on the light. We smiled collectively at the sight of a massage table. Illuminada exclaimed, *"Caramba!"* She certainly spoke for all of us that time.

Delores had told us where to find the cleaning equipment that she kept on site, and after completing our tour, we dutifully assembled the necessary pails, mops, cleansers, and rags on our carts. Pulling on rubber gloves, we set off in different directions. Betty and I each slouched toward one of the bathrooms while Illuminada made for the kitchen area. When I had scoured the fourth toilet, I paused briefly and thanked God for my day job. After scrubbing the fourth sink, I made a solemn vow never again to complain about reading and responding to student papers. By the time I had mopped the seemingly endless bathroom floor clean enough to see my reflection in the tiles, I promised myself that nevermore would I gripe about boring committee meetings, mindless administrators, or even nepotistic trustees. And, at long last, when I had polished a conference table and six chairs and vacuumed a carpeted area the size of a city block, I sank into the nearest chair to catch my breath.

Just as I was promising myself to get in shape by dieting and doing more yoga, I noticed the nameplate on the door of the room adjacent to the chair where I had collapsed. It read, "Troy Tarnoff, CEO, Director of Special Projects." The name acted like a shot of adrenaline, and galvanized me into taking the action I did, the very action we had all agreed not to take. Trying the door, I found it locked. That didn't stop me. A quick glance at the lock told me it was like the one on our inside front door at home, cheap and easy to pry open. I pulled my trusty Visa card out of my bra where I'd stowed it just in case I needed to buy myself a beer later. Sliding the card into the space between the doorjamb and the lock, I jiggled it around until I felt it edge under the movable part of the lock. When that little gizmo retracted, I turned the doorknob and the door opened.

Running my fingers along the burlap-covered wall in search of the light switch, I stepped inside. Suddenly I was careening through space and then crashing into several pieces of furniture. In seconds I was on my butt on the floor. My heart was beating loudly, but the throbbing in my head was louder. When I dared to open my eyes and look around, I made out a scooter illuminated by a shaft of light from the open door. Apparently that soon to be trendy toy was the vehicle that had transformed me from an expert lock picker into a thing that went bump in the night.

Slowly I tried untangling my legs and arms, and they seemed to work. I wiggled my hips. Nothing felt broken. This wasn't the first time my aging bones had stood up to a bad fall. Grimly I recalled being sideswiped by a thug in a pickup truck who thought I'd look better in the gutter. Did I owe my survival to divine intervention or to my estrogen patch and all those calcium supplements I swallowed so religiously?

Pondering this question, which never would have occurred to me before I began my bat mitzvah studies, I was still sitting there rubbing my arms and legs with one hand and holding my head with the other when Illuminada charged in, backlit by the glow from the hallway. Neck muscles rigid, eyes narrowed to wary slits, she had her right hand in her pocket where I knew she kept her gun. Betty was right behind her. Even in semidarkness it didn't take either of them more than a second to see what had happened. "Joy riding again," whispered Betty, picking up the scooter and moving it out of my way so I could get up.

Illuminada held out her hands and effortlessly

pulled me to my feet. I always forget how strong she is. I knew she was angry that I had entered the office, but all she whispered was, "If you're okay, tell us where to put this damn thing. Where was it?" She held the scooter in one hand. I pointed to the spot on the floor near the door where I thought it had been, and Illuminada carefully placed it there. Betty suddenly stuck a rag under the rubber-gloved hand I'd been holding to my head. She had moved just in time to prevent the blood that was dripping from my fingers from staining the floor. Losing no time, Illuminada pulled a Kleenex out of her pocket and plastered it to the side of my head where my blood was in danger of ruining my blond wig. Silently we closed and locked the door and left the room. A few minutes later we walked by the yawning security guard and found ourselves once again outside. At the curb Delores was waiting in the van. She looked at her watch. It was exactly eleven o'-clock. She smiled.

Eyes on the road, Delores noticed nothing amiss, and it wasn't long before she dropped us off at Illuminada's house. We pulled off our wigs. I was in no mood for a lecture from the new no-nonsense Illuminada, so I was relieved when, she said, *"Como mierda,* Bel, you can't go home looking like that. If Sol sees you bleeding, he'll have a coronary. Besides, he won't let you come out and play detective with us anymore. Come in. We're going to play doctor now." She sounded like her old self.

"Listen, girl, Bel isn't the only one who needs medical attention. I haven't worked so hard since the last time we moved. Tonight I used muscles that I haven't heard from since I gave up tae kwon do classes over two years ago," said Betty.

"Yeah, and tomorrow you're going to really be hearing from them, believe me," I said. "We all are." Reaching into my book bag, which I'd been reunited with when we got to Illuminada's, I took out a large bag of M&Ms, ripped it open, poured myself a handful, and offered the bag to the rest of the night shift.

Betty wrapped some ice in a towel and handed it to me to apply to my eye while Illuminada swabbed the cut on my ear with antiseptic and bandaged it. While she worked, she said, *"Dios mio,* you got pretty banged up. Probably by the time you take off that uniform, you'll be black and blue all over the place, like an overage S&M queen." She actually giggled. "Better put some ice on those bruises too." I knew she was right although the infusion of chocolate and sugar had already worked its customary alchemy, and I was feeling much better. It occurred to me that maybe it wasn't God or estrogen, but rather my steady diet of chocolate and sugar that had kept my bones from cracking when I crashed into the corner of Troy Tarnoff's file cabinet, his desk, and his floor. I helped myself to another handful of M&Ms.

As Illuminada finished treating my ear, I instinctively put my hand up to my other earlobe, reaching under my hair for the plain gold stud I had worn instead of the more flamboyant hoops and spangles I favored when I was not cleaning toilets. I felt my stomach muscles tighten and my heart rate increase as I fingered the tiny gold nub. "Oh Oh."

"What is it? Did you get cut on the other ear too?"

As she spoke, Illuminada brushed the hair back from the other side of my face and saw the gold stud. "*Caramba,* Bel," she said, dropping my hair as if it were on fire. "Your other stud tore off when you hit your head, didn't it? That's why you have this gash. And now the damn thing's in that office somewhere. On the floor. You might as well have left your business card."

I lowered my head, ashamed by what I'd done and chastened and hurt by the sharpness of Illuminada's reproof.

"It's okay, Bel," said Betty. "A stud like that could belong to anyone who works there. Even guys wear them. It won't matter." Turning to Illuminada, Betty directed, "Lighten up. I'm telling you it won't matter." I could have kissed her for trying to reassure me that I hadn't blown the whole deal, but I didn't believe her for a minute.

my application, they'll think I'm well rounded (which I'm not)
and not some unathletic dork (which I am). I have to do community service every week too, so they realize I'm compassion-
ate and concerned about my fellow humans. And, on top of all
that, I have to go to Hebrew school three afternoons a week
AND go to services on Shabbat AND memorize a whole lot of
Hebrew prayers and chants AND write a brilliant speech that all
my relatives will love. I have to do all this before December because my bat mitzvah is on December11. I don't even have time
to surf the Net much anymore. I don't believe God would want
me to go through all this, do you? So who's got problems?

I had problems. Not surprisingly, one of them was
Sol. Having given up nagging me about my safety after
I figured out how to apprehend Louie Palumbo's killer
without getting myself killed, he was now focusing his
anxiety-driven attention on my health. Worried about
the impact of my latest extra curricular activity, domestic servitude, he was constantly on my case. Every
week when I came in after cleaning, he'd be waiting in
bed. He would look up at me over his crossword puz-
zle and ask, "Bel, how can you expect to stay out half
the night working like a peon and then teach at RECC
all day? You'll get overtired and then you'll get sick."
Or he'd call me at RECC and leave a message on my
voice mail saying, "At least take a few minutes and get
a flu shot, will you? You're going to get run down."
My all-time favorite was a fax he sent me at work saying simply, "Sweetheart, you're just a few years south
of sixty. You can't stay out until all hours anymore." I
asked him if he wanted to take out an ad trumpeting
my age in the *Jersey City Herald*.

My mother was also making me nuts. She had a different fish to gefilte though. Ever since we'd talked about it during that Sabbath dinner, she had been after me to have a will and advance directives drawn up. "Sybil, what if you're run over by a truck on the way home from work?" Or, even better, "Sybil, what if you're mugged and you end up in an irreversible coma?" Or the one that never failed to push every button I had and then some, "Sybil, remember poor Sarah Lenz, the thirty-five-year-old woman who had an aneurysm in the shower and dropped dead?" Finally after I gave in and promised her that I'd get a lawyer and do a will, her only response was, "I'll believe it when I see the piece of paper."

Sol didn't believe me either when I assured him that after a few sessions on the night shift, I had started to toughen up. The exercise actually felt good. I may have been getting older, but I have very young endorphins. Betty and I agreed that even the imposed silence was beginning to feel meditative rather than punitive. The whole experience was taking on a very Zen quality, and this was good because I was certain that if we hung out there long enough with our eyes open, we'd notice something or hear something that would help us figure out who killed Chris Johanson. The techno zombies in the office, including the nocturnal tai chi practitioner and the guy we dubbed Rip Van Winkle, were getting used to us as were the others who drifted in and out all evening.

I hadn't even minded the night Delores asked us to clean up what we'd taken to calling the polka.com cubicle in preparation for a quick paint job and a new oc-

cupant, and that task fell to me. I went at it with the
gusto of a born-again housewife trying to impress her
mother-in-law. First I chucked the jaunty cowboy hat
into the trash where it crowned the debris until I de-
flated the plastic saguaro and tossed it after the hat.
Then I wiped down the walls, dumped the trash, and
vacuumed the floor and the butterfly chair. Finally I
actually sat down in the chair for a few minutes to rest.
The seat was a lot lower than I remembered it being
when I was in college, and there was no Harry Bela-
fonte crooning in the background now, but I settled my
weary bones into that familiar fabric sling and leaned
back. Stretching luxuriously, I found myself staring up
at the spot where the gray overhang of the climbing
wall met the white of the ceiling.

I began speculating about what had happened to the
previous occupant of that surreal cubicle. I reasoned
that she or he was some techie whiz kid who had grad-
uated from a Southwestern high school or college in
1998 and headed East to cash in on the profits to be
made in Silicon Slum. Now this millennial migrant
worker had probably moved on to an even more lucra-
tive position in the wired and wild world of e-commerce.
Or maybe the child prodigy had tired of life in this la-
la land that was half FAO Schwarz and half science fic-
tion and, homesick for Big Sky Country, returned to
the desert and a low-tech career lassoing livestock on a
ranch. This extended reverie bought me a few minutes
of much needed sitting.

When I finally heaved myself out of the chair, which
had been much easier thirty-odd years and, alas, pounds
ago, I looked around at the now pristine pink splotches.

Delores would be pleased with my work. And Delores was. She was pleased with all of us. She'd gotten a call from the facilities manager at scoop.com commending her for the thoroughness and efficiency of her work-force, and she planned to raise her rates on the strength of the excellent job we were all doing.

We certainly were thorough and efficient. Betty and I finished early one evening and, in accordance with Delores's instructions, began an assault on the interior of the fridge. Delores had asked us to empty it, chuck anything that moved, and scour the shelves and draw-ers. Expecting the worst, we opened the door. It wasn't bad. There was no overpowering reek or mag-goty food. It looked a lot like anybody's fridge in that there were enough doggie bags of half-eaten take-out food to feed a good-sized village somewhere and enough cans of beer to slake the thirst of a good-sized fraternity.

Following Delores's instructions to get rid of all leftovers, we put the soft, often squishy sacks into a big plastic trash bag. As we did this, I remembered Ashley tossing Chris's climbing gear, photos, and allergy meds into a bag to bring to his wife, and that flashback intruded on my Zen state for a few sad seconds. While Betty scoured the interior of the fridge, I scrubbed and rinsed the drawers. We intended to do the freezer next week unless someone else got to it first. On our way out, I was surprised to see Betty carrying the large plastic garbage bag. Then I recalled that, since our reg-ular inspection of the trash receptacles had revealed nothing of interest, we had agreed to bring the contents of the fridge home to examine. There was always the off chance that among the moldy and/or desiccated sushi, mesclun, and three-cheese pizza slices, we'd find whatever it was we were looking for.

In a way we did. Spreading the contents of the plastic bag on Illuminada's kitchen table, we opened two of the seven identical brown bags and found that they contained the now putrid remains of partially eaten roasted veggie wraps. The roasted veggie packets rang a bell. "That's what Greg had the day I visited e-media.com," I exclaimed.

"Yeah, but he's not talking to Troy, right? There's no way he'd come over for a cozy lunch, is there?" Illuminada was right, but that wasn't what I had in mind.

"No, according to Ashley, they're not tight anymore at all. But maybe this is Troy's wrap." I spoke tentatively, and both Betty and Illuminada looked puzzled. To their credit they waited patiently for me to finish thinking my thought, knowing from experience that only then could I tell them about it. Finally I continued, still choosing my words carefully and then saying them slowly. "You know, Sandi and I used to eat tuna melts all the time in college. We got them at a deli in Poughkeepsie. I still love them and make them a lot. So does she. Greg and Troy used to be close. Their friendship goes way back. Maybe they both got onto a veggie wrap kick. Maybe Greg still orders those when he can. I think it's a long shot, but it'll be easy to check out who ordered these at the place where they got them. There ought to be a receipt in at least one of the bags. If not, there aren't too many places around here and . . ."

"And what? *Dios mio,* Bel, I mean Sherlock," said

Illuminada, her voice gruff with impatience. "It's not bad enough you've got us cleaning a place as big as the Coliseum all night, now you want us to go on a wild goose chase tracking down some geek's leftover lunch. Why? Just tell me that? Why?"

Although Betty wasn't articulating the same question, it was very clear from her drawn brow that she too harbored grave doubts about the significance of Troy's lunchtime leavings. "Well, Ashley thinks Troy was clued in by somebody that Chris was a snitch. And she said Troy was the one who probably talked too much to Chris. And Troy and Chris happened to be rock climbing together when Chris died. So I'm trying to get a handle on Troy and besides, we haven't got anything else to go on. And after all, we are what we eat," I ended rather feebly. Nobody said anything.

Illuminada finally spoke. "Okay, but count me out on the lunch hunt. Instead, I'll go get a copy of the police report." Now I looked puzzled. "Even though this went down as an accident, there still had to be an investigation and some paperwork. I'd rather spend my time reading something into that than trying to read something into this guy's food fetishes."

"That's okay. Betty and I can handle the lunch detail, right?" I turned to catch Betty's eye, knowing that she loved an excuse to break away from her office at noon and do lunch.

That's why I was surprised when she said, "Sorry, Bel. You're on your own. Nothing personal, but I'm going to take up rock climbing on my lunch hour."

 **Chapter 14**

Bel,

Where the hell have you been? You missed the meeting of the Discipline Committee yesterday and I can't seem to catch you in the office. Neither could the student who came by for a conference he had with you this morning. He left a note. Do you still work here?

Wendy

I guess I wasn't as alert as I thought if I'd completely forgotten about the Discipline Committee meeting and my conference with Nathan. The Discipline Committee had met on the same day at the same time each month during the five long years I'd been a member. I don't think I'd ever missed a meeting before. And I certainly didn't make a habit of missing conferences with students. In fact, I prided myself on my accessibility, my commitment. I checked the October 19 page of my indispensable date book and saw big as life, "DC mtg. 9-10" followed by "conf. w. Nathan 10:45." I'd just never thought to check it when I got home at midnight the night before after trolling through the trash of scoop.com. Maybe the late nights of hard labor *were* taking a toll. And my old friend and office mate, children's literature professor Wendy O'Connor, was certainly right. She and I were long overdue for a reunion. It was time for us to do lunch.

I scrawled her a message, and when we actually ran into each other in the ladies' room, we agreed to get together the next day. Wendy and I are close in the way that only two people who have shared a tiny cubicle for years are close. We'd learned early on that the best way to maintain our friendship was to stagger our time in the office so that we were there together often enough to stay connected and not often enough to crowd each other. But recently, my late nights often had me sleeping in and rushing directly to my first class. By the time I finished teaching, she had already left for her class. Before I realized it, those occasional breaks when Wendy and I could sit around over our mugs of tea and coffee exchanging RECC gossip, family crises, and teaching problems had become a casualty of my work with Delores Does Dusting.

"Bel Barrett, do you mean to tell me that you are cleaning offices at night? You, a full professor who's just a dissertation away from her Ph.D.? You, who had your kids doing laundry before they were potty trained and who fell in love with the first man you met who vacuumed?" Wendy's eyes widened. As I opened my mouth to explain, she put her finger to her lips and shook her head. "No, don't tell me. I know. This has to do with your belated discovery of religion. God is telling you to clean offices, right? You're hearing voices."

Ignoring the sarcasm in her pronouncement, I tried to explain. By the time I finished, we were at Elysium, the restaurant named on the receipt in one of the bags of fungal food that I intended to prove had once belonged to Troy. ". . . so that's why I'm cleaning offices. It's only temporary." We entered the trendy eatery on the ground floor of one of Newport's new luxury office towers, a block from Silicon Slum, and gaped. Like much else in this neighborhood, it would have been at home in Manhattan, specifically in Chelsea. A shiny metal bar snaked all the way from the front door to the back of the handsome mirrored dining room. The bar acted as an S-shaped divider, with circular tables in the curves on either side. Business people in suits and techno types in full grunge regalia eagerly chowed down on what looked like gourmet sandwiches, soups, and salads, eating at the bar as well as at the tables. Wendy was unimpressed. "Is that why we're here," she asked, "instead of at the RIP or someplace closer to school that we can afford? Because you think somebody's month-old lunch will reveal the killer?" She rolled her eyes and turned her back on me as we both followed a chatty young man carrying two enormous menus to a table.

Perched rather precariously on one of the round backless stools suspended on large coiled springs that were Elysium's modish approach to seating, I prayed for balance. The tables were bar height, and bobbing diners risked vertigo while perusing the menu, a study in vegan and veggie delicacies that was as high concept as the decor. Each dish was titled with an acronym important to dot com culture. "Welcome to Elysium. I'm Paul and I'll be your server." Paul turned out to be the same chatty young man who had seated us. "Would you like to hear the specials?" Before we had a chance to even nod, Paul had launched into a recital of the various concoctions the chef had dreamed up for that day. The acronyms for the far-out food combos made the entire list sound like an exotic alphabet soup, and Wendy and I had to avoid each other's eyes and stifle our giggles. I ordered the veggie wrap on the regular lunch menu, where it was dubbed IPO, for initial public offering. According to Paul it was one of Elysium's more prosaic and yet most popular items. He was about to offer an explanation of this phenomenon when Wendy opted to lunch on one of the specials, a glamorous salad of julienned zucchini with walnuts and blue cheese drizzled with balsamic vinegar, which was titled VC, short, I figured, for venture capital. In deference to all the work we had to do later that afternoon, Wendy ordered a Sprite and I ordered cranberry juice with tonic and lime. When Paul finally said, "I'll be right back with your drinks" and left, Wendy and I were relieved.

I watched him take our orders to the endless bar and hand them to a young woman with her back to us mixing drinks. I was surprised when, after hearing our orders, the bartender turned in our direction, smiling broadly. Like most of her patrons, she was in her early twenties. Her long black curls were barely restrained in a ponytail low on her neck. She had the deep-set dark eyes of the dashing Raoul Gutierrez and the straight nose and strong chin of the lovely Illuminada Gutierrez. This made perfect sense since she was Lourdes Gutierrez, former future pharmacist turned bartender. As soon as I recognized her, I smiled back, carefully descended from my stool, and went over to say hello.

We managed an awkward hug over the bar and then Lourdes said, *"Dios mio,* Bel, you're still the only one I know who drinks cranberry juice and tonic with lime, so when I eyeballed the order, I knew you had to be here."

"Clearly you've got your mom's propensity for detective work. It must be in the genes," I replied. I was curious to see how she'd react to the mention of her mom after Illuminada had given her so much grief about dropping out of school.

"Must be," Lourdes said pleasantly enough. "It's good to see you, Bel. It's been a while. What brings you down here?"

"Just needed a change of scene and a good lunch. How do you like working here?" The question was unnecessary. Lourdes looked terrific. Her eyes glowed and her warm smile stayed put as she poured and measured behind the bar, mixing drinks effortlessly even as we chatted. Clearly her new lifestyle agreed with her.

Like my kids' friends, my friends' kids retain a special place in my heart. Invariably considerate and affectionate, they never blow up at me, question my sanity, or criticize my weight or wardrobe the way my own kids do. That's why I was unprepared for Lourdes's next words. "Are you okay, Bel? You look a little, uh, tired. A little drawn. And I don't remember you with those circles under your eyes. Are the students giving you a hard time?" The corners of her mouth had turned down and she actually looked worried.

"No, I'm fine, really," I reassured her, resolving to check myself in the ladies' room mirror. And maybe instead of going back to the office to read student papers, I'd go home for a nap. "But I'm tying you up here," I said, leaning over the bar again to give Lourdes a quick peck on the cheek. "I'll let these folks get to you." I moved out of the queue of servers that had formed behind me and rejoined Wendy at our table.

"How's Sol taking this latest bout of postmenopausal madness? Has he issued an ultimatum yet?" Sol's penchant for overreaction to my sleuthing was well known ever since he'd walked out on me once in the middle of a murder investigation. I had nearly died of misery, and none of my friends wanted to see a repeat performance.

"He's not worrying about me becoming the target of crazed killers this time. Now he's worried about my health even though I feel fine." As I spoke I ran my fingers lightly over the skin beneath my eyes, feeling for new circles, new lines. Then, eager to shift the focus of the conversation, I asked, "So how are your kids?"

"How is everything? Are you enjoying your sandwich?" The lunch crowd had thinned and Paul hovered, apparently free now to discuss the pros and cons of the roasted veggie wrap that I hadn't even started yet. Wendy and I both nodded, unwilling to encourage him by saying so much as a single word. He left.

While Wendy filled me in on the latest doings of her grandchildren, who lived close by and whom she saw several times a week, I thought sadly of Abbie J three thousand miles away and comforted myself by greedily devouring my wrap. There was no question that it was identical to the ones that had fossilized in the fridge at scoop.com. Now I just had to figure out who ordered it. When our plates were clean, Paul came back, and this time I engaged him in conversation. "I know the bartender," I gushed. "Her mom's a friend of mine. That's why she recognized me by my drink. She knows I always order the same drink . . ." I ignored the look of incredulity Wendy shot me as she clambered down from her stool to go to the ladies' room. We'd shared too many bottles of house red over the years for her to envision me on the cranberry juice wagon for any length of time. I was glad she'd decided to leave for a minute so she didn't laugh out loud.

"Yes. We've got folks like that. Always order the same thing. I used to be like that with peanut butter and apple sandwiches. That's all I ever ate for lunch for years when I was in middle school I think it was. My mom was real worried even though it was a healthy combination. She . . ."

Before he got too far into his Proustian reverie, I deftly refocused him. Not for nothing had I been devising essay topics and tests for all these years. I know how to get information out of people. "Well, my wrap was so great I wish I could order it every day. I bet a lot of people actually do that." This was going to be easy. It was all I could do to keep from grinning.

"Oh yeah, for sure. There's this one guy from one of the dot com companies still has his mother ordering his. Can you believe that? She says he's addicted to these things. I at least outgrew my peanut butter and apple sandwich phase." He scratched his head.

"Well, this was a great sandwich. I bet he's not the only one who gets it on a regular basis." I paused, a little nervous now, hoping Paul would make this easy.

"Yeah. I do the deliveries sometimes. We got another guy in some other dot com company. You know, over there." He pointed in the direction of scoop.com. "And you know what? The sandwich you had is called the IPO. But I think we should rename it either the CEO or the DSP because the guy whose mom orders it for him at e-media.com is the CEO there, and the other guy who gets it all the time is the CEO and director of special projects at scoop.com."

"What a good idea," I said, grinning at him, at Wendy who had just returned, and at myself for having gotten what I wanted with a minimum of hassle. "I think DSP would be perfect because it's a really special wrap." Energized by my small but real triumph, I felt no need for a nap and went back to RECC, where I inhaled a bag of M&Ms and spent a productive afternoon responding to a set of journals.

# Chapter 15

To: Bbarrett@circle.com
From: Futura@recc.nj.edu
Re: No problem
Date: 10/22/99

Dear Professor B,

It cool about you missing the conference. We can set up another one. I know I need help with them verbs. Sometimes the computer tell me my grammar lame, but I don't know how to correct it. So how bout we get together next week and go over all my journals. I give you another chance:-).

Meantime I got me some good news. Ashley (she work at e-media.com but she only in onceandawhile) she say she gonna give me her computer soon as she get a new one. Now she working on getting me a printer! This gonna make a big difference in my school work, you'll see. And my sister, she can use it too.

I feel funny there sometimes you know. Like these dudes aren't much older than me, but they already got so much money and so much business experience. The marketing people they all got 4 year degrees. I'm the only community college person there. But the techies like Greg, he drop out of Brown University. I don't get it. I read that college grads make more money than people with no degrees and people been telling me I need to finish college ever since I can remember. But Greg he drop out and he got rich anyway. I don't think it's a color thing either cause there's a techie brother here black as me who also drop out of college and he drive a lexus. Something tell me if I drop out (don't worry, I won't) I end up driving a garbage truck:=). . .

Leave it to Nathan to raise complex issues of social class and social mobility. I'd have to have a talk with him about more than verbs, although they played a part in the pattern he was describing. I made a note to myself to ask Professor Jones, Nathan's adviser, to steer him into a sociology course and to help him make the connection between social class and upward mobility in millennial America.

By the time I got home, I knew it was going to be tough to gear up for another night of slave labor. When I entered the house, I smelled brisket. Sol was putting the finishing touches on a noodle kugel. The table was set for two. There were candles and a vase of chrysanthemums. A Scarlatti sonata sounded softly in the background. "God, I wish I could stay home tonight!" I exclaimed, sinking into an easy chair.

"You can and you are!" Sol said, "It's Friday! Remember? You don't have to go anywhere on weekend nights." Of course I hadn't remembered. The rigors of dusting with Delores had combined with my postmenopausal short-term memory loss to blur the hours of the day and the days of the week into one long triathalon of teaching, cleaning, and sleuthing.

I spared my already worried life partner all that and said simply, "TGIF!"

"We're having a cozy Shabbat dinner a deux and then you're going to bed. Here." Handing me a glass of red wine, he quickly blessed it.

"Amen!" I sighed, sipping the wine and easing out of my shoes. I found myself easily slipping into Shabbat mode. Virginia Woolf, my black cat, did also. She leaped into my lap and placed her paws on my chest, her purring complementing the pianist's efforts.

An hour later after several glasses of wine and two helpings of Sol's excellent brisket, I felt up to doing the dishes, but Sol wouldn't hear of it. "Just talk to me while I put them in the dishwasher," he said. "I miss you." Then, gesturing toward the garbage bag of leftover lunches from scoop.com that I'd stashed in the catproof cabinet beneath the sink, he asked, "By the way, can we get rid of this? It's pretty foul."

"NO! Don't touch that! That's my garbage! I have to go through that one more time!" I practically screamed, leaping out of the chair and grabbing the bag. The fumes wafting through in spite of the twisttie nearly knocked me out. Without benefit of refrigeration, my collection of doggie bags had devolved into something that smelled like doggie do. "Yuck," I commented pithily. "I see what you mean."

"What the hell do you have in there, anyway?" Sol bent over the dishwasher rack as he spoke. By the time I finished explaining, he'd loaded all the dishes, put away our leftovers, and wiped off the countertops and the table. I was still standing, holding the bag, so to speak. "Here. Let me have that. I'll put it outside."

"No! A cat or a squirrel or even a rat might get at it," I said, picturing our urban fauna feasting on my hard-earned evidence.

"Trust me, Bel," Sol said patiently. "I'll put the thing in a covered trash can in the backyard, and we won't put the can out front until you're prepared to face life without this stuff." Reassured, I relinquished the bag and washed my hands. When Sol came in, he washed his hands, poured us each another glass of wine, and said, "Well, you haven't asked me, but do you want to know who I think killed that poor bastard?"

Instantly I realized that I should have asked Sol what he thought long before this. He was a brilliant man, and he had been really helpful in solving the murder of Louis Palumbo. Besides, Sol was obviously feeling left out. "So who do you think killed Chris Johanson?" I asked, joining Sol on the sofa. He put his arm around me and we both extended our shoeless feet up onto the coffee table.

"First of all, I think you and your friend Ashley are totally off base to assume that this was a work-related crime. I think it was a crime of passion." Sol proclaimed this opinion with all the certainty of the white male professor that he used to be.

"Huh? And just how do you figure that?" I asked, a bit taken aback and really curious.

"Okay. Look at it this way. Here's this young couple, Ashley and her husband, right?" Sol took a sip of wine and looked at me. Reading my puzzled expression correctly, he went on. "Ashley spends a lot of time at work with this Chris, talks about him like he's real special. Maybe he was. Get my drift, honey?" Sol elbowed me gently in the ribs and faked a leer to emphasize his "drift."

"Ashley insists that she and Chris were not having an affair," I replied.

"Neither was Bill Clinton." Sol's smartass gotcha left me without an argument. In the resulting conversational void, he continued to lay out his theory. "But that's not the point. It doesn't matter if Ashley and Chris were getting it on or not."

"So why are we talking about it then?" The question seemed logical to me.

"We're not anymore," Sol said. "Now we're talking about how Ashley's husband feels about his wife's relationship with this Chris guy and how he perceives that relationship. If he thinks his wife and Chris are having sex, he's going to be jealous. It doesn't matter if they are or not. Get it? I'm talking about jealousy, Bel, passion."

"You think Ashely's husband suspected her of having an affair with Chris and somehow or other contrived to have Chris killed while rock climbing at work? Is that what you really think?" When I heard Sol lay out his suspicions of Ashley's husband Howard, they sounded plausible. When I heard myself articulate the same scenario, it sounded unlikely.

"Bel, since the beginning of time jealous men have killed for less reason than Howard had. The jealous husband is a cliche." Sol sounded so rational. I vaguely recalled he had postulated the revenge-of-the-jealous-male theory in the Louie Palumbo case too.

"But Ashley says—"

"I don't care what Ashley says. I think you have to at least eliminate Howard as a suspect in order to have a credible investigation." Sol spoke with such assurance, such certainty. I yawned. "That's one of the reasons I've made an appointment with him to draw up wills for both of us. We can check him out. But not tonight. Come to bed." I barely heard Sol's last words as I staggered up the stairs behind him.

Chapter 16

*2 It happened late one afternoon, when David arose
from his couch and was walking upon the roof of the
king's house that he saw from the roof a woman
bathing; and the woman was very beautiful. 3 And
David sent and inquired about the woman. And one
said, "Is not this Bathshe'ba, the daughter of Eli'am,
the wife of Uriah the Hittite?" 4 So David sent mes-
sengers, and took her; and she came to him, and he
lay with her. (Now she was purifying herself from her
uncleanness.) Then she returned to her house. 5 And
the woman conceived; and she sent and told David, "I
am with child."*

2 SAMUEL 11

In spite of my hard work Friday afternoon, I still had
a full set of papers to read Saturday morning. Even if I
were an observant Jew, reading student papers, a sacred duty of English profs, would seem important
enough to justify working on the Sabbath. So it wasn't

until after lunch on the day before my presentation that I was finally able to turn my attention to Samuel. I skimmed both books to get the plot outline and then, following Sandi's advice, gave a close reading to the snippets of text about my foremothers, the women who married and/or mothered the earliest Israelis.

There was Hannah, barren until she begged God to open her womb. When he did, she gave birth to Samuel, the first of a dynasty of rulers. Then I read of the kindly medium at Endor, sought out by a beleaguered Saul, the very king who had banished mediums from the land. Although only my mother called me by my given name Sybil, I had of late begun to identify with wise women of the past, so I was curious about the much maligned medium. Saul sought from her reasons for hope in his upcoming battle against the Philistines. Taking pity on him, the softhearted seer tempered the bad news she brought with food and drink.

Next came poor Rizpah, Saul's concubine, political pawn, and, finally, a grieving mother. She must have suffered terribly when her two sons, sired by Saul, were impaled on stakes by order of David, who feared their claim to the kingship. Empathizing with Rizpah's pain triggered thoughts of the agony Chris Johanson's mother must be experiencing in response to the loss of her son. I quickly repressed this grim association and resumed reading.

The story of Micah followed. Daughter of Saul, loyal wife and wily protector of David, Micah was traded back and forth in marriage like a Pokemon card. She is remembered for castigating the prancing and polyga-mous David for dirty dancing in public. As I reread

Micah's story, I noted a few questions. Was her scathing harangue a result of PMS? A bad hair day? Or, more likely, an enraged protest against the ungrateful patriarch who had, like her father, exploited her? Micah remained childless, a dire fate in biblical times.

Abigail, another smart survivor, fared a little better. I hoped my granddaughter, Abigail's namesake, would someday find strength in her story. Defying Nabal, her lout of a spouse, in order to wine and dine the visiting David, Abigail saved her household from the king's wrath. When Nabal died ten days later, I had to wonder if it was her defiance that did him in. Abigail became one of David's wives and the mother of one of his sons. Finally, there was Bathsheba, the comely wife of Uriah, a Hittite general in David's army. At the moment that David summoned Bathsheba from her ritual bath to his bed, the death knell sounded for the unsuspecting Uriah.

My head whirling, I took notes, not trusting my midlife memory to retain the details I had read. I typed up my jottings with the intention of organizing them and practicing my speech a few times in the morning. I planned to give short shrift to my already famous forefathers and, for a change, concentrate on my neglected foremothers. I thought I had the makings of a dynamite feminist presentation and went to bed fully expecting to sleep the sleep of the truly tired. But I didn't. My rest was troubled by dreams of women as wombs, as property, as seers, and as survivors. I awoke first, relieved to be in bed with Sol and not guarding the impaled body of Chris Johanson from wild animals and vultures. When I slept again, it was to awaken whimpering in protest as my daughter Rebecca was married off to an unsavory suitor to satisfy her father's lust for a crown. The pudgy face of Lenny Barrett, CPA, my first husband and father of my children, grinning beneath a diamond-studded crown, was not an image I would soon forget. Later still I tossed and turned myself awake to expunge images of Sol as a soldier, deserted by his own men, and under attack by hordes of spear-wielding Philistines.

Near dawn I awoke in a sweat from a nightmare in which a snowy-bearded old man carrying a shepherd's staff and wearing a trailing white robe was inscribing for posterity on a parchment scroll the history of my family. Every time I asked him to change a word or add something, he ignored me. As I crawled out of our warm bed, pulled on some sweats, and unrolled my yoga mat, I vowed to describe the lives of those women as they might have described them had they ever been asked. They would no longer be bit players and walk-ons in the epic drama of Jewish history, but stars of their own stories.

Sandi came over about an hour before class, and she and Sol and my mother assembled in our living room to be an audience for my final run-through. Sandi volunteered to tape the actual presentation for me. "You know, I'm really nervous," I said with surprise as I stood near the dining room table, my notes in my hand. "You'd think after teaching speech for so many years and helping hundreds of students prepare speeches and presenting at scores of academic conferences, I'd be a little less anxious. After all, there will be only four people in the audience."

"Well, one of them's a rabbi, and another is a former student of yours. I know you want to show her how it's done," commented Sandi. "Besides you're the first one of us to make a presentation." I was glad Sandi wasn't trivializing the butterflies playing tag in my innards. "And you do have one of the longer readings," she went on. "But you'll do fine. You always do." Sandi knew her lines and was saying them convincingly. If anyone could talk me through my preperformance jitters, she could, and I was glad she'd be one of the four audience members.

"This is good preparation for your doctoral defense too," Sol reminded me. "Think of it as a warm-up exercise." Defending my as yet unwritten dissertation seemed remote, but I was determined to get that degree, and, as usual, Sol was right. At my defense I'd have to present my argument and face faculty whose job it was to question it. Today's exercise was similarly organized. I'd review the Book of Samuel then take comments and questions. "And when you four actually are bat mitzvahed, you'll have to make a speech," Sol continued. "So this is just for drill."

"Oops, I almost forgot," I said, looking at Sandi. "When I'm done, if there's an awkward silence, please be ready to ask a question, okay?" I was taking the advice I give students about ensuring a lively exchange after a talk by arranging ahead of time with someone to initiate the discussion.

"So talk already," Ma said. "Then later we'll discuss what you're wearing." Sandi, Sol, and I exchanged a knowing look. To Ma's inner Pygmalion, her postmenopausal fifty-something daughter, currently clad in jeans and a black turtleneck, was still a work in progress, and so Ma continued to offer tips on shaping and draping my body and making up my face. This morning I wasn't going to let her get to me. Instead of snapping at her, I leaned over and kissed her on the forehead before I began to speak. "I'm betting on you to knock 'em dead today," she asserted, and, since the woman would bet on anything, I believed her and smiled.

The practice session went well, but if I do say so myself, my actual presentation was even better. I was wired on the subject of those women! I spoke for almost an hour, and was tickled to see everyone, including Rabbi OK, taking notes. When I got to the part about David ordering his soldiers to desert Bathsheba's husband in the thick of battle, leaving him surrounded by enemies, I dropped my voice in horror. Then, abruptly shifting mood, I practically shouted, "How would you feel if you were Bathsheba and you had to sleep with the king when he snapped his fingers, and then you got pregnant?" Without waiting for my audience to answer, I went on. "How would you like it if you later learned that this action had resulted in the death of not only your husband but also your child?"

By the time I finished, I was flushed with moral outrage and high on my own oratory. I was relieved to be pressed to answer a barrage of questions and then, finally, indecently gratified to hear eight hands clapping. "Here! Here!" called Mildred, stamping her feet on our classroom floor in the time-honored manner of enthusiastic audiences.

"Good job, Bel," said Janet, her thin lined face enlivened by one of her rare grins. "You tell 'em," she added, raising her fist in the air.

"I give you an A+ on that," said Ashley with a wink. "Now those of us who come after you have to live up to the standard you set." When she frowned and added softly, half to herself, "Times haven't changed much," I noticed Rabbi OK glance quickly in her direction and frown.

But when the rabbi turned to me, she was smiling and said, "You've gotten us off to a fine start, Bel. And I've got a list of feminist interpretations of biblical writings for you to read if you'd like to continue this line of exploration." We spent the rest of the session in a spirited discussion of the lifestyles and values of Old Testament women.

Later, after treating me to lunch, Sandi presented me with the tape she had made and said, "See. I told you you would ace this."

I floated home, feeling pretty good until Sol, having congratulated me on my oratorical success, brought me back to earth. "I'm going to take the Odd Couple grocery shopping now," he said. We called Ma and Sofia the Odd Couple because they were so different in background and interests and yet so completely compatible. Either Sol or I took them grocery shopping every Sunday since we had revoked Ma's driving privileges. Sofia's daughters had long ago convinced their mother to leave the driving to them. "They weren't ready earlier. Do you want to come or would you rather stay here and sift through that garbage you're so uptight about while it's still light out? Tonight's trash night, so after you're done, we could put it out for pickup." That was Sol's not so subtle way of letting me know that a can full of somebody else's putrefying refuse was not his preferred form of yard enhancement.

"Okay, okay. I'll do it," I agreed grudgingly. I was annoyed at being distracted from reliving the triumph of my rant against the transgressions of the tribal patriarchy to ferret about in a bag of yucky trash.

"If you find anything useful in there, I'll buy you dinner," Sol challenged, his deep voice booming after him as he headed to the front door and I made my way toward the back door leading to our tiny yard.

 *Chapter 17*

To: Bbarrett@circle.com
From: Mbarrett@hotmail.com
Re: Tierra del Fuego or bust
Date: 10/24/99 09:28:31

Yo Ma Bel,

It was a little daunting to find six messages from you when I finally made it to a cyber café to check my e-mail. Just because you hadn't heard from me in a couple of weeks is no reason to come all unglued like that. I told you everything is a long bus ride away from everything else here, so I'm always riding to classes or teaching classes. Stay cool, huh? Hello, Mom, Buenos Aires is very safe. Anyway, I'm working too hard to get into trouble.

I wish I could say the same for you. Rebecca tells me you're playing detective again, only this time instead of going undercover as a religious fanatic, you're now out of the closet as a real religious fanatic and masquerading as a maid. Seriously, Mom, I don't know what to worry about first, some psycho pulling a gun on you or you pulling a muscle. Please be careful. Why don't you act like a regular grandmother and spend your time digitizing photos of my niece, the awesome Abbie J?

Here's some good news to ponder while you're scrubbing floors. My Spanish is pretty fair now, and the teaching really rocks. Best of all, the months of teaching extra classes, living on rice and beans, and sharing a shack in the boonies with the dudes I met in the hostel are paying off. I've saved up enough to stake a serious road trip. Check this out. On November 15, Aveda, Elise, Marcello, and I are off to Tierra del Fuego, the end of the world! We'll be gone awhile 'cause it's a haul to get there.

Oops, I'm running out of time, and I have to watch those pesetas now. More next time. Hasta luego.

Love,
Mark

"*Caramba!* He's going to the Land of Fire!" Illuminada translated. "Well, good for him. That kid is seeing the world. When he finally settles down, he won't have any regrets, that's for sure."

"Lourdes didn't look like she had any regrets either," I said. "And she's a lot closer. *She'll* be home for Thanksgiving."

"So when did you see Lourdes?" Illuminada asked, ignoring my most recent bitter reference to the childless holiday looming ahead of me.

"Wendy and I had lunch at Elysium, which is where a lot of Silicon Slum tyros get their take-out. They have the biggest and busiest bar scene this side of the river and your daughter was working it single-handedly."

"Dios mio, she should be able to mix a few drinks since her father and I have paid for most of an advanced degree in pharmacology for her," was Illuminada's pained rejoinder.

"Well, she looks very well. It was good to see her. I think you ought to go down there and say hello," I said, unable to resist foisting my advice on my friend.

"When you go to Tierro del Fuego for Thanksgiving, I'll go to Elysium, Bel," snapped Illuminada, obviously not pleased with my suggestion and not above striking back with a reminder that Mark's latest itinerary did not include Thanksgiving in Hoboken.

"Now, now kids," Betty said, apparently deciding to rein in a discussion that she could see was going nowhere useful. "Play nice." Smiling at each of us, she then turned back to me, scowled, and asked, "Bel, why are we gathered here for dinner on a week night? What is so pressing that it couldn't keep until the weekend?"

I removed the last circle of fried calamari from the bowl we'd been passing around the table at Laico's, dipped the crisp tidbit into the marinara sauce, and ate it before I replied. "Yesterday afternoon I finally went through all the doggie bags we scooped up at scoop.com the other night." I paused while they both wrinkled their noses at my puny pun. Illuminada looked at her watch. "In one of them I found a crumpled note. It said, 'Beware of geeks bearing gifts.' " I stopped, waiting for a reaction.

"So?" Illuminada's upturned palms accompanied by a shrug and a widening of her eyes reinforced Betty's monosyllabic query.

"It goes on to read, 'Don't wait till the horse e-merges

to close the barn door.' So," I said, removing the wrinkled piece of paper from my purse and smoothing it out on the table. "So," I repeated, "I think this note was sent to Troy from someone at e-media.com to warn Troy that someone was spying on him." To their credit, my two friends looked thoughtful as, in spite of their skepticism, they entertained my hypothesis.

Betty spoke first, her response evidence that her skepticism ruled. "You can't be serious, girl. You think that somebody at e-media, that citadel of cyber dudes, wrote this out by hand and somehow smuggled it to Troy in his lunch? And then Troy, realizing that his new friend might be the spy to whom he had revealed too much, killed him in broad daylight while they were rock climbing indoors at the office *and* made it look like an accident?" She was a little breathless when she finally came to the end of her question.

"Yes. That's exactly what I think," I responded calmly. "It's what Ashley has been saying all along."

"Ashley has never had any evidence for this theory. That's what she wants you to come up with. *Chiquita*, how do you propose to prove this?" asked Illuminada, looking smug, as if she enjoyed making it rain on my parade. "As an explanation it's way out there, but this whole case is way out there," she said with a dismissive shrug. "I have the police report here," she added, reaching into her briefcase and extracting several folders. "What you're postulating just doesn't jibe with the police report. First of all, Betty, it didn't happen in broad daylight. The accident occurred at 10:34 p.m."

"Read us the whole report," said Betty, as usual completely at home in the imperative mood.

"I made a copy for each of you, but it doesn't say anything we don't already know from Ashley or, for that matter, the newspaper," said Illuminada handing us each a folder. "In brief, the deceased, Chris Johanson, was climbing with his friend Troy at the climbing wall at scoop.com. They were both experienced climbers. Troy was on the ground belaying Chris—"

"*Bewhatting* Chris?" I blurted out, interrupting her in midsentence. My manners were no match for my confusion and curiosity.

"Belaying. I think it means acting as a kind of spotter or safety net for your partner," said Illuminada. "But I'm not sure. I haven't studied this yet. I just got it this afternoon and skimmed it before I came over here. May I go on?" Illuminada's not so veiled reference to my interruption served as a tongue-in-cheek warning.

"Please do," I said, lowering my head and opening my palm in an exaggerated bow.

"As I was saying, Troy was on the ground belaying Chris, who had reached the highest point on the wall and climbed out onto the overhang. He had not clipped in, whatever that means, and he lost his grip and fell the whole two stories, breaking his neck. Someone called 911 but Chris was dead before the EMTs arrived. All the climbing equipment was checked over at the lab and none of it was defective. Troy, the only witness, was devastated. It went down as an accident."

"I'm going to call and arrange for a student intern from RECC to go to scoop.com for the rest of the semester." Betty's nonsequitur pronouncement was ill-timed because, as she spoke, the linguini with white clam sauce, eggplant parmagiana and shrimp Francese we'd ordered arrived and distracted all of us for a few minutes.

Only after we'd worked out the complex exchange of tasting portions that had become de rigueur at our shared meals did Illuminada react. "Why, Betty? What does a student intern have to do with the police report? You've lost me." Her exasperation was barely concealed.

"Duh," said Betty, clearly relishing her moment in the limelight. After my brief moment of glory on Sunday, I could identify completely, so I let her take her time.

Illuminada, however, exploded, "*Como mierda,* Betty. I'm not in the mood for your games tonight. You know we worked all day and we have to be out half the night cleaning after dinner. Just say what you have to say."

Stung by the uncharacteristic vehemence of Illuminada's scolding, Betty spoke quickly. "Well, I'm going to pose as an intern at scoop.com and see if I can get what's-his-name, Troy, to teach me rock climbing while I'm there. That way I can figure out how he killed Chris, if he did." Having spoken, she turned her attention to her plate. Catching each other's eye, Illuminada and I began to giggle. The picture of Betty rock climbing was hilarious but not nearly as funny as the image of our take-charge friend in the guise of a student intern. "What's so funny? I'm in pretty decent shape now. I might even enjoy it." Betty looked a little hurt as my giggles grew into guffaws and I automatically scanned the restaurant in search of the nearest ladies' room, ever

mindful that after fifty, the funny bone is directly connected to the bladder. Meanwhile the usually dainty Illuminada nearly expelled the mouthful of eggplant she
had been struggling to chew ever since Betty had
dropped her bombshell.

"You'd be running scoop.com in less than a week,
that's what's so funny. You might scale Everest, but
you'd never last a day as a student intern," I explained
stifling the smile that was the last trace of my laugh attack. Betty's chin jutted out, and her eyes gleamed
with what I had learned to recognize as her "try-and-
stop-me" look. My mocking words had only served to
reinforce her determination. Beneath the table, I
kicked Illuminada, signaling her to provide a reality
check.

"*Dios mio,* Betty, what about your day job? Remember? RECC would fall apart on the days you were
gone. Besides, you get three weeks of vacation a year.
Don't tell me you were planning to use your precious
vacation days?" A glance at Betty's sheepish smile indicated that Illuminada had guessed right. Seeing her
advantage, Illuminada pressed, "Vic would just love
that. I thought you two were planing a trip to Italy this
spring." Illuminada's tactful intrusion was working. I
could tell from Betty's next words that the thought of
missing out on a Roman holiday with her beloved Vic
Vallone was less than appealing.

"Isn't there some less time-consuming way you
could check out rock climbing?" I asked, hoping Betty
would still pursue what I saw as a potentially fruitful
line of inquiry. "I think it's very important for us to
know more about it."

"Okay, okay, I give up. I'll just take a couple of climbing lessons on the weekend and do some reading." A sigh of resignation followed this statement. In two seconds, however, Betty had resumed running the show. Her voice crackled with authority. "Illuminada, you're going to Elysium for lunch, and you're going to make nice to your daughter and invite her home for Thanksgiving dinner." Illuminada opened her mouth to reply, but Betty reached over and gently put her index finger to Illuminada's lips. "Hear me out, will you?" she insisted, her finger rendering her query purely rhetorical. She continued, "And while you're there, girl, you're going to ask Lourdes to nose around and find out how that note from somebody at e-media.com could have gotten into the lunch order of somebody from scoop.com." Betty retracted her finger.

"Betty, you drive a hard bargain. You really think I should visit her there? She won't think I'm approving of her dropping out of school?" Illuminada spoke the questions slowly. She looked at me, then at Betty. Slightly older than my two friends and with children also slightly older than theirs, I had navigated the rocky waters of most of the passages facing parents of young adults by the time Betty and Illuminada reached them. And my friends knew that my hard-earned wisdom was exceeded only by my pathological need to give advice. So it didn't surprise me to find myself once again in the role of parenting pundit.

"Of course not. You let her know loud and clear what you thought about her dropping out, right?" Illuminada nodded. "And you and Raoul are insisting that she pay back the tuition for the semester she refused to

finish, right?" Illuminada nodded again. "And you
have been snotty to her since then, so if she has something to say about her hopes, dreams, fears, and plans,
you, her mother, are, right now, the last person on earth
she's going to say it to, right?" Now it was Illuminada's turn to look sheepish. She held up her hands,
wrists bent, palms toward me, signaling me to end my
diatribe. To my credit, I shut up.

"*Dios mio,* enough already. I'll go. Raoul's actually
stopped by there a few times. She invited him to visit
her apartment, but he said he'd wait to go with me." Illuminada smiled, perhaps envisioning her reunion with
Lourdes and the resumption of normal relations between them. Betty and I exchanged a glance and emit-
ted a simultaneous "whew." We knew this was the best
course of action and we also knew that now there was
a good chance Illuminada would stop projecting her
anger onto us. I felt pretty pleased about the way this
was working out. Maybe I'd have a second career as a
family therapist.

But Betty interrupted my thoughts, bursting that
particular balloon before I had even selected a color
scheme for my new office. "Whoa! Hold on!" she ordered. "Won't Illuminada be jeopardizing Lourdes's
safety if she involves her in this mess?"

"Are you kidding?" Illuminada replied. "Lourdes
probably already knows the answers to most of what I
want to know. She's very nosy and very manipulative."
Now Betty and I had to smile at the unmistakable note
of maternal pride in Illuminada's voice as she spoke.
"Every year since she could talk that kid got her father

to tell her what we had bought her for Christmas without the poor man even realizing it."

"It's in the genes," said Betty and I at exactly the same time.

"There is just one small problem, though," said Illuminada, ignoring our chorus. She went on speaking slowly, as if explaining something to a couple of mentally challenged two-year-olds. She never failed to infuriate me when she spoke that way because it usually signaled that she was onto something I had missed. "If Betty figures out how Troy committed this murder, and if I find out who ratted on Chris, we still don't know why somebody from e-media.com would want to assure the death of their own spy. There's still no motive. And, *chiquitas,* without a motive, all we've got is one weird *hombre* sending weird notes to another weird *hombre*." Illuminada sighed.

"That's my problem," I heard myself asserting with much more confidence than I felt. "I'll figure out the motive. There's got to be one."

Chapter 18

To: Bbarrett@circle.com
From: Nhimm@aol.com
Re: Software solution
Date: 10/25/99 10:18:12

Bel,

I know how you feel about having to give up your Sunday mornings to meet with your Hebrew tutor. It sounds like you have a pretty busy schedule what with the two jobs and all. I've been going to Sunday school for years, and lately it's getting pretty lame for me too, especially after a sleepover or a party. Besides it must be mortifying to be tutored at your age. But I've got a solution for you! If you're asking for help on-line in a bat mitzvah chat room, you must be computer literate. (Some older people are a little behind when it comes to computers.) Anyway, check this out. You can learn to read and write Hebrew on the computer! My father sent for this totally awesome software from Florida for me. It has three different fonts: print, script, and

Torah script. One program even has all 54 haftorah portions as well as all the blessings. It even makes the vowels disappear and reappear so I can practice my Torah reading without them and then check myself. The coolest part is it plays at every musical key, fast or slow, and can transliterate from Hebrew into English AND Russian even. So if you're from Russia like this girl in my Sunday school class you can still get bat mitzvahed. I don't know how much the software costs, but my mom always jokes about how my dad is the last big spender (ha! ha!), so it can't be too expensive. My dad got it because he said he didn't want me to have to go through what he went through when he was bar mitzvahed.

Good luck!
Nicole Himmelfarb

It was too late for me to short-circuit the Hebrew tutor Ashley had threatened to find. Now thanks to Ashley's persistence and efficiency her well-intentioned threat had become reality. Hebrew tutorial was now inscribed in my date book at the only time all four of us could meet, just before our regularly scheduled Sunday sessions. Much as I needed help learning Hebrew, I really didn't welcome another incursion into my few unscheduled waking hours.

I was not the only one in our little group burning the proverbial midnight oil. One night that week, bewigged and uniformed as usual, I'd been at scoop.com dusting as Delores. I'd just started scouring the last sink when a thin bespectacled blond wearing Doc Martens, black jeans, a black T-shirt, and a black leather collar studded with nails walked into the

women's bathroom and entered a stall, closing the
door behind her. This was the first time I'd noticed this
apparition at scoop.com, and at first I assumed she was
the new temp now ensconced in what had once been
the polka.com room. But she looked oddly familiar, so
I scrubbed slowly, eager to get another glimpse of her.
When she emerged, she made for a sink, apparently
one of those few Americans who, researchers report,
does wash her hands after using the toilet in a public
restroom. I checked her reflection out as best I could in
the mirror across the room, noting her sallow com-
plexion, gaunt cheeks, and deep-set circled eyes. On
leaving the room, she turned and finally acknowledged
my presence with a wan smile. That's when I recognized her. She was Ashley, born-again blond, and looking a lot the worse for wear. She did not appear to have
recognized me. I forced myself to return her greeting
with a mumbled *"Buenos noches,"* and a deferential
nod of my head.

Although Ashley had indicated that she was being
sent to finish Chris's job at scoop.com, it felt odd to see
her there. When Delores dropped us off at Illuminada's
that night, I mentioned that I'd run into Ashley, whom
I assumed had been working late undercover. "And she
looked terrible, really awful. I didn't notice before how
thin she's gotten and how unhappy she looks. I wonder
what her problem is now," I mused aloud, throwing the
question out to see what insights my cohorts might
offer.

"Well, she could just be tired. She may have been at
work all day," speculated Betty.

"Besides that, these kids all wear themselves out at

the gym too. Lourdes calls them body Nazis 'cause they work out all the time," chimed in Illuminada. "Or maybe she's in the early stages of a difficult pregnancy. You said she wanted to have a family."

"More likely the stress of this whole mess is getting to her. She must feel very vulnerable there in the enemy camp. Plus which, keeping those hours can't be very good for her marriage. Maybe her husband is getting fed up with playing second fiddle to a computer." I was not above trying to answer my own question. "You know, last week in our bat mitzvah class, I thought the rabbi looked worried about Ashley. I bet she knows what's on her mind. They're very close."

"Well the rabbi won't tell you, so forget about even asking her. Father Santos is the same way," said Betty, referring to her beloved parish priest. "You know, they're like shrinks, the clergy. Their lips are sealed."

"I know," I replied. "But I still wonder about Ashley. I wish I could read her mind."

"You know, Bel, she didn't recognize you this time, but if she sees you again, she may. And I still feel funny about her. We should shift our cleaning operation over to e-media.com for a while at least and see what we can come up with there." I responded to Betty's latest dictum with a mock salute, acknowledging her leadership even though I didn't see poor Ashley as a danger.

"Good idea," Illuminada agreed. "I already asked Delores, and her firm does do the cleaning for e-media.com. She said no problem. Anytime we want to make the switch we can. *Dios mio,* Delores says we're doing such a good job, she wants us to take on two or three other assignments!" Illuminada was laughing, but she already had her cell phone out and was punching in numbers. Before the long night finally ended, Illuminada and Delores had arranged for us to replace the regular cleaning crew once a week at e-media.com.

There the drill was very similar to that at scoop except for two things, the dog hair and the basketball court. We each tackled a third of the bathrooms, the kitchen areas, and the common areas, and scrubbed and vacuumed away the dirt, debris, and dog hair left by the youthful e-merchants who worked there and the long-haired pet of one of them. This pooch's shedding fur defied even the industrial strength vacuums we used and turned carpet cleaning into a rigorous calisthenic that left us winded and sore. At Delores's suggestion, we agreed to share the onerous labor of applying Murphy's Oil to the hardwood floor where the techies played basketball. So near the end of the night's work, we gathered beneath the deserted hoops to swab in self-imposed silence, like three exhausted jitterbuggers going through the motions in the final hour of one of those marathon dance contests.

Recovering and playing catch-up over the weekend, I was unprepared for a cheerful call from Illuminada's husband, Raoul, the following Saturday afternoon inviting us over for dinner and a movie that evening. "I'm cooking and I've made too much, so, if you're free, just come. Betty and Vic are coming," was how he worded the impromptu invitation. Sol was delighted at the prospect of one of Raoul's meals. Sol also looked forward to spending a Saturday night with people who were not pacing the bedroom muttering letters of an ancient alphabet to themselves in an attempt to cram a week's worth of Hebrew study into a few hours the night before the tutoring session.

"Tell him we'll bring bread and wine," I said, knowing that a couple of loaves of crusty, still warm brick-oven baked Hoboken bread were always welcome and were available 24/7 at the bakery around the corner from our house. Having established our contribution to the evening's festivities, I put aside the student papers I was working on and reached for the Xeroxed sheets featuring the Hebrew alphabet that our tutor had distributed. Once again I struggled to associate each consonant and vowel with the appropriate signifying squiggle and sound and remember the combinations. When Sol shook me awake an hour later, there was just enough time to shower before we left for Illuminada and Raoul's.

The minute we entered, I felt better. A lyrical yet bouncy serenade from one of the maestros on the CD of the *Buena Vista Social Club* and savory smells from the kitchen acted as instant mood elevators. "Here's to our children," Illuminada said, raising her glass of wine with more than a touch of her usual good humor. We raised our glasses, and Betty and I exchanged looks. Both of us were eager to hear the story of the mother-daughter reunion. We suspected Raoul had organized this impromptu meal so we could all celebrate with him the reconciliation of his warring women.

Our host had begun heaping our plates with ropa viella and rice and beans, and Vic was serving a tossed salad he and Betty had brought. As I was about to pass a plate to Illuminada, I made a pretense of withholding it, saying, "Okay, Illuminada. You want this dinner, you better tell us what happened when you went to see your daughter."

"*Caramba!* It was really amazing, wasn't it, honey?" Grinning, Raoul looked over first one shoulder and then the other, as if searching the room for "honey." Betty and I widened our eyes simultaneously. Illuminada made a point of never addressing Raoul as anything but Raoul.

"It was beautiful, Mina," he answered, finally filling his own plate and taking his seat opposite her at the other end of the table. "You were so good," he said. "The kid's gonna be fine. She just has to make us a little crazy is all."

"Tell us what happened. When did you go? Lunch or dinner?" Betty's specific questions served their purpose.

Looking up from her plate, Illuminada said, "We went to Elysium for a late dinner last Friday night. The place was full of young people. Raoul and I were practically the oldest people there by twenty years." The fact that anyone over forty dining in a restaurant in Hoboken or downtown Jersey City stands out among the resident yuppies like a chaperone at a high school prom was not exactly news.

Following Betty's lead, I attempted to remind Illuminada of her obligations to her audience. "Did you tell Lourdes you were coming?" I prompted.

Illuminada balanced a mouthful of rice and beans and meat on her fork while she answered. "Yes, of course. I called her two days before and left a message that her papi and I wanted to come to Elysium Friday night and, if possible, we would like to buy her dinner. What time was convenient? Could she get some time off? Would that be a good idea?" Illuminada grinned at the memory of her diplomacy.

"No joke. You would have thought Mina was arranging a summit conference in the Middle East or something, the way she worded it," Raoul interjected, taking advantage of the pause that occurred while Illuminada was swallowing a few bites.

"That's the way you have to talk to these kids, though," said Sol, looking serious. "It's not like it was when we were their age. Nobody used psychology on us."

"You better believe it. I got smacked so much I thought it was normal. My old man almost broke my arm once throwing me across the room 'cause I told my mother to stay outta my business," said Vic, pausing between mouthfuls of food to share this particular slice of his life.

"Yeah. I used to get bounced off the walls regularly. My nose got broken once when I forgot to put my head down," Sol said, inspired to add his own two cents to the catalogue of childhood horrors.

I was worried that Illuminada's story would get lost in the ensuing competition between Sol and Vic about which of them had received harsher punishment from his psychologically challenged old-school parents. I needn't have. Betty interrupted them, saying, "Okay, dudes, save the stories of your abused boyhoods for when you're doing the dishes. Right now, Illuminada, we still want to know what response you got to this phone call."

"Lourdes left a very sweet message saying *she* would make *us* a dinner reservation for around eight Friday night and that, while she couldn't eat with us, *she'd* treat *us* to a drink on the house." The way Illuminada pressed those pronouns out really made it clear that in her mind some sort of major upheaval in the Gutierrez family dynamic was taking place.

"The first time I dropped in to visit Lourdes there, before Mina had calmed down about the Rutgers thing, Lourdes treated *me* to a ginger ale," added Raoul, letting us know that he too had experienced the seismic effects of his daughter's new lifestyle on family roles. "It's like her way of saying she's an adult in this place. In that restaurant, they treat her like an adult." He shook his handsome head and ran his hand through his wavy black curls.

"So what happened when you got there?" I queried, not ready for the parental spin on the event until I'd heard all about the event itself.

"Nothing really," said Illuminada. "It was like you said. She's running this big bar, mixing drinks, chatting people up, taking cash. She was doing a great job. She seemed totally cool and in control. When she first saw us, she came around the bar and gave us both a big hug just like nothing ever happened. Later she introduced us to the owner when he showed up and to the customers and to the poor guy who was our waiter . . ." Illuminada paused, pushing her empty plate a few inches away.

"Why is he a 'poor guy'?" asked Vic, who had

served himself another helping of food while Illuminada was talking.

"Oh, you can see he's got the hots for her and you
can also see that she's not that interested in him," answered Illuminada in that dismissive way that mothers
of attractive daughters speak of the young men those
daughters reject. "Poor *hombre*. It's sad."

"He's a jerk anyway," said Raoul predictably. "Too
tall, too blond, and too soon. She's not there to meet
guys, anyway."

"Right," said Sol. "What gorgeous, healthy, single,
twenty-two-year-old woman in her right mind would
want to meet guys?" he asked with feigned innocence,
having long ago lost his only daughter to a suitor
who'd caught him unawares.

"Did she ever buy you two that drink?" I asked.

"She had a bottle of chilled champagne waiting at
our table," said Illuminada. Was that a tear I saw her
brush away with her napkin? I felt my own eyes tear-
ing up. Somehow the symbolism of that bottle of bub-
bly had gotten to me, triggering thoughts of every
argument and reconciliation I'd ever had with my own
mother and my own daughter.

"And she'd reserved the best table in the house,"
said Raoul proudly.

As the men stood and began clearing the table,
Betty, Illuminada and I remained rooted in our chairs,
sipping our wine. "And how were things today?" asked
Betty.

"Lourdes told us to pick her up at two in the afternoon for breakfast! *Como mierda!* That girl used to be
in the library at Rutgers at eight every morning of the

week," Illuminada exclaimed, seeming surprised that a young woman might opt for a different schedule. Both Betty and I had long ago survived the return to the nest of adult children and knew what it was like to get home from work in the late afternoon to find a yawning kid in his underwear having breakfast. This was old news.

"Yeah. Did you see her apartment? Did you have a chance to talk?" I was eager to know if in the first flush of their reconciliation, Illuminada had thought to enlist Lourdes's help in tracing the path of the note I was so curious about, but I didn't want to interrupt Illuminada's story. She was usually the impatient one, waiting for me to get to the point, and now I knew how she felt.

"Her apartment's a joke," Illuminada said, smiling. "Three girls share one bedroom with twin beds, and they're building a loft for the third. Right now they take turns sleeping on the floor next to this pile of wood they bought. They have a table and an old sofa covered with a bedspread. The refrigerator has nothing but Häagen-Dazs and beer in it. But," and here she shrugged her shoulders and held out her hands, palms up, as if to cede control of her daughter's living arrangements, "it's in a fairly safe neighborhood, the other two girls seem okay, and the rent is within their collective means."

The three of us raised our glasses. "To Lourdes," we toasted. But Illuminada had more to say. "Over breakfast she pretty much apologized for not telling us ahead of time, but she was afraid she wouldn't be strong enough to leave school over our objections, so she just left and then told us." Betty and I nodded, understanding all too well the do-it-now-tell-them-later strategy. "And I apologized for the way I spoke to her when I found out," said Illuminada. "She gave us a check for a hundred dollars toward the semester's tuition." We raised our glasses again in recognition of the fact that, like the bottle of champagne, the small sum stood for something big.

"I guess you all had too much going on to ask Lourdes about that note," said Betty, managing to sound disappointed and understanding at the same time.

Illuminada answered in her crisp, clear, professional PI voice. "Of course I asked her. She said she'd check it out. I told her what the note said and she started laughing. It seems scoop.com had a really high-end party at Elysium after their IPO. The staff is still talking about it. It had a Greek theme. The restaurant served Greek food, and they hired Greek dancers who performed on the bar to live Greek music. It just happened to be this guy Troy's birthday that day, so they had a huge cake with a digitized photo of some famous rock he climbed on it and one of them presented him with a solid gold paperweight shaped like a carabiner."

"A what?" I asked.

"It's rock climbing gear. A carabiner is the doohickey a climber uses to fasten herself to the rope and the rock or wall. They call them biners for short." Betty threw this in casually. Only the turned-up corners of her mouth betrayed how pleased she was to have the answer to my question.

"Oh, somebody's been doing her homework," I said. "Thanks for the translation."

"Yeah. Lourdes said it was something only rock

climbers would want." Illuminada was less interested in the trees than the forest, so, leaving the nomenclature of rock climbing gear to others, she went on. "Lourdes seemed to think she could find out not only how the note might have gotten delivered to Troy, but how it actually did get to him. She may never get a degree in pharmacology, but she's got real *cojones,* that kid."

We heard the loud hum of the dishwasher. "*Senoras!* Come on upstairs and watch the *Buena Vista Social Club*," called Raoul. "No flan until after the movie."

 *Chapter 19*

To: Bbarrett@circle.com
From: Rbarrett@uwash.edu
Re: Abbie J
Date: 10/31/99 17:09:35

Dear Mom,

Isn't that awesome about Mark going to Tierra del Fuego? I hope
he takes lots of pictures. Speaking of pictures, did you download
the latest batch we sent you of Abbie J eating solid food? We sent
one of her eating banana and one of her eating oatmeal. Which
one do you think she likes better? Now whenever she sees the
camera, she smiles. Got to go. I have to take her all the way out
to Issaquah to stay with Louise while I'm in class. Keith's got an
important meeting with the new owners that he can't miss and I
can't bag another physics class. (I missed one last week when
Abbie J had a little ear infection. Don't worry. She's fine now.)
Keith will pick her up on his way home. Thank God Abbie J and

Louise have bonded. Why haven't you answered my last two
e-mails? Are you okay? I love you anyway.

                                                    Rebecca

There was not even time to download the latest
snapshots of my only grandchild or to worry about Rebecca as she juggled classes, waitressing, and mothering. That's how hectic things had gotten and how tired
I was. As it turned out, there was not even time to type
a quick and mendacious message to Rebecca reassuring her that I was fine because the phone rang just as
my index finger was poised to click on reply. Who
could be calling at seven in the morning? "Bel?" The
voice was low. I could hardly make out my name.

"Yes, this is Bel. Who's this? Please speak up. I can
hardly hear you." Very few of my students called me
Bel, so I doubted that it was one of them. Perhaps a bad
connection was muffling the words of a friend.

"Bel, Ashley here." Her voice was audible now, but
surprisingly nasal. Maybe she had a cold. What could
Ashley possibly be calling about at seven o'clock on a
Monday morning? Was she phoning from a cubicle at
scoop.com? Was that why she had spoken so softly?
Was she in danger? Damn. I'd gone looking for God or
at least a Jewish spiritual life and what I'd found was
poor Ashley, a Jewish Calamity Jane.

"Hi, Ashley. How's it going?" I tried to mask the
concern her early morning call triggered.

"Bel, I need to talk to you. Can I meet you for just
a few minutes before you go to class? We could have
a quick breakfast. How about the RIP? Please? I can

be there in fifteen minutes. Please? It's really important." Remembering how truly terrible Ashley had
looked in the mirror of the women's room at
scoop.com, I agreed. I hoped I wouldn't catch her
cold. Surely she wasn't calling me at that hour to enlist me as a study partner to memorize Hebrew with
as she had threatened. Could she be calling to ask me
for a progress report on the murder investigation that
she had initiated? Or to tell me that her worst fears
had become reality and some underage techno trash
millionaire was threatening her safety. None of these
prospects appealed to me at all as I drove to Jersey
City.

Ashley was waiting for me in a booth when I arrived
at the RIP Diner, the eatery RECC students and faculty
frequented, since RECC boasted no cafeteria. She was
blowing her nose, and when she looked up at me over
the Kleenex, I saw that her eyes were red. Instinctively,
I leaned away from her and the germs I imagined she
carried. I needn't have worried. Taking one look at me,
she burst into tears. Perversely I relaxed a little, realizing that I was not breakfasting with Typhoid Mary, but
rather with Madame Butterfly.

"Oh Ashley, what's wrong?" I asked, signaling the
waitress and reaching across the table to pat Ashley's
shoulder at the same time. I ordered OJ, a fried egg
sandwich, and tea for myself and tea for Ashley, realizing just in time that she probably wouldn't eat anything at the decidedly unkosher RIP. Was she still
sobbing over Chris? Or had someone else died? Or
had she been fired? I ran through these possible explanations for Ashley's misery as I waited for my

breakfast to arrive and for Ashley to collect herself
enough to speak.

That may be why I was completely unprepared for
what she said. "It's Howard." The two words came out
in a gulp and precipitated another long session with the
Kleenex, which gave me time to recall that Howard
was Ashley's husband, the man for whom she had
agreed to give up not only Jesus but also shellfish.
What had happened to Howard? Was he dead too?

"What's wrong with Howard? Is he ill? Ashley, pull
yourself together and talk to me. You may work on dot
com time, but I have a nine o'clock class." I was
halfway through my sandwich by the time Ashley finally stopped weeping and began to speak.

"He's having an affair." So there it was. I mentally
kicked myself for not having included this timeworn
husbandly hobby in my speculations.

"Now Ashley, don't jump to conclusions. What
makes you think Howard is having an affair?" I
couldn't imagine that the devoted-looking young man
smiling at Ashley in the snapshot I'd seen in her cubicle was running around. They hadn't been married for
more than a couple of years.

"He's never home. He leaves the house really early
and he gets home really late and—"

"Well, he's a young lawyer. And he's probably ambitious. Everyone knows lawyers trying to build their
practices work long hours," I interrupted. I spoke
soothingly, convinced of the truth of my words.

"He never returns my calls either. I leave messages
and his secretary takes them or at night I put them on
the machine. Most of the time he doesn't call me back

and when he does, he sounds really distracted." I was about to offer a word or two about how not everyone feels a sacred obligation to return calls or has good telephone skills when she reached across the table and put her hand on my arm with surprising firmness. "Listen, Bel, I'm not stupid." That was certainly an understatement. Ashley's intelligence was not at issue. "I followed him a few times. He's got a woman in Bayonne. He doesn't even go to the office. He goes right to her place. And I've seen his car there at all hours of the night. And when he comes home, he's so wound up. He's not interested in me . . . you know . . . sexually." Then apparently rethinking this declaration, Ashley said, "Well, actually he's like a totally different person on the weekends. He did try to come on to me Saturday night when I finally got home from work, but I told him I was too stressed out. Which I am." Ashley's version of a rueful smile turned up the corners of her mouth for a millisecond. "He does this really bizarre Jekyll-Hyde thing on the weekends. His new squeeze must be out of town then." Sarcasm clipped the words in her final sentence and they hung in the air etched in acid.

My heart went out to the stricken young woman sitting across from me. She had been driven to use her formidable arsenal of espionage maneuvers to tail her own husband right to the illicit love nest where the creep was shacking up with some bimbo from Bayonne. The poor girl didn't even have the comfort of denial to shield her from the hard fact of Howard's betrayal. "What should I do, Bel? I'm so upset I can't function. I love Howard." How did I guess? My former student wasn't the first nor would she be the last to waste her love on a no good, philandering jerk.

"Did you talk to Rabbi OK?" I asked, not really sure what other course of action to suggest. "She'll have some good ideas."

"I did talk to her once," Ashley said, an air of resignation in her voice. "She said we should consider couples counseling." I saw her eyes fill and her lip tremble. "She said I should confront him with my suspicions and, depending on what he said and how I felt about what he said, maybe we should go for counseling. But that was before I followed him." Tears running down her face, Ashley rummaged through her purse looking for a Kleenex. I handed her one. Her thank-you was barely audible as she blew her nose and wiped her eyes in a valiant struggle for control.

"She's a client. I checked his client list the other night to see if he has one living at that address." Mata Hari had nothing on Ashley Solomon. "There's a Rosa Suarez living there. Maybe Rabbi OK thinks he should bring Rosa Suarez to couples counseling too. And I thought Jewish men were supposed to be such good husbands." Bitterness lent a hard edge to her voice. Was bitterness better than just plain despair? I wasn't sure anymore. I just knew that I was tired of listening to the sad tales of women whose men cheated on them.

"Listen Ashley," I said with a glance at my watch. "I've got to get to class. But I think you should go back to Rabbi OK with this information and see what she says now. Meanwhile I'll give this some thought too. Don't do anything crazy. I'm sorry you have to go through this." I patted her shoulder and stood. I took my check to the cash register, leaving poor Ashley sitting in our booth hunched over a pile of wadded-up Kleenex crying her eyes out. It was not an auspicious beginning for the day.

Chapter 20

NEW STUDIES DISPROVE ESTROGEN'S EFFICACY AGAINST HEART DISEASE

New studies of the long-term effects of estrogen replacement therapy, touted by physicians as a deterrent to heart disease and osteoporosis in menopausal and postmenopausal women, now challenge this belief. Recent research shows that, on the contrary, taking estrogen may even slightly increase such a woman's chances of suffering heart disease . . .

"Look at this, Sybil. It's a good thing you're going to make out a will. You may need one sooner than you think." With these words, my mother—the breast cancer survivor—greeted me as she climbed into the backseat of our car and handed the news clipping to me. I scanned the article, my first contact with newsprint in weeks. My new tripartite identity as professor–maintenance worker–student of Judaism precluded frivolous activities like keeping up with the news, paying bills, and taking care of my health. Plagued by guilt at being three thousand miles away when my own daughter needed an emergency baby-sitter for my only grand-daughter and at being unable to come up with a solution to Ashley's latest dilemma, I had hardly slept. "Right, Ma. Thanks," I said, stuffing the unwelcome article into my purse. The last thing I needed en route to the lawyer's office to draw up wills, medical directives, and any other depressing papers Sol and Ma decided that we couldn't die without, was to be told the patch on my butt pumping hormones into my overworked body was user unfriendly. I made a mental note to discuss the latest research on ERT with Dr. Bodimeind. Of course making mental notes had become an increasingly futile endeavor since even the patch was powerless against my midlife memory loss.

Desperate to change the subject, I said, "Good morning to you too, Ma. So how did you and Sofia make out in Atlantic City yesterday? Did you blow my inheritance? Is there anything left to will to me?" It is hard to banter after a sleepless night, but I was doing my best.

"Don't worry, dear. Your mother did all right." Ma only spoke of herself in the third person when she did not intend to say very much. Sure enough, she changed the subject. "Sofia lost a few dollars, but we had a good time. The bus was full." Ma was unusually close-mouthed about the details of her win, and I lacked the energy to grill her at six-forty-five in the morning.

The reason I was having another early morning rendezvous was simple and, as it worked out, timely. The night before, when I was telling Sol about Ashley's husband's infidelity, Sol was delighted to have his low opinion of Howard confirmed. "See, Bel, I told you he was no good. Maybe Howard's screwing around with this Rosa Suarez to give Ashley a taste of her own medicine, you know, to get her attention. A little sauce for the goose, you know." Sol had looked almost gleeful at the thought of Howard Solomon's adulterous revenge.

Then he really surprised me by saying, "But listen, Bel, remember that many moons ago I made an appointment with Howard Solomon, attorney-at-law. We're finally going to do our wills and get started on our pull the plug papers. And since the love of my life is in thrall to Delores Does Dusting at night, the appointment is for seven a.m. tomorrow!" Sol smiled with smug satisfaction much like that of the proverbial feline who has just breakfasted on a succulent yellow songbird. I was appalled at the prospect of having to think about my will at all, let alone at such an early hour. But I have to admit I was pleased at the prospect of meeting Ashley's wayward spouse. That way I could size him up and get some sense of what kind of advice to give my heartbroken former student.

"So, Sadie, did you bring your old will and a list of what you want to ask this legal eagle?" said Sol, maneuvering the car expertly into a sliver of a parking space on a side street near Journal Square.

"Yes. I've got everything here," said Sadie, patting her black kid purse.

"Bel, what about you? I reminded you about this when you got home last night, remember? While we were talking? Do you have your paperwork and a list of questions?" Sol knew damn well I had no idea where my previous will was or what it said. He also knew I didn't want to think about medical proxies or advance directives or any of that grim stuff he and Ma discussed at such great length. He also knew I wasn't crazy about the idea of actually making Ashley's two-timing husband privy to my preparations for death or incapacitating terminal illness. I didn't deign to reply.

As it turned out, it didn't matter what any of us had brought. When we got to the eighth floor in the reno-vated art deco high-rise at the address Howard Solomon's secretary had given Sol, there was nobody there. The sign on the door read "Howard Solomon, Attorney-at-Law," but the door was locked and the room behind the clouded glass window was dark. We waited for a few minutes, during which time Sol called Howard's office on his cell phone and got no answer. We could hear the phone ringing in the empty room be-hind the dark door. Sol left a message reminding Howard of our appointment. We waited some more.

But Ma couldn't be on her feet for too long, so we took the elevator back downstairs and approached the hefty security guard who had barely noticed us when we entered the building. "We have an appointment with Howard Solomon on eight," Sol said, "but there's no one there. He must have forgotten. What time does he usually get here?"

"Solomon?" The security guard repeated the name and consulted his roster of tenants. "Mr. Solomon no here no more."

"What?" Sol's one syllable query resounded in the

building's marble-walled lobby. It was as if he had funneled all his incredulity and indignation into that single word. In spite of working for years with unreliable Rutgers undergraduates and temporally challenged Eastern European bureaucrats, Sol was still surprised when someone stood him up. "We had an early morning appointment. I booked it with his secretary." Uttering these words as if repeating a mantra that would make Howard Solomon materialize, Sol glanced repeatedly at the doorway, expecting to see the missing lawyer walk through it.

"Did he leave an address?" Tired from standing around, Ma spoke in her court stenographer's voice, matter-of-fact, courteous, and imperious all at once.

Galvanized into action, the security guard began leafing through a small black loose-leaf notebook he had pulled from his back pocket. "Mailman," he said, pointing with a surprisingly delicate index finger to the words *Solomon Mailman* followed by *44 Avalon Avenue, Bayonne, 07002.* Sol and I exchanged glances. While we stood gaping at one another, Ma was still on the case. She whipped a pen out of her purse, noted the address on the corner of what looked suspiciously like a copy of her will, and said, "Thank you so much." We followed her back to the car.

"At least he left word where his mail was to be forwarded," she said. "He must have moved his office since you called and they forgot to tell you." Sol just grunted. I could tell he was furious, and I knew if he weren't so eager to check out Howard Solomon, Sol would have abandoned this early morning goose chase then and there and found another lawyer.

It was almost eight before we stood outside the door of a duplex in Bayonne. The name *Solomon* had been scrawled on a tab and inserted in a slot over the mailbox. Sol gave the bell a decidedly antagonistic poke. A few seconds later, the door opened and we were face to face with a barefoot, heavyset, unshaven man of about thirty-five, wearing jeans and a T-shirt. Standing on tiptoe, I looked behind him, straining to catch a glimpse of Rosa Suarez, Ashley's competition. "Yes," he growled, not inviting us in. Maybe Rosa was still in bed. The only thing Howard Solomon had in common with the young man in the photo I had seen in Ashley's cubicle was that he wore glasses. It was hard to imagine Ashley losing her heart to this slob.

"Are you Howard Solomon, the lawyer?" Sol asked.

"Yeah. Hold on a sec, will you?" Leaving the door ajar, our reluctant host darted back inside the unfurnished foyer and made a beeline for what should have been the living room. We followed him at a discreet distance, quietly closing the front door behind us. On the large-screen TV a male talking head was rattling off some figures. Copies of the *Wall Street Journal* and *Barron's* covered the table where the PC sat and many others lay in untidy heaps on the floor. The elusive Rosa was certainly not much of a housekeeper, I concluded. Our lawyer sat hunched in front of his flickering computer screen staring at some charts until suddenly he jumped to his feet, gave a big thumbs-up, and did a little jig of exultation, yelling, "Yes! Yes! Yes! I just made eighteen hundred dollars!"

I thought he was daft and looked uneasily at the door. But it didn't take Sol long to interpret the scene correctly. He smiled at the ecstatic figure in front of us and said, "So you're a day trader now, counselor?" I did a double-take. Ma had moved some magazines from one of the two chairs in the room onto the floor and seated herself. Mesmerized, she looked from the TV to the PC to Howard Solomon, somehow gleaning that the stubble-faced, shoeless person hopping up and down in front of her was a kindred spirit, a fellow traveler, a man after her own heart, another hard-core gambler just like she was. She wasn't sure exactly what his game was, but, forgetting for the moment her precious last will and testament, she was ready to learn.

"I'm Sol Hecht. This is my partner, Bel Barrett, and Bel's mother, Sadie Bickoff," said Sol, extending his hand. Ma and I nodded. Howard shook Sol's hand and then dropped it. Turning suddenly back to the PC, he said, "Hold on a sec, will you? I gotta put a stop on something. Just take a minute." He gave no indication that he recognized my name. While he typed and muttered, I looked around the room. A bag of golf clubs leaned against one wall, apparently held up by the cobwebs that had formed on the leather. The wastebasket was a cornucopia of empty take-out containers. By the time Howard was ready to talk to us again, I had also glanced into the bedroom, where I saw, on the floor next to the unmade bed, a large plastic bag probably containing Howard's wardrobe. There was no sign of Rosa. Suddenly the duplex was depressing. All I wanted to do was leave and try to grab some breakfast before my first class.

But Sol, thoroughly relishing this unexpected turn of events, had other ideas. He was playing detective and determined to interview the suspect. "What about your law practice? Do you still have one?"

"No way!" replied Howard. "I bagged that. Now I don't have to pay a secretary and rent an upscale office. I don't have to follow the court's schedule or suck up to clients. I work by myself, put in the hours I want, and dress the way I want. Every day is dress down Friday!" he exclaimed, rubbing his hand fondly over the tufts of hair sprouting from his chin. Howard clinched this paean to American individualism and independence by saying, "Plus, I'm beating the odds! I'm making good money."

"This must be a fairly recent shift," Sol said. "I made an appointment with your secretary several weeks ago to come in and redo our wills. No one saw fit to inform me that you were no longer practicing law." Howard would have had to be deaf to miss the disapproval in Sol's tone.

"Sorry about that. It *was* a recent decision. I haven't even told my wife yet. I want to surprise her with a big bundle so she can quit her job. I don't think she likes her work anymore. Besides, we want to have a family," said Howard, the future father. He swiveled his chair around to face the computer and scrolled up and down the screen for what seemed like an hour before twirling back, a frown creasing his forehead. "Damn. Now I'm down twenty-one hundred dollars. I'm in the toilet. I should have had a stop on that one too."

I saw Ma shaking her head in sympathy. Sol pressed on. "Won't your wife be upset to learn that you've changed careers without even telling her? What if she calls the other office?" I realized Sol had noticed the bedroom too because he remarked, "It looks like you're pretty much living here."

"Well," Howard said, "the lease on the other office isn't up until the middle of the month and my secretary's still there from nine to five Monday through Friday to take calls during business hours. So I'll get phone messages for a few more days anyway. I did a will and a prenup agreement for one of my clients and in return she let me stay here for free until she gets back from her honeymoon. Maybe then I'll pay her a modest rent.

"You're right. I do spend a lot of time here. I like to get news of the world markets at six a.m." That said, he whipped around to face the screen again. "I'm canceling that one," he announced as if we had asked. He continued the earlier conversation as if there had been no interruption. "I don't want my wife to know that I bagged my practice 'cause she'll get all bent out of shape. But I know she'll go along. My decision is part of a well-thought-out business plan. I researched it. I read how a lot of money is moving on-line. And I saw some guys I know, young guys, make out real well trading on-line. I don't see any reason why I shouldn't be one of them." He spoke as if Ashley was in the room and he was pleading his case. Perhaps he was rehearsing. He turned back to the computer.

"May I use your bathroom, please?" These were the only words I had uttered since we arrived. Howard pointed in the direction of the bedroom. I followed his hand and, stepping over the plastic bag, made my way to the john. There was definitely no sign of a woman anywhere. The nearly empty medicine chest contained no cosmetics or aromatic bath products. The reading material next to the toilet consisted of a much high-lighted copy of *The Complete Idiot's Guide to Making Money on Wall Street* and a dog-eared copy of *Trading for a Living*. When I reentered Howard's private trading floor, he was explaining to my mother how to drive up the value of a stock by bidding against yourself.

When we left, Sol apologized to Ma and promised to find us another lawyer, this time one recommended by friends. Ma, whose gambling had been limited to bridge and, lately, the casinos in Atlantic City, spoke to a different point. "What he was doing doesn't look like nearly as much fun as playing cards with the girls or getting on a bus with your friends and going where there are a lot of people, a lot of excitement. Who wants to stay at home alone all day talking to a machine? His mother must be a wreck." Sol and I had to smile.

As soon as we dropped Ma off, Sol said, "You know who he reminds me of?"

"No," I answered. "Tell me."

"That day trader who went postal last summer and killed his wife and kids and then killed eight or nine people who worked in the trading shop he used. Remember? Got time for breakfast?" Sol was never one to get hung up on transitions. His query caught me by surprise, though, and I tried to imagine Howard Solomon as a homicidal day trader. It was not a pretty picture.

"No, of course I don't remember. And yes, I have a little less than an hour."

Sol parked in the lot at the RIP. Once settled into a booth, we ordered, and Sol said with a grin, "Well, beautiful, when you drop dead of fatigue, just remember you're intestate."

"I'll be fine after I have breakfast," I assured him. "So I gather from your reference to the day trader who ran amuck that you still think ex-counselor Howard Solomon is a jealous husband who arranged for the murder of a man he imagined to be his rival?"

"Well, the man is certainly missing a few links in his chain," said Sol. "You know, I asked around. He was an up-and-coming attorney with a decent practice. He gave that up. And he didn't even tell his wife, let alone discuss it with her. But he seems to care about her in a weird sort of way."

"Well, he is weird. But homicidal? I doubt that he'd leave the computer long enough to arrange a murder. I'll have to call Ashley with this news. No wonder the poor kid thinks she has a rival."

"She does," said Sol as he attacked his omelet.

sister's name. Even her name is better than mine.) did so well."
You want to know what she looks like? She's tall and thin with
straight brown hair and big green eyes and NO zits. She already
wears a 32A. My mom tells me I'm pretty, but how can
I be? I'm short and not thin. My hair is frizzy and black and I
have freckles. Today I have two and a half zits. Some days I
have as many as four. I wear a 28AA, but I don't need it. What
do you look like?

Cynthia Sachs

I was beginning to look quite frightful. Permanent
purple circles outlined my eyes. Since I'd begun
cleaning offices, I'd lost five pounds, but this loss
was most apparent in my newly sunken cheeks and
the loose folds of flesh that had suddenly formed beneath my chin. I had not yet made time for a flu shot,
and my sinuses had finally checked in with a
vengeance. As a result my runny nose was always
red and my watering eyes perpetually glassy. When I
did finally collapse into bed, I was too stressed about
how behind I was with student papers and my bat
mitzvah studies to sleep well. It had been weeks
since I'd done any yoga. In short, I was running on
empty, but like most workaholics, I denied this reality and/or felt that I could cope even though I was
overtired, overworked, and sick. I recalled other
times when I had managed to get the job done while
in the throes of various work, health and family
crises that had left me sleep deprived but functional.
That was then. Now my previously endless reserves
of energy were tapped out.

Sol was losing patience. He nagged me all the time. "Bel, I'm serious. You said this weekly cleaning business was only temporary. But it's still going on and you're exhausted. You've given up sleep, civil conversation, and sex, and you're neglecting your students, your Hebrew classes, and me. You look terrible and you snap at everybody. You know, you're not a kid anymore. When are you going to reclaim your life?"

"Sol, I'm only there one night a week. Don't get so dramatic. I'm not absolutely sure we've learned everything we can, so I'm not quite ready to turn in my mop and pail just yet," I'd reply, trying to sound peppy and pert. "Give me another week."

"Bel, that's what you've been telling me for the last two weeks. You must think I'm stupid." That particular afternoon though Sol came to the end of this diatribe and suddenly wheeled around and strode out of the house, slamming the door behind him. Rushing to the window I could see him stalking through the few autumn leaves scattered on our city sidewalk. There at the window I trembled slightly, recalling the last time Sol had stormed out of the house. And here I was, driving him away again. What was my problem? He was right. Besides, Betty, Illuminada and I had damn little to show for all those hours of scrubbing and mopping. Tonight I'd talk with them about calling a halt to our exhausting and debilitating charade.

Maybe that's why I was so desperate that night. There were quite a few more e-media people working late that evening, so it took longer than usual to get everything cleaned. At one point I noticed a figure in a denim jacket and jeans exit Greg's office carrying what might have been a printer and leaving the door ajar behind him. I glanced around to make sure nobody was looking and darted inside in spite of the fact that the private offices and cubicles were off limits. I shut the door behind me as quietly as I could.

In an instant I was at the desk. I knew that without a password I'd never get onto Greg's computer, but I would settle for handwriting samples, pieces of paper, anything that could be used to trace that note to his office. I spotted a gold paperweight shaped like an anorexic pretzel weighing down a few scraps of paper covered with scrawls. I had just folded one of these sheets of scribbles and stashed it in my bra when I heard a noise and the door opened. Brandishing my feather duster and humming an upbeat melody vaguely reminiscent of a song from the soundtrack of the *Buena Vista Social Club,* I whipped into my best imitation of a cheerful tone-deaf person dusting a computer monitor.

"Hey! How'd you get in here?" It was Greg himself who had glided silently into the doorway on his Rollerblades. Holding onto a doorjamb with each hand for balance and leaning into the room, he filled the doorway, making escape impossible. "What're you doing here, huh? Calling your relatives all over the Caribbean like the last one? You people never learn, do you?"

I realized that he thought I'd been using the phone to place long distance calls. This was a fairly common practice among homesick evening maintenance workers and even security personnel in Jersey City, who couldn't resist making "free" calls to relatives, friends, and lovers they had left behind in places like Miami, Dominica, Haiti, and Ecuador. At RECC this unauthorized activity had resulted in some pretty high phone bills, so the administration had blocked long distance access on most of the college's phones. "What's your name? Answer me?"

I smiled idiotically. I did not have to mimic fear. I was terrified. What I had to mimic was Spanish, so I kept muttering, *"No comprende"* and then, in a desperate imitation of Illuminada's accent, I whispered, *"Dios mio,"* lowered my head as if awaiting the guillotine, and crossed myself. Gliding over to the other side of the desk, he picked up the phone and punched a number. "Jack, send someone from security up here to escort one of Delores's girls downstairs. She can wait for Delores outside. I don't want her in the building. I'll call Delores myself and tell her I caught her girl using the phone in my office." I struggled not to let my face show that I understood what he was saying as I moved tentatively from behind the desk in the direction of the doorway.

It took a few minutes for the security guard to get upstairs, so I was able to hear Greg bark into Delores's message machine. "Delores, Greg, CEO at e-media.com here. I just caught one of your girls using the phone in my office tonight. Those offices are off limits. I don't want to see her here again." I was livid. This underaged and underbred techno tycoon had pushed most of my buttons. He'd called me a girl. My blond wig and uniform did not mask the obvious fact that I was, literally, old enough to be his mother. He'd referred to nonnative speakers as "you people," lumping all immigrants together as, at the very least, petty criminals. And finally, he'd lied about me using the phone, and his lie would have gotten me fired if I'd been a real employee of Delores Does Dusting.

By the time the security guard arrived, Betty and Illuminada had finished the basketball area without me and were putting away their equipment. I pantomimed to my keeper that I too wanted to stash my maid props, and I did. As it worked out, my escort and I went downstairs in the same elevator as Betty and Illuminada. But there was no question about it. For me it was a one-way ride. From now on Delores would be dusting without me. I had been canned.

I figured Delores had gotten Greg's message, so as soon as I got in the van, I gave her my version of the story and my apology. I had, after all, violated our agreement. "Delores, I'm really sorry. Somebody left the door to Greg's office unlocked and I just slipped in for a quick look. Then Greg came in and found me. He accused me of making long distance calls on his phone. I swear I didn't even touch the phone. I know he doesn't want me back. He doesn't know I speak English, so I overheard him leaving you that message." Even though I had addressed my narrative to Delores, Betty and Illuminada were all ears.

"No problem," said Delores, her voice low and tired sounding. "Don' worry. What's done is already done. Lon' as he didn't break our contract. Tha's the importan' thin'. I got plenty girls want that job. Somebody else be there in your place next time. No problem." She was already pushing buttons on her cell phone as she pulled to a stop in front of Illuminada's house.

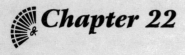

Chapter 22

Nathan Futura
College composition III
November 2, 1999

Journal

Thank you for the help with my verbs last week and for lending me that phat grammar book. Now when the computer tells me there's a mistake, I got some idea how to fix it. I appreciate the help especially since you got that cold. I hope you are feeling better. See how you think I'm doing.

Well, things are getting seriously intense over at e-media. They are gearing up to launch a new B2B product and lots of people are working late and all. They even asked me to work overtime, but I got to stay with my sister. Nobody is shooting hoops or taking naps this week, that's for damn (sorry, Professor B) sure. Even Greg Mr. Cool himself is all wired. He lost it and totally dissed one of the women in sales. Right in front of everybody at Matties sales meeting he told this woman that her numbers weren't good enough. He made her cry. That same day he called me in his office and asked me if I was using the phone to make personal calls long distance. I told him no, but I'm not sure he believed me. I didn't notice him asking anybody else.

And that dude is tightening up on security. He said how somebody got in his office and was snooping around. I wonder what he got in there. Most of the stuff for the new software launch is in the tech dudes computers. And man you need a password from God hisself to get in those things. Maybe all this stress is too much for King Greg. It still makes me mad how that dude is so close to my age and how he got so much money and babes and whatnot . . .

I was only halfway through Nathan's journal when I arrived at RECC one morning not long after I had been relieved of my responsibilities at Delores Does Dusting. To my great relief, Sol had returned home. But he had not been waiting up for me, and he had not left the usual snack and funny note on the sink island. When I finally crawled into bed, I noticed no change in the even rhythm of his snores. He slept the sleep of the righteous.

I, on the other hand, hardly slept. Although I welcomed the reprieve from my exhausting regimen of scrubbing and vacuuming, I would have preferred to have defected from my drudgery voluntarily. I felt guilty for having been canned, for having violated the agreement we'd made with Delores, and for having jeopardized our investigation. I felt guilty for making Sol worry and for neglecting my students' papers and my Hebrew studies. Guilt is self-perpetuating, so it wasn't long before I was also castigating myself for having neglected my faraway daughter, son, and granddaughter, my dead father, and, of course, my mother. And I still had a cold that I felt guilty about too. Clearly if I were a better person, the germs would have avoided me. When my conscience and my congestion did let up enough to permit me to doze, I dreamed of being chased across the deserted basketball court at e-media.com by a gigantic Rollerblader in a denim skullcap intoning Hebrew prayers. A little later in another bout of fitful slumber, I dreamed of being fired from the faculty at RECC for not having baby-sat for Abbie J and then begging Delores for another chance to dust my way to heaven.

Small wonder that I stopped trying to sleep and got out of bed long before sun-up. I was just about to throw the clothes I'd worn the day before into the hamper when I caught myself. Carefully I extracted from my bra the scrap of paper I'd managed to swipe during my ill-fated foray into Greg's office. Smiling through my sniffles, I smoothed it out and filed it in my wallet. I had high hopes for that purloined piece of paper. After a hot shower and a cup of tea, I greeted the dawn by reading and responding to College Comp III journals in the hope of being able to return them when I met the class later that morning. Before I headed for RECC, I express-mailed the scrap of paper to Illuminada, asking her to have the handwriting on it compared with that on the note in the leftover lunch bag. Then I left the sleeping Sol a note of my own explaining that I'd cleaned my last toilet in Silicon Slum.

As tired, congested, and unprepared as I was, I still

expected the morning to be fairly straightforward. I was meeting the nine o'clock College Composition III class in the Writing Center where they had access to computers for one hour each week. The lab assistant would open the lab, boot up the PCs, and offer technical assistance, leaving me free to confer with students over the developing drafts of their internship analysis essays. I looked forward to these conferences and the students looked forward to using the computers in the Writing Center. For those who didn't own PCs, these sessions were their only hope of bridging the digital divide.

I knew something was wrong when I approached the Writing Center at a few minutes before nine only to find seven or eight of my students lined up outside a locked door. "Where's Melissa?" I asked rhetorically. It didn't matter where the missing lab assistant was. What mattered was how to get the door open. I lowered my armful of books and journals to the floor of the corridor outside the door, saying, "Jonah, keep an eye on these please. I'll try to scare up a key." Jonah, a lanky young man who was just learning to use the spell check and had yet to master rudimentary editing maneuvers on the word processor, nodded agreement. I knew he hated to lose even a minute of his precious lab time. Unfortunately it took me ten minutes of phoning and running around the building to round up a security guard and persuade her to come upstairs to open the lab.

"Just give me a minute and I'll boot up these machines," I announced as cheerfully as I could. "Nathan, will you give me a hand?" It had suddenly occurred to

me that Nathan was in this class, and he had been a lab
assistant for several semesters. He'd help. When
Nathan didn't answer, I looked frantically around at
the faces entering the room. Nathan's was not among
them.

"Nathan's not here, Professor Barrett," said Jamala, putting her books down at one of the dormant
machines and preparing for what she could see was
going to be a long wait. I was moving from machine
to machine as fast as I could, but it was still a good
ten minutes before I had all but two up and running.
For over two semesters those two PCs had had frayed
and yellowed notes taped to their monitors warning,
"Do not use."

To my horror, almost all the students registered for
the course had shown up. We had twenty-three working computers, and twenty-four students were already
in the room. This was the eventuality that the geniuses
who mastermind our cutoff figures at registration
every semester always insist will never happen because of the notoriously erratic attendance patterns of
community college students. They had registered
twenty-seven students for a class that meets weekly in
a lab with only twenty-three working computers.

There was still no sign of Melissa or Nathan, so I
was flitting from student to student doing my best to
resolve technical glitches that are the inevitable result
of combining old computers and new users. One of my
most technically proficient students, Ramir Singh, saw
the problem and immediately acted to make himself
part of the solution. "I help, Professor Barrett," he said,
offering his computer to Jamala and then waving me to

the table where I customarily conferred with students.
"I be lab assistant today." But Ramir was first on my
list for a conference and he knew it. He had yet to pro-
duce an outline or any journals on which to base his internship analysis essay. I would have to talk to him, but
how would I manage it without someone to assist the
students as they mastered cutting and pasting, cus-
tomizing margins, line spacing, fonts, printing, and the
crucial act of saving their drafts onto floppy disks?

It was now almost nine-thirty, and I was furious.
Where the hell *was* Melissa? Why hadn't she at least
called in to let the director of the Writing Center know
she wasn't going to show so he might have made some
effort to arrange a substitute? And where the hell was
Nathan when I needed him? After all, I'd gotten him a
great internship and started him on the road to writing
standard English and what did I get in return? In a
growing frenzy, I continued to circulate around the
room, helping students as best I could. Jonah's PC was
inexplicably frozen. Jamala realized that she'd left her
disk at home. Ramir, resignation souring his normally
cheerful expression, seated himself at the conference
table, to wait for me. Two other students put up their
hands, indicating that they needed help.

At exactly twenty minutes to ten, a grinning Nathan
sauntered into the lab. He was forty minutes late.
"Well, look who finally decided to show up. I hope you
enjoyed your beauty sleep." The public rebuke flew out
of my mouth and across the room and wiped the smile
off Nathan's face. He gave his head a startled shake
and then narrowed his eyes and mouth in a grimace I'd
never seen before. The other students looked a little

shocked as well since I had thus far managed to repress my inner drill sergeant, and Nathan was known for his easygoing humor.

Wordlessly, Nathan assessed the situation and, noting Melissa's absence, began assisting his classmates with their technical problems, leaving me free to confer with Ramir. That seemed to me the very least Nathan could do. With my head pounding and my nose running, I abandoned my customary conference modality, a time- and energy-intensive exercise that requires engaging the student in a dialogue, finding out why his work is late, and enabling/manipulating him into producing it. Instead, I stood over the young man, wagged my index finger at him, and barked, "Ramir Singh, if you don't get the missing journals into my mailbox by the end of the week and schedule a conference with me to go over them, you are looking at an F for this course."

Before the brief and fragmented session drew to a close, Jonah had lent Jamala a floppy disk, but he had somehow lost his own morning's work by pushing one wrong button. It was Nathan who stood over the distraught young man and coached him through a salvage effort while the other students and I left the lab. I snuffled, snorted, and snapped at people through two more classes that day, trying not to breathe on anyone. I excused myself from a committee meeting and was in the office gathering up books and papers in preparation for going home when Wendy appeared, partly hidden behind a pile of colorful children's books. "Yikes, Bel. Halloween is over. You look worse than awful. And I thought you'd be all happy and excited. I can't believe how bad you look." Wendy had never been known to sugarcoat the truth.

"Thanks, Wendy. Now why don't you tell me what you really think? What is there to be excited about?" I was pulling on my jacket as I asked.

"One of your College Comp III students won the Faculty Senate Scholarship. Futura." She came up with the name before I'd even articulated the question. "I saw him in the dean's office this morning with Harold. The two of them were giving him the good news. The kid had a grin a mile wide. Isn't he the one you got the internship for?"

"Oh my God. That's why he was late. I bet he left me an e-mail message telling me he had an appointment with the dean and would be late for class. I never even checked my e-mail this morning." With a sick feeling in my stomach that had nothing to do with my head cold, I sank back into my chair, letting my armful of books and journals slide onto the desk. Again I pictured Nathan's grin disappearing in the aftermath of my public rebuke. Again I saw his eyes and mouth narrowing. In his opinion, I was now no different from "King Greg," an abuser of power who had nothing better to do than humiliate my subjects.

"Now what?" Wendy had left the door open and was maintaining a healthy distance from my aura of infection.

"I dissed him in front of the class for being late." I didn't think twice about using the urban abbreviation for the newly coined verb *to disrespect*. It had entered the discourse of RECC faculty, where it was universally understood and appreciated for its terse accuracy.

"He looked crushed. He probably expected me to be happy for him and congratulate him and all that. And what did I do? I blindsided him. 'Well, look who finally decided to show up. I hope you enjoyed your beauty sleep.' " I repeated my greeting to Nathan, exaggerating my sarcasm. "He looked so confused and hurt." I put my throbbing head down on my arms.

"Bel, let's try for a little perspective here. You can apologize to him. I'm sure he'll understand. You're blowing this up way out of proportion because you're sick and tired. Go home. E-mail him right away if it'll make you feel better. Then go to bed, for God's sake. And consider taking a sick day tomorrow. From both jobs. You're a mess."

"I got fired from the cleaning job," I said, my head still pillowed by my arms.

"Thank God," exclaimed Wendy. "Now go home."

Chapter 23

To: Bbarrett@circle.com
From: Futura@recc.nj.edu
Re: Good news!
Date: 11/02/99 21:08:23

Dear Professor B,

You the first person I e-mailing on my new computer right here
in my house! You the first one in my address book too. Because
I know it really thanks to you that I got it. So it be only right that
you get the first e-mail from me :=). And I got something cool to
rap with you about too. Today I got a letter from the Dean and
from Professor Furguesson you know, the President of the Faculty Senate. They said they got something good to tell me and
they sceduled a meeting with me first thing tommorow morning.
Man, I hope it got something to do with that long aplication I
filled out for the Faculty Senate Scholarship. My moms be on her
knees talking to God about it right now 'cause without a scholarship to buy books and whatnot with I can't transfer to State.

But I guess they didn't look at my scedule to see that I got your class, so that's why I'm telling you now, I be a little late tomorrow. Please excuse

Your student,
Nathan Futura

There was Nathan's e-mail message big as life waiting for me when I logged on to my PC at home. Reading it, I felt ashamed. I should never have allowed myself to get so wigged out that I didn't even check my e-mail. That was simply irresponsible. One had to be accessible to one's students practically 24/7. Private time was a quaint relic of a precyber age, like black and white TV, rotary phones, and vinyl records. Nevertheless, ignoring all the other messages, I summoned a spurt of energy and e-mailed Nathan an apology, promising to explain my nastiness during a conference with him next week. I congratulated him on winning the scholarship. It occurred to me that Ashley had won that same scholarship when she was a RECC student. Then I realized that Ashley hadn't returned my call, so I e-mailed her too, asking her to get back to me. Physically and emotionally exhausted, I went to bed and, oblivious of the imperatives of a full bladder, an empty belly, and an unexplained killing, slept until the next morning.

There was still no word from Ashley by Sunday afternoon when our entire bat mitzvah class was scheduled to meet at Symphony Space, that venerable showcase for writers and musicians on the Upper West Side of Manhattan. Mildred had wowed them at her audition and was now a bona fide Klezmama. This was her first gig with the group and we had agreed to turn out in force to support her. Rabbi OK was going too and I was bringing Sol and Ma, who, of course, had invited Sofia.

"So tell me again, what is klezmer? Did Frank sing any klezmer songs?" Sofia asked.

Before Sol or I could answer, Ma was lecturing, "You know Sofia, everything is not always Frank Sinatra." I winced and poked Sol in anticipation of one of the Odd Couple's typical squabbles, but Sofia didn't take the bait this time, and Ma continued. "Originally in Eastern Europe klezmorim, that's Yiddish for traveling musicians, would play these songs at weddings and other celebrations. The tunes come from synagogue chants and other very old songs. Then wherever Jews lived, Russia, Poland, Romania, the Ukraine, we added the folk songs sometimes from the gypsies even." Ma actually hummed a phrase or two of some melody only she could recognize. "My Ike, he loved klezmer music. My mother too." Lost for a moment in nostalgia and sadness, Ma concluded her tutorial with a sigh.

"You'll enjoy it, Sofia. Think of the wedding music in *Fiddler on the Roof*. When the Jews came to America, they added jazz, blues, and even rock." Sol was unable to resist contributing his two cents.

"The violin is pretty important in a klezmer band, and my friend Mildred is the group's new violinist, so this is a big day for her, like an opening night. The Klezmamas are an up-and-coming band. They're actually planning a European tour," I said, realizing that by now Sofia was probably regretting her initial question.

"Sybil, you've still got that cold, haven't you?" Ma's comment on the residual nasality in my voice signaled her timely return to the present. Sol was pulling up in front of Symphony Space to let us out and then park. I was about to respond to Ma when I spotted Ashley approaching alone from Ninety-fourth Street.

"Ashley! Ashley!" I called, leaping out of the car. She turned and, seeing me, walked toward us while I helped Ma and Sofia out. I felt a familiar pang of sympathy for the younger woman as I introduced her to the Odd Couple, who gave her the once over, noting her pallor, her skeletal frame, her barely brushed hair, and her haunted eyes. All she needed was a Styrofoam cup and a sign saying, "I Have No Food," and she could pass for a homeless waif on leave from a mental hospital. Sofia and Ma exchanged glances. I ushered us all inside.

Once we were shown to our places in the block of seats Mildred had chosen for us, Ma and Sofia studied their programs. I turned around and addressed Ashley, who was conveniently seated in the row behind ours two seats to the left. "Ashley, why haven't you returned my calls. I have something important to tell you. It's good news, I think, about Howard."

Only when I mentioned Howard's name did Ashley look up. "What about him?" she responded.

"Well, he's not having an affair in Bayonne." There was no change in Ashley's expression. It was going to take more than my simple say-so to convince her of Howard's fidelity. "He's established an office there. He's given up his law practice." Now Ashley blinked and turned her head a little. At least I had her attention. "He's become a day trader. He's got an office in a duplex in Bayonne that a client, Rosa Suarez, let him have while she's away."

"Run that by me again. Howie gave up his law practice? To day trade? This is my Howie Solomon we're talking about?" Incredulity gave her voice a higher than usual pitch. Understandably Ashley was having a hard time matching the husband she'd thought she knew with the man I was describing. While she struggled to take in my revelation, Sandi and Janet arrived and took the two seats next to her. Rabbi OK and her husband were behind them, and Sol was making his way across the row to his seat next to me just as the curtain parted and the musicians took their places.

"I'll talk to you again at intermission," I said, turning around and focusing on the stage where the Klezmamas were warming up. They all wore black pants and red shirts, and they looked fabulous. Mildred appeared calm, her face and body language bearing no traces of the anxiety she had professed to feel about her debut performance. In fact, she looked downright beatific. But she played like a demon. Sometimes her bow moved so fast that it blurred. Then Sofia and Ma tapped their feet. At other times Mildred stroked the fiddle in a slow mournful caress. That's when I saw Ma wipe away a tear with a Kleenex Sofia handed her. The Klezmamas played dances and dirges, a rich legacy of melodies sung in the language of our shared past. By intermission the audience was clapping wildly.

When we stood to stretch our legs, I turned around to signal Ashley that I wanted to continue our conversation. She was looking slightly less peaked and fairly bristled with curiosity. While many others lined up to buy CDs or a snack, Ashley and I stood outside on Broadway just out of range of the cluster of diehard smokers and continued our conversation. "Bel, how do you know that Howie is day trading in Bayonne and not shacking up with Rosa Suarez?" I was not exactly unprepared for Ashley's question, so I recapped the story of how Sol, Ma, and I had attempted to employ his legal services at his former Jersey City office. Talking fast, I detailed our brief visit to Howard's hideaway in Bayonne, the sparsely furnished scene of his liaisons with his new love, the stock market.

By the time an usher signaled us to reenter the concert hall, Ashley's entire demeanor had changed. Relief flushed her cheeks and brightened her eyes. Her shoulders were straighter and she was running her fingers through her short hair. She gave me a big hug before taking her seat, and as I moved toward mine, she smiled a smile that transformed her.

Not surprisingly Ashley was among the most enthusiastic members of the group surrounding Mildred when we gathered for a quick celebratory drink in the lobby after the concert. Looking triumphant, and clutching a bouquet of yellow roses, Mildred stood among us, modest and composed, asking, "Oh, did you really like it?" "Isn't that clarinetist something?" "Wasn't this a great audience?" and "Thanks so much for coming" over and over in between hugs from her family and friends. Unable to take photos during the performance, the shutterbugs were now at it and someone snapped a picture of Ashley embracing Mildred.

The combination of wine on an empty stomach and the exploding flash bulb stunned the already dazed Ashley, who stood there blinking as Mildred went on to greet another well-wisher. It was at that moment that I chose to pull Ashley aside and ask, "Do you have any idea why Greg would have wanted Chris dead?"

Chapter 24

**"ONLY 13 DAYS UNTIL THANKSGIVING!
ORDER YOUR FRESH KILLED TURKEY NOW!"**

The prospect of a childless and grandchildless Thanksgiving had not inspired me to rush out and order a turkey even though Sandi, Josh, and Ma were going to be sharing the holiday with us. I just couldn't get into it, so Sol had taken over the planning and provisioning. This left me free to catch up on student papers and preparations for classes, memorize the Hebrew alphabet, read the Hebrew Bible, and speculate on what motive Greg might possibly have had for wanting his own employee dead. On this last point I was eager to compare notes with Betty and Illuminada, so I lured them over for take-out on a Friday night when Sol was shopping and I was not searching for my Jewish identity in a plate of brisket or at a Sabbath service.

Betty surprised us by arriving with a carton containing three aluminum foil pans, one of veal Marsala, another of baked ziti, and a third of salad, the leftovers from a RECC Board of Trustees luncheon meeting that afternoon. Two loaves of still warm brick oven bread from Marie's were tucked under her arm. In the time it took to open a bottle of Chianti, and displace my cat, Virginia Woolf, from the bowl in the center of the counter, General Ramsey had commandeered the kitchen and was reheating this incredible feast. Normally I might have objected to being relegated to the sidelines in my own house, but there were times when Betty's need to control and my need to collapse meshed, and this was certainly one of them. Soon the three of us were huddled around the sink island in our customary places and Virginia Woolf was purring from her new nest in the empty carton on the floor.

"It's good that you didn't let these goodies get away," said Illuminada, daintily spearing a mushroom.

"It's even better that a few of our trusty trustees didn't show up, so we had a lot of leftovers. I couldn't let them go to waste," Betty said, ripping off a hunk of bread and carefully mopping up her Marsala sauce. "Nothing but the best for us!"

"Here's to the end of our careers with Delores Does Dusting," said Illuminada, raising her glass. "*Dios mio,* I'm glad that's over." She sighed and sipped her Chianti.

"Amen," Betty chimed in, tapping Illuminada's glass with her own. "You can say that again, girl. It's going to be a long time before I pick up another mop."

"You mean you're not still cleaning? What happened? Did you get the axe too?" I asked. "How are we going to get information about what's going on there?"

"No, *we* weren't fired," Illuminada said. "At least not exactly. It was mostly mutual. I have to go out of town on business for a few days this week, and when I told Delores, instead of offering to replace me, she handed me this."

"You've got to be kidding," Betty exclaimed, leaning over so that her dreads momentarily obscured both Illuminada's hand and the tiny object twinkling in her palm. "Bel's earring!" Betty sounded amazed, as if she were staring at the Hope diamond instead of my little gold stud. Illuminada closed her palm, inverted it in my hand, and loosened her grasp. My stomach coiled as my fingers closed around the small metal sphere. Quickly I filed it in the change compartment of my wallet.

Before I could even ask how she had come into possession of the missing bauble, Illuminada said, "Troy's secretary Kathy gave it to the security guard to give to Delores. Kathy told the guard that Troy found it under his desk and asked around to see whose it was. When none of the women who work there claimed it, he figured that one of Delores's "girls" had been in his office and he got really mad. I had to explain to Delores about Bel and the scooter. So now Delores thinks we should all cool it for a while. She's afraid of losing her cleaning contracts," Illuminada explained. "I told her we'd give up that gig for the time being anyway. We need a rest."

"Ain't that the truth," said Betty, covering her mouth to hide a yawn. "This body was not made for so much hard work."

"Well, was it made for rock climbing?" I asked, glad

to change the subject from the errant earring that had returned to haunt me.

Betty giggled and helped herself to a second portion of ziti. "I'm sure glad I don't have to haul these bones up walls anymore either. I'll stick to tae kwon do, thank you very much." Betty was very proud of her black belt in the Korean martial art. "My boss has me climbing the walls at work, and that's enough high altitude for me."

"So? What did you learn in rock climbing school? Anything useful?" Illuminada asked.

"Yes, as a matter of fact, I did. At least I think I did." Betty pushed her now empty plate away and walked over to her purse. She extracted a strange but oddly familiar-looking metal object and a length of plaid nylon rope. "Look," she said. "This is the carabiner. And here's how you hook it up." While she talked we watched, mesmerized, as her short brown fingers nimbly manipulated the rope through the metal oblong ring. "See, you have a buddy system and you and your buddy are connected by rope attached to both of you with these." She held up the carabiner. "When you climb, your buddy belays you. That means he stays on the ground and cuts you slack or tightens up on the rope if you slip." Betty stood there holding the carabiner and the rope like a flight attendant demonstrating how to use a seat belt.

"Caramba," Illuminada drew out the word with a slow exhalation. "It's perfect," she pronounced.

"Huh?" I said, feeling left out of the collective aha moment my two friends seemed to be sharing.

"Listen." Again Betty was pressing one side of the

metal device and the rope was sliding through the resulting opening. "Whoever was belaying Chris could have either deliberately pulled on the rope, causing him to lose his balance and fall, or could have waited until Chris lost his balance and instead of pulling him up, could have simply let him fall."

"See?" asked Illuminada, knowing I didn't. "That's why it's perfect. The police report says the equipment used was not defective. Nobody cut the rope or tampered with the carabiner or greased the handholds or footholds on the wall. They checked all of that. But this . . ." Illuminada paused, savoring the macabre scenario she and Betty had conjured up.

"So now you're both saying that Troy Tarnoff killed Chris Johanson by either allowing or causing him to fall two stories from the top of that wall and break his neck?" I asked, as much to hear the proposition spoken as to test its accuracy.

Both Betty and Illuminada nodded in unison, their faces grim. Betty returned to the table. In silence each of us carried her empty plate into the kitchen and I loaded the dishwasher while they covered the leftover food and stowed it in the fridge. Desperate for the psychic energy to contemplate a killer who deliberately sent his buddy to a fairly certain and very sudden death, I took out three small bags of M&Ms from my stash behind the Saran Wrap in a kitchen drawer. Wordlessly I emptied each one into a small dish and popped the dishes into the microwave for a few seconds. Betty was brewing decaf.

"Then I guess Ashley was right all along," I said when we were seated once again. "Troy told Chris something, probably about the new software they're launching. Then Troy found out Chris worked for e-media.com and killed him to prevent him from revealing what he had learned." With a few warm M&Ms melting in my mouth, I continued, "And what clued Troy in to Chris's real identity may very well have been that weird note we found in his lunch, 'Beware of geeks bearing gifts.' "

"I didn't think so at first, but I do now," said Illuminada. "Listen to this. Lourdes has been asking around at Elysium and the server, Paul, the one who likes her, he heard her asking the kid who expedites the take-out orders . . ."

"Wait a second. You lost me. What was she asking?" demanded Betty, who had separated her M&Ms by color and already eaten all the brown ones.

"She wanted to know if anyone had asked to have a note put in Troy's lunch, right?" I interjected.

"Well, actually she asked if anyone had gotten a big tip lately for putting a birthday card in someone's lunch or something like that," said Illuminada, obviously proud of her daughter's cleverness. "And guess what, *chiquitas*? The expediter didn't know anything about anything, but Paul did. He said a nice-looking gray-haired woman had tipped him fifty dollars to put a note in Troy's lunch one day. A belated birthday card she said it was." At the end of this bulletin, Illuminada, who was, of course, eating her M&Ms one at a time, deliberately placed one in her mouth.

"Did he say anything else about what this 'older' gal looked like?" I asked, picturing the silver haired and sweating Mattie Mollifer as a menopausal messenger of death. Had she known the intent of the note? Was she an accomplice? A conspirator? Or an innocent victim just following orders?

"Just that she was very pleasant and well dressed. He remembered that she wore glasses around her neck and she was complaining about the heat," said Illuminada with a grin.

"What about the gifts?" asked Betty. "What's the meaning of that part of the note?" Even as she framed the question, her eyes widened with understanding. She reached out and touched the carabiner she had left on the counter. "Lourdes told you that one of them gave Troy the birthday present, remember? A solid gold carabiner. 'Beware of geeks bearing gifts,' " she repeated, suddenly withdrawing her hand from the metal device as if it were a coiled snake. "It all fits now. Chris must have been the one to present him with the carabiner."

"Well, I'm sorry to say it doesn't all fit," I asserted, popping my last M&M. "We've got a theory on method and even opportunity, but what about motive? We know why Troy would want Chris dead, but not why Greg would betray his own agent. That's what I tried to get Ashley to tell me."

"*Como mierda*, Bel. I thought we agreed you weren't going to say anything to Ashley about our investigation." Illuminada sounded mad. I couldn't blame her. I'd violated every pact we'd made since we had started looking into this death. First I'd entered Troy's office, nearly broke a leg, and left my earring as a calling card. Next I'd invaded Greg's office and come close to blowing our cover completely. And now I'd questioned Ashley. I tried to reassure Betty and Illuminada by reviewing for them the whole story of Ashley and Howard's marital misunderstanding, its resolution, and how my question had caught Ashley off guard at Symphony Space.

"I didn't tell her anything about us or our investigation," I assured my collaborators. "I simply asked her if she had any idea why Greg might want his own employee killed."

"So what did she say?" asked Illuminada, managing to look both mollifed and piqued at the same time.

"She looked totally bewildered and said she had no clue," I answered. "And I don't either. I just can't imagine why Greg would set up his own man for a hit."

"Well, you better figure it out, *chiquita,* 'cause without a motive, this little Greco alpine execution we've reconstructed doesn't make any sense at all. It's just too zany to fly."

"Well, I told you what Sol thinks." I felt some obligation to at least remind them of Sol's theory, especially since I had none of my own.

"Yes, but remind us," said Betty.

"Sol thinks A: Howard Solomon got jealous and arranged somehow for the murder of his rival Chris and then became a day trader to deflect suspicion. Or B: Howard Solomon got jealous and arranged for the murder of his rival Chris and went off the deep end and became a day trader. He thinks Howard is a clever but insecure psychopath, quite capable of murder." I leaned back in my chair, satisfied that I had represented Sol's opinion fairly.

"But how would Howard have gotten Greg's mother

to do his dirty work for him? Or Troy for that matter? Maybe Howard is a nut, but this is so obviously an inside job, a dot com killing, a family affair, sibling rivalry really. If Howard wanted Chris dead, he would have killed him himself. He wouldn't go to the trouble of arranging a complicated corporate conspiracy resulting in a fatal rock climbing 'accident.' Or would he?" Betty shook her head, acknowledging her own confusion.

"I doubt it. But then who would? And why?" Illuminada's question echoed in my brain long after she and Betty had said good night and Sol and I had put away the groceries, unloaded the dishwasher, and gone to bed.

Chapter 25

To: Bbarrett@circle.com
From: Sandig@calgal.com
Re: Out in the cold
Date: 11/12/99 18:08:01

Bel,

So what happened to all those deep discussions we were going
to have about our spiritual identity? Our Jewish roots? Can we
go to services together on Saturday morning and then have a
nice long lunch just the two of us? Like old times? And don't tell
me you have another cold or you have to clean toilets or read
papers or solve some dumb murder. I haven't seen you in ages.
Come on, Bel.

Sandi

"So what do you think about the bat mitzvah experience?" Sandi asked as soon as we sat down at a quiet

225

table at Beta Kebob, a landmark Turkish restaurant in
Weehawken. We'd decided that even though we were
not having a traditional Sabbath meal, we could have a
Middle Eastern one, so I'd driven us to this old riverside town just north of Hoboken. At tables around us
diners chatted amiably in Hebrew, Turkish, Arabic, and
English. Here we could feast on a smorgasbord of delicacies and then linger for hours over Turkish tea and
rice pudding or pastry stuffed with pistachio nuts and
oozing honey.

"Truth?" I asked, knowing that Sandi would settle
for nothing less. "It hasn't made a believer of me. The
more I read about God and the wars fought in His
name in the Bible or, for that matter in the newspaper,
the less inclined I am to believe. I envy my students
their faith sometimes, but I don't share it."

"So you'll still be a Jewish humanist. That's okay,"
Sandi pronounced. "But now you'll be a well-informed
Jewish humanist."

"Thanks for your permission," I teased. "But reading biblical history can be pretty disillusioning too.
Those patriarchs were not only misogynists, they were
also jealous, conniving, power hungry—"

"That just makes them more human, doesn't it? And
it sure makes for good stories. I mean, who'd want to
read about a clan of virtuous, saintly, holier-than-thou
folks falling all over themselves to do good works?
Sounds boring, no?" Sandi closed her copy of the
magazine-sized menu. "You order. You've been here
before."

After I'd selected an assortment of appetizers and a
salad, I said, "You know, Sandi, the truth is, I really

don't have time for religious study, reflection, or ritual in my life. I'm American. I rush around all the time. I'm a workaholic. Practicing Judaism takes time and energy that I don't have." I sighed. "What about you? Are you still glad we're doing this?"

"Yes. And right now, we're having our own version of a Sabbath meal, reflecting together on our spiritual lives. Right here. Right this minute. You and I. It's just that our personal celebration doesn't conform to the traditional way of celebrating the Sabbath. Those rituals are continually evolving." Sandi spoke earnestly. It was good to be with her. She brought so much energy and creativity to everything she did. Now she was single-handedly reconstructing Jewish ritual life! You had to love her.

"I take it you're enjoying the bat mitzvah preparation experience?" I asked again. She glowed with health and well-being. Clearly something agreed with her. Was it New York? Her new job? Studying Judaism? Was there a new guy in her life? The important thing was that the anxious and lonely California transplant of a few months ago had evolved into this radiant model of midlife fulfillment.

"Yes. I really am. I spend a lot of time on the weekends studying. By the way, I promised Ashley I'd get together with her and go over some Hebrew. I've e-mailed and called her a couple of times and she hasn't responded. Maybe she's working round the clock and when she calls me back, she'll be a millionaire." Sandi's tone was light, but I knew it was unlike Ashley not to return calls, and a frisson of anxiety disturbed our private Sabbath meal.

Unaware of my mental digression, Sandi continued. "You know, I enjoy the little community we're becoming, the four of us. I loved going to Mildred's concert. I really like Ashley and Janet too." Sandi's eyes widened as the first few dishes we'd ordered arrived. For a few minutes we passed them back and forth, helping ourselves to strips of warm pita bread.

"Yes, I like them too. You know, it's funny, I don't have that many close Jewish friends. I never thought much about it." I pictured Wendy, Betty, and Illuminada. Would we be any closer if they were Jewish? Sarah Wolf and I had forged our friendship in a long-ago aerobics class, and our bond was based on our age and our very secular mutual interests. Aloud to Sandi I said, "But I feel so guilty that I can't put more time into learning Hebrew and reading. And I promised to take you to the Lower East Side, to Ratner's and the Tenement Museum. Maybe during my Christmas break." The baba ganoush, hummus, and stuffed grape leaves had all but disappeared when a plate of stuffed eggplant and another of tzatziki, a garlicky yogurt dip, arrived. Instinctively, Sandi and I slowed down.

"Well, you always feel guilty, so what's new? Christmas break will be fine. You'll be relaxed, your cold will be completely gone, and we'll make a whole day of it," Sandi said graciously.

"Sounds good," I said. "I just hope we get to Ratner's before it closes. Can you believe somebody wants to make a club out of that old dairy restaurant? I hope they save the chocolate pudding recipe."

"I hope so too," said Sandi. "You've been talking

about Ratner's chocolate pudding for over thirty years." She rolled her eyes.

"Can you believe we're planning Christmas break when we haven't even gotten through Thanksgiving yet?" I asked, marveling as always about how fast the semesters that I measure my life in whiz by.

"I know. Time really does move faster out here. I'm so excited about Thanksgiving. So is Josh. We're really glad you invited us," Sandi smiled at me across the table and gave my hand a squeeze. "I told Sol we'd bring the wine. How many people will there be altogether?"

"Just you and Josh and Ma and Sol and me," I said miserably. I know Sandi didn't mean any harm, but I really hated thinking about the upcoming holiday.

"By the way, I just want to remind you that I'm borrowing your car on Thanksgiving morning so I can whip out to Newark Airport and meet Josh's plane. That means you won't be able to run out for that one last thing you forgot to buy. I'll be over to pick up the car at about eleven." Sandi's words seemed to bubble out of her mouth, propelled by her excitement at the thought of meeting Josh.

"Sure. That's fine. We don't have to drive to get what we forgot anyway. I could pick up the ingredients for a whole Thanksgiving dinner that morning within a five-block radius of home if I wanted to. That's one of the beauties of Hoboken. Remember, this is not California where people live to drive." I guess I sounded a little edgy because Sandi just nodded. "You know what really bothers me about Judaism?" I asked, eager to move the conversation back to a less painful topic.

"So tell me," said Sandi obligingly.

"It's frozen in the past. It doesn't seem to have any application or relevance to modern life, to my life anyway. The language is ancient, the legends are archaic, the morality is so absolute. I mean, 'Thou shalt not kill.' That just doesn't allow for the complexities of modern life. What about a woman's right to choose? A dying person's right to opt for assisted suicide? The Ten Commandments and the biblical legends have become simplistic . . ." I was on a roll and would have ranted on, but Sandi interrupted.

"Give me a break, Bel. The stories in the Old Testament certainly are reflected in our everyday lives. Look around. Take your King David. He reminds me of Bill Clinton—you know, a smart, ambitious leader with, if I may understate, an eye for the ladies. And there's a woman I work with who I swear is a prophet. She's that good at predicting how each member of the board of directors will react to changes in personnel policies that we're trying to introduce. She calls them right every time."

I mulled this over while I tried to imagine Ron Woodman, president of RECC, as a king of Israel or my office mate Wendy as a seer. "Well, that kind of application would be a reach for me," I said, smiling. "RECC doesn't lend itself to biblical projections. And let's face it, there are no prophets in Jersey City."

"Don't bet on it, Bel. Take it from that hip California girl who predicted that if you learned to use Tampax you'd be happier," Sandi cracked, grinning at the recollection of coaching me on the niceties of tampon insertion from an adjoining stall in the dorm bathroom. "There are prophets everywhere."

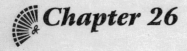

Chapter 26

LOCAL E-COMMERCE COMPANY
LAUNCHES LANDMARK SOFTWARE

scoop.com, an e-commerce company based in Jersey
City's Silicon Slum, unveiled a revolutionary new
software product today called e-merge. Designed to
streamline and facilitate business-to-business trans-
actions on the Internet, the new product is expected
to earn mega profits for the fledgling company and
its major stockholders. According to Troy Tarnoff,
scoop.com's twenty-six-year-old CEO and director of
special projects, e-merge will revolutionize the way
on-line business is conducted . . .

Illuminada had spotted the article and faxed copies
to Betty and me, but I didn't have time to read all of it
because I had a department meeting after classes and a
conference with Nathan after that. I was tired when the
interminable meeting finally fizzled into wrangling

over the date for the department's annual multicultural millennial festival, which had replaced our annual holiday party of the eighties, which had replaced our annual solstice be-in of the seventies, which had replaced our annual Christmas party. I ate a chocolate chip cookie Wendy had left on my desk and felt a little more energized.

It was not hard to greet Nathan with a smile when he entered. "I hope you'll accept my in-person apology for my nastiness last week," I said before he had settled his lanky frame into Wendy's chair. "I hadn't read your e-mail about the scholarship meeting, and Melissa wasn't around, and I had that cold . . ."

"No problem. We still cool, Professor B. I got your e-mail and I figured it was somethin' like that." Nathan put out his hand in a classic gesture of forgiveness, and I shook it. That simple action wiped away the last of my anxiety and guilt. I knew that now Nathan would not harbor a grudge or seethe with resentment on my account. Like the man said, we were still cool.

Free to revert to our former relationship, I said, "And Nathan, I'm so happy for you about the scholarship. It's such an honor. The Faculty Senate gives out only one of those each year, and the committee that awards it is quite strict. You must be very proud of yourself."

"It cool. Now I can go to State. What you think? This class be the only one I'm worried about. Ashley, you know the one who got me the PC? She was tutoring me once and awhile, but she out in the field now I guess. Think I'm going to make it with a B?" Nathan's tone was light but his query was serious. For a minute I wished I did have the gift of prophecy.

"Well, here's the way the situation stands now. When you use the computer, you see the green lines underlining your grammatical errors and you're getting pretty good at fixing them. So if you get the paper drafted in time to really proofread it carefully, I'd say yes, easily. But . . ."

Nathan's smile faded as I reached the end of my pronouncement. "But what, Professor B?" he asked.

"But I want you to start working on your speech and the writing you do that doesn't get green-lined, for instance, your e-mails. You're going to be talking and e-mailing a lot in your classes at State and when you get a job. So we need to start working on making you truly bidialectical." I paused to give him a chance to absorb this information.

"You could be right. But that gonna be hard, Professor B," he said as if I needed convincing. "Got any ideas on how I gonna do that?"

"Yes. And it is hard, but lots of people not half as smart as you are become bidialectical, so you will too. You're going to start paying attention to your spoken grammar and consciously imitate the standard English speakers you hear like me and the people at e-media.com." I spoke with certainty, hoping to hook into Nathan's own youthful optimism and enormous determination.

"Man, I'm not sure anymore I wanna sound like King Greg. That dude think he cool. He got too much money and too much attitude. Yesterday I saw him in that car of his wid a phat red-haired babe. But just 'cause he got a lot of money and a cool car don't give him the right to diss the rest of us. Hell, he even give his moms a hard time the other day. He tol' her to F off right in front of me and the whole sales staff just because she said how scoop.com's stock was worth more than e-media's right now. He said she sounded like some Chris." Nathan shook his head, still talking. "Can you believe that? Someday he gonna have a kid and that kid gonna diss him." Nathan shook his head again. "Man, that dude don't deserve to have no kid." Nathan was venting, and I wanted to steer him back to the difficult task of learning to code switch to standard English when it would serve him to do so.

"Nathan, let's take that last sentence, 'He don't deserve to have no kid,' " I prodded, jotting it down on a piece of paper. "What grammatical problems do you see here that the computer would green-line?" I asked, venturing into new territory. I'd never tried this approach before, but I didn't have many students with Nathan's cybersmarts and determination either.

"He doesn't," Nathan answered promptly.

"Anything else?" I insisted, pleased so far with the result of my crash course in code recognition. Then in an inspired moment, I asked, "How would I say it?" After all, generations of students have been sending up their profs by aping our accents, grandiose word choice, and intonation. It was high time someone made constructive use of this overlooked resource.

Hesitating for only a minute, Nathan grinned and said, "He doesn't deserve to have a child," in a flawless imitation of my diction, voice, and level of animation.

I was jubilant. "Exactly! You got rid of the double negative and the slang and fixed the subject-verb agreement, which, by the way, you're getting really good at. That's what you have to do. Start with your e-mails 'cause they're written. Then you'll gradually begin to edit your speech without too much thought." I knew that the task I had set Nathan was not easy, but I was eager to see him take charge of his language and have a couple of dialects at his disposal as he went out into the larger post–community college world.

"Now let's take a look at that paper," I said.

At home that night I recounted to Sol what I considerd a groundbreaking pedagogical encounter, the ultimate synthesis of technology and teaching, Bill Gates meets Our Miss Brooks. "So you think you're gonna get that homeboy to talk and write like a Rhodes scholar by having him imitate a computer and then imitate you?" Sol was chuckling. "What makes you think this Nathan even wants to sound like a middle-aged white woman on speed?" Sol was kneading my shoulders as he spoke. He hadn't been too impressed by my account of Nathan's conference, but even his gentle jibes couldn't dim my enthusiasm.

"Did you get the phone message from Rabbi OK?" Sol asked. "I left it on the machine."

"No. What did she want?" I didn't feel like getting up to play the message myself.

"She just wondered if you had seen or heard from Ashley lately. Ashley didn't show for an appointment they had and Rabbi OK couldn't reach her at home or at work. Apparently Ashley's husband still doesn't return calls. The rabbi sounded worried." Sol stopped kneading my shoulders. "That's it for tonight, love."

The message from Rabbi OK quickly undid the soothing effects of Sol's back rub. I felt my shoulder muscles spasm into familiar knots as I contemplated my worst fears about Ashley. Had Troy or one of his colleagues at scoop.com discovered that she was really a spy for e-media.com and done away with her and hidden her corpse? Or had the mysteriously motivated Greg done her in for whatever macabre reasons moved him to do in his employees? Or had she confronted Howard with her anguished suspicions and recent discoveries and thus provoked a fight? And in the heat of what the cops always dubbed a "domestic dispute," had Howard killed her and disposed of her body? None of these scenarios was conducive to a good night's sleep, and so, not surprisingly, I had a doozy of a nightmare.

But when I woke up sweating and shaking, I was pretty sure why Greg Mollifer had orchestrated the death of his own lieutenant, Chris Johanson.

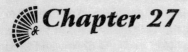

Chapter 27

*Nathan said to David . . . 9 "Why have you despised
the word of the Lord to do what is evil in his sight? You
have smitten Uriah the Hittite with the sword, and
have taken his wife to be your wife, and have slain him
with the sword of the Ammonites . . ." David said to
Nathan, "I have sinned against the Lord." And Nathan
said to David, "The Lord has put away your sin; you
shall not die. 14 Nevertheless because by this deed
you have utterly scorned the Lord, the child that is
born to you shall die."*

2 SAMUEL 12

"*Como mierda,* Bel, what the hell were you going on
about in that crazy message you left with my secretary
this afternoon? Maribel thought you said something
about a prophet and a king? Did your estrogen patch
catch on your pantyhose again?" Illuminada looked
tired when she got to my house that night, but she was
smiling when she spoke.

"She told Gina the same thing," said Betty, kicking off her shoes. "I figure that sinus infection you had went to your brain. What's the big hurry? What's going on, girl? All I know is I'm double-parked, and I'm going to get a ticket in this damn town. I don't need a prophet to tell me that." Betty looked drawn and tired too. Our weekly cleaning sessions had taken their toll on all of us.

"Well, I figured out why Greg Mollifer wanted Chris Johanson dead," I proclaimed, passing around the box of pizza from Benny Tudino's. Sol had dropped it off before he left for a meeting of the Citizens' Committee to Preserve the Waterfront, a group working tirelessly to fend off the developers from what little was left of Hoboken's magnificent riverside vistas. "I hate to miss your tête-à-tête tonight. I'd love to see Betty and Illuminada's faces when you spring this one on them," he'd called over his shoulder as he left the house. "I don't need a prophet to tell you how they're going to react. Don't let them commit you before I get home."

"Okay, here goes. Let's see if I can tell you the whole thing before a cop tickets your car." I took a deep breath. "I had this conference yesterday with my student Nathan. Actually, his last name is Futura." I paused. "Think about it. Nathan Futura. He's an intern at—"

"*Dios mio,* Bel. Spare us the biography. What about him?" Illuminada's customary impatience with what she saw as digressions and what I saw as narrative had transformed her smile into a tight-lipped scowl.

I tried another tack. "Well, last night I had a dream about—"

"Bel, tell it to a shrink like everybody else. You did not get us over here on a Tuesday night to tell us your dreams." Illuminada was making me nuts. I wanted to shake her.

Betty walked to the window, raised the blind, and peeked out at her car. "Well, I've got all night now. He just put a ticket on my car. So talk, girl. What's on your mind?" Back at the sink island, she helped herself to another slice of pizza.

What's on my mind is that if you two want to hear this, you'll have to hear it the way I tell it. So please just be still and listen, okay?" I hoped that the question at the end of my mandate would take some of the bite out of my words.

They nodded. I continued. "Okay, so last night I had this incredible nightmare in which my student Nathan Futura stood up at his graduation in his cap and gown and prophesied the death of David and Bathsheba's baby in standard English." Realizing that the liguistic metamorphosis of my student was not really germane here, I hastened to add, "I couldn't fall asleep again because a few of the details Nathan had mentioned in our conference started to come together and lead to a couple of possible motives." Illuminada couldn't resist motioning with her hand for me to go on, but she remained quiet. "Nathan said he'd seen Greg drive off with an attractive redhead. I met Norma Johanson, the victim's widow. She is an attractive redhead."

Now I had their attention. Encouraged, I continued, determined to explain the whole deadly diorama as I had constructed it during my nocturnal stint as a one-woman think tank. "According to the Book of Samuel . . ." I saw

Illuminada roll her eyes, but she stifled her knee jerk impulse to belittle my reference. "King David saw Bathsheba, wife of Uriah, a Hittite general in David's army, bathing on an adjacent rooftop. He desired her, commandeered her to his bed, and impregnated her. Her pregnancy posed the usual PR problems for both the politician and the general's wife. In an effort at damage control, David summoned Uriah home from the battlefield, assuming that Uriah would sleep with Bathsheba and so establish himself as father of her baby. But Uriah refused to have sex with Bathsheba while his men suffered on the battlefield. So David sent him back into battle and ordered his generals to desert Uriah when the enemy surrounded him. They did as the king ordered and Uriah was killed in battle. Nathan prophesied that as punishment to King David, his child would die." I paused for a swig of apple cider.

Betty was nodding, indicating her familiarity with the story. Illuminada sat quietly, listening, but not reacting. Grateful for her restraint, I resumed talking. "I am willing to bet that Norma Johanson is pregnant. I also think that Greg Mollifer knew his old buddy Troy well enough to know that Troy would kill to protect his stock options at scoop.com. I think Greg alerted Troy to the fact that Chris was a spy and then Troy killed Chris and made it look like a rock climbing accident."

"But why would they care about the pregnancy? The baby might just as well have been Chris's. He wasn't away on some battlefield." Betty's question had troubled me too, so I had given it some thought and was prepared to put it to rest.

"Ashley mentioned to me that Chris had joked that he and Norma hadn't had sex for months. He thought she had turned him off because she wanted to move to the burbs and he didn't. More likely, she'd gotten involved with Greg and either had some notion of fidelity to him or she was confused about how she felt about Chris. Maybe her thing with Greg was even a reaction to Chris's friendship with Ashley. I don't know." Betty was shaking her head at the antics of these rich young marrieds.

"Just one thing, *chiquita*," said Illuminada. By hearing me out, she had earned the right to cross-examine me. "In the heat of your bat mitzvah studies perhaps you have not noticed that we do not live in ancient Israel. We live in the year 1999 and this is America. First of all, why would a pregnancy be such a big deal? She could end it. In fact, she could end the marriage too."

I knew I wouldn't have to speak to this point. Betty, more Catholic than the pope, chimed in almost before Illuminada had finished her sentence. She spoke in the measured tones of one accustomed to making the same point over and over as, indeed, she was. "Illuminada, even in America in the twentieth century not every woman experiencing an unplanned pregnancy chooses to abort. Even as a lapsed Catholic, you should know that. And not everyone leaps out of the wrong bed and into divorce court either."

"Right," I said. "Especially super conventional types who long for homes in the burbs."

"Okay, okay. As my daughter says to me, 'Let's not go there tonight.' I haven't the energy to argue with both of you." As she spoke, Illuminada smiled at Betty.

"But what about the possibility that there is no pregnancy and Greg just wanted Chris out of the way? Maybe Greg was afraid that Norma would ultimately prefer Chris. Maybe he didn't believe that Chris and Norma weren't having sex and was jealous."

"Could be," I said. "But there's another little thing I noticed when I met Norma that leads me to believe she might be pregnant."

"Are you planning to share or do we have to beat it out of you?" Betty made mock fists. I was relieved to see a trace of a smile brighten her face.

"The afternoon Ashley and I visited Norma, someone, I think it was her mother, mentioned that Norma wasn't sleeping well and that the doctor had prescribed a sedative. She suggested that Norma take it. First Norma asked her mother to bring her the bottle of pills, and then, after her mom came back with them, Norma abruptly decided not to take them." Illuminada and Betty were both nodding again, indicating that they understood the connection I was about to make. "You know how the kids today are such purists when they're pregnant. They really watch what they ingest."

"*Dios mio,* when I think about what I inhaled and ingested when I was pregnant with Lourdes," Illuminada said, suddenly grinning. "No wonder she's such a rebellious kid." Then her grin disappeared and she sighed. "Frankly, I think the whole Norma connection is a long shot whether she's pregnant or not. But it's all we've got."

"No, it's not. But it's a big part of what we've got," I said. "Illuminada, would you be willing to have someone in your office check area hospitals and

OBGYNs, including those in Manhattan, to see if anyone answering Norma's description is receiving prenatal care?" I knew that this was the kind of task that Illuminada could delegate to a member of her staff who would perform it swiftly and accurately. Illuminada nodded and typed something into her Palm Pilot.

"So what else do we have?" asked Illuminada when she finished typing.

"According to both Ashley and now Nathan, Greg is extremely paranoid," I said slowly, thinking as I spoke. "Ashley once said that Chris used to stand up to him, and according to Nathan, he's still talking trash about Chris. Maybe Greg was worried about the fact that Chris had formed a social relationship with Troy and feared he would defect to scoop.com." Betty and Illuminada didn't react, so I rephrased my suspicion. "So maybe Greg set Chris up because he imagined Chris was going over to the other side, to Troy. Spies do that sometimes, you know. Maybe Greg even hit on Norma to get back at Chris."

"*Dios mio,* that's a reach, but suppose you're right," said Illuminada. "Greg has known Troy long enough and well enough to realize that he'd do something crazy to keep Chris from blowing his big launch."

"Yeah, but it's really hard to believe that he'd kill somebody," Betty chimed in. "I mean, we're not talking here about some two-bit drug dealer protecting his turf."

"No, but we might as well be," I said. "It's the same principle." I was annoyed at what I saw as her naiveté and her class bias.

"You know, I sure wish there were witnesses," Betty

continued. "It's maddening that with all those folks working weird hours and with that wall right out in plain view, nobody saw anything."

"That's what I thought," said Illuminada. "But you saw the police report. Apparently nobody was in the cubicles under the place where he fell, so nobody saw anything." In my mind's eye, I saw again the place where the gray overhang of the climbing wall met the white of the ceiling that I had noticed from my seat in the butterfly chair the night I cleaned the polka.com cubicle. I almost missed Illuminada's next words, "And, *chiquita,* it *0* maddening, but nobody heard anything either, until he landed."

Suddenly I wasn't so sure Illuminada was right.

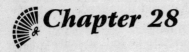

Chapter 28

"Sol, stop waving that paper in my face. What does this have to do with what I'm talking about?" I asked. "I'm trying to tell you that I think I know who might have witnessed Chris Johanson's murder." Sol and I were attempting to enjoy an early morning cup of tea together before I left for class.

"I know. I heard you. Because of some magical

chair, a plastic cactus, and a cowboy hat, you think some recently weaned computer cowboy witnessed Johanson's murder and got so unhinged that he fled the cube farm for the Sonora without saying sayonara." Sol looked very pleased with his command of cyber slang and his snippy alliteration. I chafed as I always did when he made fun of me while I was being serious.

But, of course, once again, he was right. That was more or less what I did think. "Okay. You're right. Except for the part about the chair. The chair's not magic. It just happened to be in this cubicle, and I sat in it to rest and to see what it felt like because Sandi and I used to have one. And when you lean back in that chair and look up, you can't help but see the overhang of the climbing wall . . ."

"So who says that kid was even there that night? Why didn't the cops talk to him when they looked for witnesses?" Sol's questions were fair. Illuminada and Betty would ask them too.

"Here's the scenario. Try to put yourself in this kid's position," I said, mustering up the patience to once again explain my version of what had happened. I was relieved to note that Sol had finally put down his damn newspaper. "You're a kid, probably a boy of somewhere between seventeen and twenty-two, and either way still pretty moist behind the ears. You were born with a silver mouse in your hand and your idol is, let's say, alpha geek billionaire Bill Gates. You grew up and/or went to school in someplace like New Mexico or Texas or Arizona, where they have cactus and wear cowboy hats. You get recruited by Troy Tarnoff, not Bill Gates exactly, but close enough, and he persuades you to come east. Like generations of kids before you, you're flattered and excited because you want those big bucks, a dot com adventure, and a bite of the Big Apple." I paused for a minute. "So you come east and work for Troy, who mentors you and pays you well, and then, one night, you're dozing in your chair and nobody knows you're there. You're awakened by talking, loud talking. Your boss, your mentor, is joking with somebody. You look up—"

"I hear you, Bel. Boy, you could talk the icing off a cake," said Sol.

"Wait, I'm not done. I still haven't answered your questions," I said, savoring his compliment nonetheless. Sol settled back in his chair and sipped his tea, signaling his readiness to resume listening. I picked up my narrative. "So you look up. You see what you see, hear what you hear. You stay quiet. During the ensuing commotion, maybe while your boss is checking for a heartbeat or a pulse or while the EMTs are there, you just slip out. And you don't come back. Ever. Because you can't face what you've heard and seen. You're just a kid. Troy is someone you admire. You liked Chris too. You can't really comprehend what you heard and/or saw. You don't know who to go to. So you just go."

Sol sat in silence for a minute and then said, "Bel, it's possible. But it's also possible that the kid saw the writing on the wall or, more likely, on the NASDAQ, and split. After all, in spite of their big launch, scoop.com's profit line is, as Howard Solomon would say, still in the toilet. So far they're all flash and no cash. And if you weren't too busy to read the fine print in the paper, you'd know that without me telling you."

"You may very well be right, but we won't know until we check it out. I'm going to run this by Illuminada and see if she can get Delores to get the kid's name and find out where he's from and if he went back there. If he did, I'm going to get him back here and talk to him if I have to track him across the Sonora on a camel," I vowed, reaching for the phone.

Thanks to Illuminada's efficiency and know-how, the camel was spared. Illuminada figured that just as the maintenance and security people may have made personal calls on company phones, the white-collar workers probably sent off packages at company expense. She spoke to the mail carrier for scoop.com, whose sister she'd helped nail a shoplifter in her bodega years ago. From him she learned the names of three people at scoop.com who had, in fact, sent packages regularly to the Southwest during the last year. Two of them had since left. One of those had been away at the time of Chris's murder. The other was Scot Annich.

Doing a simple Net search, Illuminada had found few Annichs, but there was a Lawrence Annich at an address in Chandler, Arizona. The news that our potential murder witness might be in Chandler had eroded some of Sol's initial skepticism. "That's Silicon Desert," he exclaimed. "That town's like a millennial version of T. S. Eliot's wasteland filled with malls and microchip manufacturers." He paused and then, seeing the puzzled look on my face, added, "Lately Chandler's economy's been driven by computer hardware companies." I nodded, appreciative of the explanation even though my puzzled expression had nothing to do with Chandler's economy. I was pondering how to get

Scot Annich back here so I could then get him to tell me what he had seen and heard the night Chris was killed.

It wasn't until later when I was sitting in my office going over some drafts of résumés submitted by Nathan and his classmates that I finally figured out how to lure Scot Annich back east. I called Sandi at work and left word for her to call me at home that night. It was about eight when she returned my call. "Hi Sandi. Thanks for getting back to me. It's time for you to do a little mitzvah for your old friend," I said.

"Oh, you mean it's payback time. Sure. What can I do for you?" Sandi's tone was light.

I resisted the urge to banter with her. Instead I said, "I think I need to explain this in person. Can I come over for a few minutes?"

"Tonight? It's already after eight. Bel, is anything wrong?" Now Sandi sounded alarmed.

"Yes and no," I said enigmatically. "I'll be there by PATH in half an hour and you'll be in bed by ten, I promise." Again I resisted the urge to remind Sandi of the long gone days when we had routinely stayed up most of the night talking. When I hung up, I headed for the PATH train a few blocks away and in the fifteen minutes it took to get to Christopher Street, I contemplated Sandi's reaction to my request. By the time she buzzed me into her building, Sandi had made skimmed milk hot chocolate and was waiting at her door.

"Okay. What brings you here so suddenly? Why aren't you home reading papers or preparing classes or chatting with Sol? Tell me what's going on. Is everybody okay?" Sandi was smiling, but her voice was sharp with concern.

"Not to worry. I told you. I need a favor. Does Classic Media have offices in Alaska or Hawaii or Puerto Rico?" I asked, throwing my jacket on a chair and settling myself on the sumptuous leather sofa.

"We have an office in Honolulu. Why?" asked Sandi.

Forgoing a slick lead-in, I blurted, "I need to lure a very bright and sensitive young computer jock to New York so I can talk to him. I thought you could offer him a job." I watched Sandi's eyebrows arch in consternation. "Wait, hear me out," I added hastily before she could register her reaction. "He just might be a murder witness, and he doesn't want to come back to Jersey City. He would never take a job anywhere near here. He wants to be far away from the scene of the crime." I winced as I heard myself use that trite phrase, but that was how I saw it. "But he just might be willing to fly in and out of Manhattan to interview for a position in Alaska or Hawaii or Puerto Rico with a classy and traditional outfit like yours . . ." I paused now, steeling myself in anticipation of Sandi's objections.

I was surprised when she simply asked, "Is he any good?"

"He was a programmer for scoop.com recruited by their president," I answered. "He probably cut his teeth in Chandler," I added, trying to sound knowledgeable about a place I'd heard of for the first time that morning.

"Okay," Sandi said. "For you, I'll put together some kind of personalized recruitment package and e-mail him. If he's a cretin, we just won't hire him. And if he's good I'll be happy to seriously consider him for a job. Now assuming he bites and shows for an interview, how do you propose to get him to talk to you?"

I was ready for this question. "Shake hands with Bel Barrett, your newest recruiter. I've been doing mock job interviews with students for years. It's time I got to do a real one." I stuck out my hand and Sandi shook it and gave me a hug.

"I knew I shouldn't have asked," Sandi said with her infectious grin. "I'll call you if and when I hear from him."

Sandy heard from Scot Annich within hours of e-mailing him and arranged an interview for that Friday. She had told him that Classic Media would pay his airfare and put him up in New York for one night. The interview was scheduled for the following Friday in the late afternoon so I could be there without missing classes. I had dressed with care in a muted gray wool dress that draped where it needed to without looking like a remnant from a toga sale. I wore simple gold earrings and a long gray and purple silk scarf Sol had given me for my birthday one year. Sandi ensconced me in the spacious and comfortable office of one of her recruiters and alerted her secretary to send in Scot Annich when he arrived.

I had barely seated myself behind the gleaming desk and launched into a daydream about having an office even half this size for myself when Sandi's secretary rapped on the door, opened it, and introduced Scot Annich. Scot had light brown hair and eyes and a solid frame. He wore a dark blue suit, an appropriately subdued tie, and the requisite pastel shirt. There was nary a trace of dot commer or cowboy in either his attire or his earnest, fresh-faced demeanor. Rather, he looked like a kid wearing his dad's clothes. He couldn't have been over twenty.

I stood and shook his outstretched hand. "Welcome to the Big Apple, Scot. How was your flight?" I asked in my most jocular manner, hoping to put him at ease.

He remained standing, looking around at the posh office and tugging at his collar. "Fine, ma'am. It was smooth and fast. It was direct from Phoenix," he replied. I saw him looking over my shoulder at the view of Times Square visible from the window.

"Quite a place, New York, isn't it?" I said. "Pretty different from Chandler?" As I spoke, I pretended to consult the brief résumé he'd faxed to Sandi. I motioned him to sit.

"Yes, ma'am. Chandler's nothing but malls and walls," he said, flashing a sudden and extremely engaging grin as he echoed Sol's estimate of the place.

"So I guess I can understand your wanting to leave there and work somewhere more exciting. But, tell me, why did you leave scoop.com?" I knew he'd have prepared a response to this standard interview query.

Indeed there was only a millisecond's hesitation before he replied, "My girlfriend doesn't want to live in New York. She wants to live someplace that's warm all year like Arizona but with beaches and, you know, culture." Again he flashed a grin, only this time it came across as a nervous twitch animating the muscles of his mouth. I decided to make my move.

I stood up and walked around the desk and took a

chair next to him. "Scot," I said gently, "I'm a friend of a friend of Chris Johanson." At once the young man's whole face shut down and his fingers gripped the arms of his chair. I was afraid he would bolt the room, so I spoke quickly. "Scot, I think I know why you really left scoop.com. I think I know what you saw and heard the night you left Jersey City. I'd like to talk to you about it. How do you feel about my taping what we say?" I inquired, just as I used to ask my kids, "Do you want to go to bed at seven-fifteen or seven-thirty?" The right to choose their bedtime from a limited set of options had prevented many a scene at our house. Now I hoped Scot Annich would focus on whether he wanted to be taped as he described what he'd witnessed rather than whether he should describe it at all.

"Are you with the police?" he asked, still wary, his fingers still wrapped around the arm of his chair.

"No, I teach English at a community college in Jersey City." But this was only half the truth, so I added, "A former student of mine was a good friend of Chris's. She wants to know how he died. She doesn't believe he fell," I said softly. "I don't either." I made eye contact with the boy in the chair in front of me. He returned my gaze, let go of the chair, and tugged at his tie until it loosened. Then he began to talk.

# Chapter 29

To: Belbarrett@circle.com
From: Rbarrett@UWash.edu
Re: Stuffing recipe
Date: 11/19/99 17:27:43

Dear Mom,

Not much time, but what is your stuffing recipe? I remember how good it always was, and even though Keith and I are both working on Thanksgiving (don't worry, Louise is baby-sitting Abbie J), we thought maybe we'd try to make a small turkey later in the weekend if we have a few hours off at the same time. I know I have to work either lunch or dinner every day and I have a paper to do, but send me the stuffing recipe just in case.

Right now Abbie J is in her bassinet playing with the mobile you sent her, and she's making gurgling noises. She talks to herself all the time just like you do. I wish you could hear her.

Have you heard from Mark? I haven't. I guess they don't have e-mail on the way to Tierra del Fuego! Love to Grandma Sadie and Sol. Thanks in advance for the recipe.

Love,
Rebecca

Rebecca's e-mail with its subtext of drudgery and starvation only served to send me deeper into the funk brought on by a renewed attack of sinusitis threatening to become bronchitis, two sets of ungraded papers, and anxiety about the still-missing Ashley. So I was especially glad to see Betty that night when she threw open her condo door to Illuminada and me. "Come in. Get out of the cold. I'm heating up some pasta fagiole Vic made over the weekend," Betty ordered and announced in one breath. A future that included hot, homemade soup was welcome news. Although I staved off her hug for fear of spreading my disease, her warm welcome made me feel better.

"I brought the bread," I reported, putting the bag down on the table next to the bowls, spoons, and napkins Betty already had out. "I'll get some plates and the butter," I said as soon as I noticed these omissions. While I rummaged in Betty's perfectly organized fridge and cabinet, she ladled out the hot soup. Illuminada hung up our coats and opened a large bag of popcorn she'd brought. Illuminada felt about popcorn the way I did about M&Ms. She was smiling as she filled a bowl and pushed it to the center of the table.

Before we even sat down, she announced, "Well, *chiquitas,* we didn't have to go too far down the alphabet before we came to Dr. Ernest French, an OBGYN in Englewood. Guess who's been showing up in his waiting room on a fairly regular basis? *Dios mio,* when Alicia told me she'd found an OBGYN with a red-haired patient living at Norma's address in Jersey City who was just a little bit pregnant, I have to admit, I was surprised. Bel, I think you should seriously consider retiring from teaching and getting your PI license." Illuminada's tone was light, but she'd made this suggestion before.

"Hell, I think you should become a prophetess," joked Betty. "You've got the gift."

A juicy hacking cough ripped from my sore chest in response. But Illuminada and Betty's words of praise and Vic's steaming and hearty soup went a long way toward lifting my spirits and soothing my cough. Illuminada took a package of cough drops out of her purse and pushed them over to me. I nodded, almost cheerful. The prospect of sharing Scot Annich's revelations also perked me up. I could hardly wait for my two friends to finish showering me with compliments so I could wow them with my latest goody. I was delighted to answer the question Betty posed as she served herself a bowl of soup. "Okay, Bel. You've got that look. What happened?"

"I found someone who witnessed Chris Johanson's murder. And it *was* a murder, a cold-blooded murder." Betty and Illuminada both looked up over their soup spoons. I knew they had been skeptical of Ashley's suspicions, and so I was perversely relieved to confirm them even if Ashley herself couldn't be present to hear me. "He's willing to talk to the police if and when the time comes," I proclaimed, trying to sound modest, but failing utterly to mask the pride in my nasal voice. Then just to make sure they got the idea, I whooped, "He heard the whole gruesome thing and saw part of it!"

"Bel, I'm amazed. Even though I helped you locate that kid, I didn't really think he'd know anything. The very idea of a witness sounded like wishful thinking on your part. So tell us the whole sordid story. Tonight." Only Illuminada's last word betrayed any of her usual impatience. The admiration underlying her comment was obvious.

"I talked Sandi into making Scot Annich an offer he couldn't refuse, a job interview for a position with Classic Media in Hawaii. I figured that would be seductive enough to draw him back east long enough for me to talk to him. I pretended to interview him and got him to talk." Illuminada and Betty exchanged glances and nodded, their respect for my ability to get total strangers to spill their secrets once again validated.

Pleased with my succinct summary, I went on. "I got him to tell me everything he heard and saw that night. Here goes." As I continued, I ticked off each sentence on my fingers, emphasizing the thoroughness of Scot's testimony. "He heard Troy engage Chris in a macho dare that actually made the murder possible. He saw Chris almost fall. He heard what Chris called out. He saw Chris actually fall. And he heard Chris's body hit the floor." I held down my pinky with my index finger for a few seconds, letting the import of what I had said register.

Then before either Betty or Illuminada could question me, I added, "Listen. Not for nothing have I been hanging around with a professional private investigator all these years." With those words and a nod to Illuminada, I pulled my tape recorder from my purse and punched play. I was gratified to see Illuminada give me a thumbs-up, indicating her approval of my savvy sleuthing technique. I was also relieved to give my voice a rest. Unwrapping a cough drop, I sat back and listened. "So tell me what happened that night, Scot?" My taped voice was calm, as if extracting testimony from an eyewitness to a murder were routine.

Scot's voice was husky but clearly audible. "I was catching a few zzz's in my chair 'cause I figured I'd be pulling another all-nighter. I don't know what time it was when I woke up, but I heard those two dudes talking—"

"Which two dudes?" I had interrupted his recitation. I saw Illuminada smile as she heard me making sure to get Scot to name names.

"Johanson. Chris Johanson. He was like a consultant. There was a rumor that he was a chainsaw consultant. That's somebody they get in to reduce the employee headcount so the CEO doesn't get blamed. And Troy Tarnoff, he's scoop's CEO and director of special projects." Scot's voice lowered. I must have moved the tape closer because his next words were louder and clearer. "They went rock climbing all the time and they were both totally awesome. I used to watch them a lot on the indoor climbing wall even though that's kinda boring. They had this contest thing going between them. You know, to see who would climb the highest up the wall without clipping pro?"

Thanks to Betty, I knew what "clipping pro" meant, but Scot didn't know that, so his next words were explanatory. "If you look up the wall, you can see places that have a carabiner dangling from a piece of nylon webbing anchored by a heavy bolt to the wall. Those are called protection. As you reach each of those carabiners, you're supposed to take the rope that's tied to your harness and clip it into them. As you climb, your partner down on the ground who's got the other end of the rope keeps feeding out just enough to let you keep climbing higher and higher. He's got the rope running through a gadget called a belaying device. If you slip and fall, the belaying device lets him instantly prevent any more rope from feeding out. So if you've been clipping pro like you're supposed to, you can't fall all the way to the ground because there isn't enough rope." Scot's words were tumbling out now, as if he were reliving the moments he was describing. "I remember Troy said, 'No way you can go all the way up and out on the overhang without clipping on, man.' And Chris . . ."

There was a pause. I remember how Scot had brushed his hand across his eyes when he spoke the next line. "Chris just laughed. That dude thought he was so cool on the wall. He was always bragging about how he had free soloed in the Grand Tetons and how the climbing wall was nothing. Free soloing means climbing without any ropes or protection. Chris never even wore his helmet on the wall. So he said to Troy, 'Watch me.' He went all the way up, and, of course, he didn't clip into any of the pro. Man, that dude was like Spiderman. He went all the way out onto the overhang where I could see him from my chair. He was using his hands and feet like he was crawling on the ceiling. And then . . ."

There was another pause when we couldn't hear anything but the whirring of the reel of the tape recorder. When Scot picked up the narrative, his voice was resigned. "The rope hanging down from his harness went taut and jerked his body hard in the middle. He held on and yelled, 'What the fuck are you doing?' He looked down and at the same time let go with one hand and grabbed for the rope and tried to put some slack into it. But before he could do or say anything else the rope jerked again and made his body twitch just like a damn puppet on a string. His other hand came off the hold and he fell, all the way to the floor from the ceiling. He landed behind the cubicles. I heard this awful thud and a crunch sound." We had to move closer to the tape recorder to make out Scot's last words, so low and husky had the young man's voice become.

"What happened next?" I remember putting my hand on Scot's shoulder as I spoke. "What did you do?"

"I didn't know what to fucking do. I was scared. I waited a few minutes until I heard Troy call out, '911! Somebody, call 911!' The few people who were around rushed over, and I just walked out in all the confusion. I was out of there before the ambulance came. I didn't know what else to do. I didn't really believe what happened. I still don't." Scot shook his head as if doing so would negate what he had seen. "Those two hung out together a lot. And Troy can be a really cool dude sometimes. And he's the honcho. If he wanted to get rid of Chris, why didn't he just decruit him? You know, like uninstall the dude? Why would he murder his friend? Why would God let him do that?" Scot's voice cracked, making him sound even younger than his nineteen years.

"Then what? What did you do next?" I had prompted, ignoring for the moment Scot's incredulity in the face of murder and a god who would allow it.

"I went back to my apartment and packed my gear. I left a note for my roommates saying I had a family emergency and took a cab to the airport. I called scoop.com from there and told them the same thing. Everybody in the scoop coops was totally into what happened to Chris, so nobody really cared much that I was leaving." I recall how Scot had shrugged his shoulders as he recapped his exit from Silicon Slum. "People go and come all the time. They even have a name for somebody thinking of leaving. He's called a flight risk. Nobody thinks twice about it if you disappear." A vision of Ashley's face distracted me momentarily from the tape. *Where the hell was she? What could have happened to her?* I forced myself to focus on Scot's next words. "They probably figured the family emergency story was bogus anyway. They probably figured I got a better offer somewhere else."

"But what about Troy? Didn't he suspect when you left right after the murder? Didn't the security guard know you were in the building?"

I remember Scot shrugging again before saying, "The security guard must have been taking a leak when I came back from getting something to eat. I didn't bother waiting. I just walked in, so I figured nobody had a record that I was there. And I'd been working the whole time until I nodded off." In spite of his shrugs and offhanded tone of voice, Scot had been pale and shaking when he finished talking. I clicked off the tape, saving for another time the story of the boy's relief at having unburdened himself of his hideous secret, and, finally, his belated decision to report what he'd seen to the Jersey City police and to testify if necessary.

Betty broke the silence that followed. "Maybe now that we have a witness we can go to the cops," she said tentatively. "He's the witness to the method and opportunity and we know the motive."

"All we've got is a tape of a kid telling us what he says he saw and heard. It's his word against Troy's," said Illuminada. Her conclusion did not surprise me. Of course Troy would deny Scot's story. In fact, I had lain awake all night coughing and working out a strategy for getting Troy to implicate himself. Only then would Scot's testimony be perceived as valid. Scot's sad tale would support a case against Troy, but it could not be the only weapon in our arsenal.

Suddenly, Illuminada began rifling through her briefcase and, after a few seconds, pulled out an envelope and brandished it in the air in front of us. "*Como mierda!* I almost forgot. This is the report from the handwriting expert! I haven't even had a chance to read it." Opening the flap with a practiced slash, she extricated the enclosed letter and scanned it. "Yes!" She exclaimed. "It's a match! The handwriting on that scrap of paper you filched from Greg's office matches the writing of the warning note Troy got. Greg wrote that note." Her tone was exultant. "Now we've got to get something on his pen pal." With that, Illuminada slammed her small fist hard on the table.

"Illuminada's right," I said. "And I've got an idea. I asked Scot to give us a few days before he goes to the police."

"*Dios mio,* for this I need the whole bowl," said Illuminada, reaching for the popcorn. "Go ahead, *chiquita*. Tell us your idea."

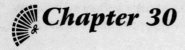 *Chapter 30*

*Troy Tarnoff I saw what you done wile I was makin a
fone call but for $500000 in cach it can be are esecret.
Bring the money in all unmark $100 beels to the leetl
room numero 16 on wendsday put the bag in the trach
can in there*

                                                    Yours truly,

The idea of gluing the gold stud that I had lost at
scoop.com to the place where a signature would be
was Betty's. I had to admit the tiny gold ball punctu-
ated the message with eerie finality. After the note was
done, we just had to get it to Troy and figure out a few
other moves. By the time we left Betty's condo, we not
only had a plan, but each of us knew what she had to
do to make it work. And to placate me, Illuminada had
even agreed to get two people in her office to stake out
Ashley's apartment and Howard Solomon's day trading outpost in Bayonne. "I don't blame you for being
worried, but there's no indication that Troy even knows

Ashley, let alone thinks she suspects him of the murder. And she never thought Greg had anything to do with it. But just for you, Bel . . ." Illuminada shrugged and, averting her head to avoid my aura of germs, gave me one of her rare hugs. "Now go home and get some sleep," she said sternly.

"This better be the last time I put on this uniform," said Betty two nights later as she buttoned the brown blouse of her Delores Does Dusting getup.

"Damn, I don't believe how tight this thing got," I said, wedging myself into my ugly brown slacks and stuffing a wad of Kleenex into the monogrammed breast pocket. Betty and I were babbling nervously as we began fussing with our wigs.

Illuminada, on the other hand, could have been primping for a day at the office. She dressed in silence, methodically tucking in her shirt and patting down a pants pocket and one ankle, probably making sure that her guns were in place. "Remember, Bel," she admonished, "no matter what, get that bag and hang on to it." We synchronized our watches.

Delores picked us up as usual and delivered us to scoop. As she had the first time she dropped us off, she produced a plastic card and flashed it at the security guard, who looked half asleep in his kiosk. Slivers of light gleamed from under the doors of several cubicles, and a few solitary figures moved purposefully about the quiet workspace. We trooped wordlessly past the climbing wall when suddenly an elongated black shadow darkened the wall's already gray surface and flickered across the floor. The hairs on my arms stiffened as I glanced up. A spread-eagled human form moved crablike up toward the overhang. Still mute, Illuminada, Betty and I gathered our cleaning equipment and headed off to where our all-too-familiar duties awaited us.

A big hand-lettered sign reading "Out of Order" on the rest room door put me off for a moment, but I entered and nearly ran into two plumbers sloshing around in a grimy pool of water beneath one of the sinks. I figured that at that hour they were probably earning overtime and that was why they were laughing and joking. Ignoring them, I cleaned the toilets and the other sinks and left without bothering with the wet floor, glad to have my load lightened if only temporarily. I was relieved to notice that the shadow on the ceiling had disappeared.

As I went through the motions of vacuuming and dusting my weary way through the familiar space, there was no sign of the tai chi practitioner or the young man who had snored contentedly from his nest of printouts on the floor. Had they been decruited or uninstalled, to use Scot's lingo? Had they gotten better offers and left? Or had they sensed something wrong at scoop.com? There did seem to be an air of general deterioration. Not only was the plumbing acting up, but the Xerox machine in the open area near the kitchen was also being serviced by an earnest-looking young woman in the familiar uniform of the company that routinely ministers to the machines at RECC. I couldn't help but marvel at how scoop.com could pay Xerox repair people overtime to come in at night while at RECC, the copier could be out of commission for a week before somebody showed up to fix it.

Hesitating only a moment to quiet my raspy breathing, I opened the door to cubicle sixteen and flicked on the task light next to the PC. The little room looked ordinary enough. There was the messy workstation with its monitor and phone, the usual gobbledygook scrawled on the white board wall, and a few photos of a good-looking young guy pushpinned into the burlap on the opposite wall. Suddenly I tensed. Was I imagining things, or had the shadow on the ceiling reappeared? From where I was located, I couldn't tell. Closing the door behind me, I moved toward the wastebasket.

Sure enough, it was nearly filled with a large plastic bag neatly closed with an ordinary plastic coated twist-tie. It looked like a bag of trash. As we had agreed, I put on my rubber gloves, opened the bag, and checked the contents. There were literally hundreds of one-hundred-dollar bills. They looked real to me. Hands shaking only a little, I refastened the sack and slung it over my shoulder, Santa Claus style. Still wearing my rubber gloves and still following our plan, I reached for the doorknob. At that moment, the door swung open and a hand closed over mine, welding my fingers to the knob in a grip of iron.

For a second I stared into the cold narrowed eyes of Troy Tarnoff. Then, taking a deep breath, I coughed in his face. Instinctively he raised his hand to shield himself from the mouthful of malignant microbes I had just fired at him. In that instant I stamped down as hard as I could on his sneakered instep. "God damn you!" he yelped, reflexively jerking his crushed foot off the ground and letting go of my hand. Clutching the bag tight to my chest, I fled the cubicle, screaming as loud as a woman with bronchitis can. Footsteps sounded behind me, so I ran faster, heading for the rest room, where, in my frenzy, I reasoned that the presence of the plumbers would prevent Troy from following. As I pushed my way into the bathroom, my mind raced. *Where the hell's the backup? Illuminada and Betty promised to be right behind me. There're supposed to be cops here. Where is everybody? Why am I always left holding the bag?*

As it turned out, almost everybody was in the bathroom. When I made my breathless entrance, the plumbers stood tensed at either side of the door holding drawn guns. One of them shoved me, bag and all, into a stall, saying curtly, "Stay here, lady." I was only too happy to huddle there, relieved that the undercover cops had indeed shown up.

"Stop! You're under arrest!" I heard a woman's voice call just outside the bathroom door. Forgoing safety for a better view of the goings-on, I slammed down the toilet seat cover and clambered onto it. From this vantage point I saw the Xerox repair person, also brandishing a drawn gun, pushing a handcuffed and, I'm pleased to report, limping, Troy Tarnoff in ahead of her. *Soon,* I figured, grinning, *he'll also be coughing.*

Chapter 31

To: Bbarrett@circle.com
From: Rabbi Susan Ornstein-Klein@jch.org
Re: Mazeltov
Date: 11/18/99 13:15:08

Hi Bel,

I finally have a moment to let you know how pleased I was with your presentation on the Book of Samuel. You brought that text to life for us all, and your impassioned oratory and complex analysis set a high standard for others to follow. As I listened to you, it occurred to me that you would have made a marvelous rabbi. Regrettably that career path wasn't open to you when you were planning your future. Perhaps if there had been female rabbis to inspire you . . . but that's a whole other topic, isn't it?

You didn't show for our last session and didn't call my office to explain, so I assume something came up rather suddenly. We all missed your insightful commentary and look forward to having you among us again next Sunday. I know the Hebrew has been something of a struggle for you, so if you need additional help, please let me know. That's what I'm here for.

Shalom,
Rabbi OK

That woman sure knew how to get to me. I guess they teach you that in rabbinical school. After reading Rabbi OK's e-mail, I envisioned myself delivering high holy day sermons from the *bemah* to throngs of devoted followers. I also vowed not to miss any more classes. That's why I dragged myself to the next session in spite of Sol's admonition that I needed another day in bed and Ma's rant about how if I didn't rest, I'd be sick for Thanksgiving. I'd done no reading or Hebrew study in weeks. I repeated the mantra I often recited to my own students, *The least you can do is attend class.* And this was an important session because, at our request, Rabbi OK would be explaining the parts of the Saturday morning Sabbath service to help us to participate more knowledgeably.

I sat apart from the others so as not to infect them. When Ashley appeared, I gaped as if at an apparition from the spirit world. But she was very real. And very healthy-looking. She did not resemble someone who had been held hostage by a ruthless killer or endured any of the other fates I'd envisioned. Her hair was sleek and elegantly styled, a soft burgundy cashmere pullover and slacks sheathed her slender body, and her nails had been shaped and tinted the same muted pink as her lipstick. And was that makeup or a tan that tinged her cheeks? I was enormously relieved to see her. But my relief was, shall we say, not entirely free from fury.

In fact, I was livid. The contrast between Ashley's air of radiant well-being and my look of Mimi meets Typhoid Mary on expectorants did not sit well with me. I fumed through Rabbi OK's distinction between an aliyah and the amidah. And after the rabbi took the last question and Janet had invited us all to a Sabbath lunch at her house in a few weeks, I approached Ashley and barked, "Ashley, where the hell have you been? You've got some explaining to do. And you're going to do it now, at my house. I'm too sick to go anywhere else." Self-pity turned that last sentence into the protracted whine of a practicing martyr.

"Of course, Bel, anything you say," Ashley responded, clearly upset by my hostility. "I'm so sorry you don't feel well. Just let me call Howard." As she held her cell phone to her ear and chatted with Howard, I noted that she blushed and blew kisses into the little receiver. Then, accompanied by Sandi, we walked the few short blocks home.

"Ashley, we've been worried to death about you. Where have you been? Why didn't you tell one of us where you were going? How could you just dump Chris's murder in my lap and then vanish? Didn't it occur to you that, under the circumstances, I might worry?" By the time I finished this diatribe I was coughing and opening the door to the house.

"Oh my God, Bel. No, honestly, you never said much about Chris's murder, so I figured you hadn't come up with anything yet or maybe you'd given up. It's just that . . ." Ashley hesitated. Sandi took charge of our coats and turned on the flame under the pot of Ma's cure-all chicken soup that Sol had left on the stove.

I spoke into the silence created by Ashley's pause. "I don't give up that easily," I said with as much dignity as I could muster while blowing my nose. "It all came together quickly though. And when it did, you were among the missing. I was very worried. We all were." Ashley's entire face was now alight with curiosity. But as far as I was concerned, it was her turn to answer questions.

She got the idea and began to explain. "God, Bel. I just didn't realize you'd worry. Howard and I spent a week at this awesome Jewish retreat for couples. You see, after you told me about Howard giving up his law practice to day trade, I was very relieved. I had been so sure he was having an affair. But I didn't stay relieved for long. When I thought about how he took such a big step without telling me, I realized that our marriage was in trouble." *Duh.* I smiled to myself at the recollection of hotshot Howard holed up in his hideaway trying to beat the odds. "And you know what? Howard *was* a little jealous of Chris." *Double duh.* Sol was right about that too.

"No thanks, really," Ashley said, passing back the bowl of soup Sandi had placed in front of her. Of course she couldn't eat anything in our house because we didn't keep kosher. *Well, that's more for me,* I thought. I felt only slightly guilty about slurping up the steaming golden potion while Ashley, soupless, repented across from me.

"So I suppose the retreat was helpful?" Sandi interjected. Her pleasant tone made my snarls sound even fiercer. But I was still annoyed.

"It was. We learned a lot of ways to talk about the difficult stuff, you know, like, like money." I almost spit out my soup. *What could a dot commer and a young lawyer possibly know of money problems? When I was your age the "difficult stuff" was Vietnam, voter registration, and women's rights. What's wrong with your generation anyway?* Oblivous to my inner monologue, Ashley continued. "There was this really cool facilitator. So anyway after the retreat was over, we decided kind of on the spur of the moment to go to St. Croix. This friend of ours has a time-share she couldn't use that week. We wanted to, you know, spend time together." At least Ashley had the good taste to redden as she mouthed this euphemism. *Great. While I was risking my life to unmask a psychopathic killer on your behalf, you and Howard were sipping rum punches and getting it on in the Caribbean.* "And it was really cheap . . ."

"I take it Howard is going to resume his practice of law?" Sandi asked. I wasn't too interested in Howard's latest career move, so I concentrated on my soup.

"I think so. We're not sure. He's giving up the day trading and I already quit my job. I can't make myself go back there anymore after what happened to Chris. Besides, e-media.com hasn't turned a profit yet and that makes me nervous. I may be old-fashioned, but I like to work for companies that make money. Somehow I don't think staying there is a good career move for me. Howie and I are both going to rethink our career options," Ashley pronounced gravely. "Maybe we'll go into business together. I'm not sure. We're open to suggestions." She suddenly smiled engagingly. I could see Sandi's human resources director persona quietly take in this factoid. I knew it was only a matter of time before Sandi devised a career plan for the Solomons. After all, Scot Annich was now designing software for Classic Media in Honolulu and Nathan Futura had an interview for a part-time job next week.

"And I apologize for worrying you two. It was totally thoughtless of me. I'm really, really sorry, Bel." Ah, there it was, the apology. I had needed to hear it and felt my annoyance dissipating a little in its wake. Ashley did look contrite. I was actually glad to change the subject when she asked, "Bel, now will you please tell me what you found out about Chris's death?"

"What we, my two friends and I, found out is that you were half right. Chris's death was not an accident. After learning that Chris was pumping him for e-media.com, Troy Tarnoff deliberately caused Chris to fall to his death from the overhang. There's a witness." Ashley had looked a bit smug when I began to speak. By the time I'd finished these few sentences, her face was grim.

"But who—"

Before she could complete her question, I was answering it, suddenly wanting to get the whole seamy story told so I could go to sleep. "The witness is a kid who worked at scoop and had a view of the overhang from his cubicle," I continued, but I knew that wasn't Ashley's question. "Greg set Chris up. You yourself said he's pretty paranoid." Ashley nodded. "Chris missed a couple of meetings and appointments Greg had scheduled. Maybe Greg was afraid Chris was going to go to work for Troy. And maybe that's why Greg was getting it on with, are you ready for this one?" Ashley nodded vigorously. "Norma Johanson, Chris's wife. Maybe Greg just moved on her to get back at Chris when he thought Chris might defect. But whatever his reason, Norma was pregnant, probably by Greg." I sat back, content to watch disbelief war with sorrow on Ashley's face.

"Was?" Sandi had not heard the latest news either.

"Was. Norma had a miscarriage. Chalk another one up to Nathan," I said.

"You see, Ashley, it's kind of like the story of David and Bathsheba, remember? From the Book of Samuel that Bel reported on?" Sandi went on to reframe Chris's murder and our investigation in biblical terms, emphasizing the role of Nathan Futura as a modern prophet. "That's why I knew Norma would miscarry," said Sandi to Ashley, who was staring at me, her eyes and mouth open wide with amazement. "According to Nathan in the Book of Samuel, taking the life of their baby was the Lord's way of punishing David and Bathsheba."

"Bel, you are totally awesome. I never would have figured Greg and Norma were hooked up," Ashley said when she could speak. "Never in a million years. Chris adored her. He would even have moved to Morristown sooner or later." I saw her eyes fill.

"I'm not sure what, if any, the charges against Greg will be yet. They may not be able to pin anything on him since he can argue that he had no idea Troy would resort to murder. But the handwriting on the note that exposed Chris matches Greg's. And the police *are* holding Troy on suspicion of murder. The witness is flying here from Honolulu to testify. The cops have already heard a tape I made, with the witness's permission, of his account of the murder." I blew my nose again, rewarded by the admiration I read in Ashley's teary eyes.

"And you haven't even heard the best part yet about how Bel and her friends cleaned offices or how Bel figured out who fingered Chris. Or, for that matter, how they trapped Troy into trying to buy Bel's silence and later trying to hurt her. It's quite a story," Sandi said shaking her head.

"And you'll hear it all before too long, I promise, but not today. Right now I just want to crawl under the covers and sleep," I said.

"Bel, thank you for doing all this for me. I know it won't bring Chris back, but it clears his name somehow. It really was a *mitzvah*."

Chapter 32

To: Bbarrett@circle.com
From: Rbarrett@uwash.edu
Re: Giving thanks
Date: 11/29/99 19:20:22

Dear Mom,

This is one thank-you note you won't have to browbeat me into writing. (Remember that heinous fight you and I had when you said Keith and I should write thank-you notes for wedding gifts on our honeymoon?) Anyway, Keith and Abbie J and I had a totally awesome Thanksgiving with you, Grandma Sadie (don't worry, I'm writing her a snail-mail note thanking her for the airfare. I hope she never stops winning in Atlantic City! And what's Wendy's e-mail address? I'll thank her for lending us the crib), Mark, Sol, Sandi, and Josh.

    The best part was the look on your face when you answered the door expecting just Sandi and Josh and saw me, Abbie J, Keith, and Mark (doesn't he look cool with that goatee?) and

Mark's laundry! When you finally stopped crying and let us in, it felt so good to be home. But I don't see how you can be such a hotshot amateur sleuth if you didn't catch on that we were coming. You totally went for my bogus e-mails about having to work and Mark's Tierra del Fuego myth. Get real, Mom.

As Mark said, the turkey totally rocked. And so did the left-overs. Mark and I didn't even mind that you neglected us to spend time with Abbie J because Grandma Sadie still thinks we're special. Thanks to you and Sol for baby-sitting so we could all go into the Village Saturday night. And BTW, Keith and I actually enjoyed the Sabbath service you dragged us to, especially after you and Sandi explained everything ahead of time. Maybe you two won't embarrass us at your bat mitzvah after all.

Gotta go now and start cramming for finals. Thanks for everything.

Love,
Rebecca

Hot Flashes and Cold Killers—
The Bel Barrett Mysteries by
Jane Isenberg

MIDLIFE CAN BE MURDER
0-380-81886-8/$6.50 US/$8.99 Can
There's nothing like a good homicide
for curing middle age malaise

MOOD SWINGS TO MURDER
0-380-80282-1/$5.99 US/$7.99 Can
When a dead legend's double gets done in,
Bel finds the killer her way

DEATH IN A HOT FLASH
0-380-80281-3/$5.99 US/$7.99 Can
She's a woman of a certain age . . .
who's just in time for murder

THE "M" WORD
0-380-80280-5/$5.99 US/$7.99 Can
In the midst of change . . .
murder is the permanent solution